YESTERDAY'S FATAL

Also by Jan Brogan

A Confidential Source

Final Copy

YESTERDAY'S FATAL

Jan Brogan

St. Martin's Minotaur

New York

This is a work of fiction. All of the characters, organizations, and events portrayed in this novel are either products of the author's imagination or are used fictitiously.

The town of West Kent, Rhode Island, is an invention of the author.

www.minotaurbooks.com

Library of Congress Cataloging-in-Publication Data

Brogan, Jan.

Yesterday's fatal / Jan Brogan.—1st ed.

p. cm.

Sequel to: A confidential source.

ISBN-13: 978-0-312-35997-3

ISBN-10: 0-312-35997-7

1. Women gamblers—Fiction. 2. Traffic accidents—Fiction. 3. Investigative reporting—Fiction. 4. Women journalists—Fiction. 5. Witnesses—Fiction. I. Title.

PS3602.R64Y47 2007

813'.6—dc22

2007008131

First Edition: May 2007

10 9 8 7 6 5 4 3 2 1

To Lannie and Spike,

my two favorite writers

YESTERDAY'S FATAL

1

It's not that fatals are beneath me.

It's just that these days, no newspaper reporter jumps into her car and rips off to an actual car accident scene. We settle for getting the facts from the cops over the phone. Partly, this is because we're so understaffed, but partly it's a sad fact that fatals are rarely front-page news anymore, just an exploitation of all-too-frequent tragedy, the ultimate senselessness of blood and gore.

I never would have even been on that road, that late, alone—except that I had to pee.

I was coming back from another assignment, a god-awful political banquet in Connecticut, and I'd taken an exit off the highway hoping to find an open service station. At the end of the ramp, I found a Mobil. But it was closed. It was raining and much too damp to squat outside. I'd run a 10K race in this area a month ago, and thought I'd remembered a Wendy's or some sort of fast-food place nearby. I headed left out of the driveway.

The road narrowed, and the trees grew fuller to form a canopy that blocked out the sky. The only source of illumination came from the weak headlights of my Honda, and I knew that the Wendy's I'd remembered was nothing more than a wishful thought, a bladder mirage. I had just about decided to turn around when I saw streetlights ahead at what looked like an intersection.

On my left, there was an old farmhouse, set back, but with a falling-down garage close to the road. As I passed, the porch lights flashed on, and I saw a woman standing in the doorway. She was in silhouette, but I could still tell she was an old lady. What was it, I wondered, the narrow shoulders? The posture? And then, before I could decide, I saw it, a weird sputter of light ahead, just beyond the intersection, in what looked like woods. A car, taillights out, was crashed into the tree. A flicker rose from the hood.

I was pretty sure that I was still in West Bay, which meant it was the bureau reporter's job to get this accident from the cops in the morning. I admit it—that was my first thought. But then I realized the cops might not even know about this accident yet. That there might be a human being trapped inside.

I crossed the intersection onto what had become a dirt road, pulled up behind the car, and jumped out. Wet, grassy air mixed with a bitter petroleum smell. My nose twitched, and I wanted to jump back into my car and seal the doors. But by now, a shot of adrenaline had boosted the caffeine in my bloodstream.

The car was a Ford Taurus, the front end crumpled with the kind of violence that makes you stop and swallow, and I could taste the smoke that rose from the gap where the hood was hinged. I ran to the driver's-side door and found it ajar, which should have alerted me that something was weird.

But by this time, I was fairly distracted. There was enough light from the interior light and my high beams to make out the form inside, a female body thrown sideways, across the console from the driver's side so that her head was on the passenger seat. The windshield was cracked at the centerline and the driver's-side airbag was deflated.

"Are you all right?" I shouted through the window. Clearly she wasn't all right. She hadn't been wearing a seat belt, and her hair was bloodied. Her head must have hit the windshield.

"You've got to wake up," I shouted at the woman. "Get out of the car." The woman did not move.

The flame at the hood sputtered. It was still small, but the clouds of smoke had grown thicker. I grabbed the cell phone out of my pocket and fumbled, trying to turn it on. Nothing. It was completely out of charge.

Think, Hallie, think. On the floor on the passenger side, the contents of the woman's purse had spilled out. I leaned into the car, trying to see if there was a cell phone anywhere. Wallet, makeup bag, date book, crumpled store receipts, a gold and black pen, and a can of Mace.

A city girl, I thought. What was she doing way out here? But at the moment, my main concern was communications.

You weren't supposed to move anyone who was injured unless you knew what you were doing. And I sure as hell didn't know what I was doing. I could feel the heat of the flame. How long before the entire engine compartment went up? Before this whole car blew?

I stepped away from the car, and my shoes sank into the wet grit of the road. I needed to get help. I ran back toward the farmhouse. Just as I got to the intersection, I spotted a flashlight making its way toward me. Behind the flashlight was the old woman, wearing a nightgown, bathrobe, and one of those clear plastic rain scarves that fold up into a bag. She was probably seventy-five years old. Underneath the rain scarf, I saw long, dark hair that couldn't possibly be real.

The woman stared at me. "Looked like that car had it out for that tree."

"What?"

"Hit it twice. I seen it from my porch."

"Did you call the police?" I asked.

She shook her head.

"Go back and call 911. There's a woman in there, badly injured!"

She turned and headed back toward her house, moving at old-age speed. "Run!" I shouted after her. "Run as fast as you can!"

Adrenaline took over, making me forget about my bladder. I raced back to the car. The flames were now blazing in the damp air.

In the backseat, I could see a soccer ball, a crumpled McDonald's bag, and a couple of Disney figurines that looked like they came from a Happy Meal. This woman might have a child. Maybe more than one.

I made one last assessment. I'm slight, barely five feet four, and not exceptionally strong, but this woman looked even smaller than me. The smoke was getting thick and my eyes burned. If I was going to do this, I should do it now.

I reached into the car. As I crouched over to lift her, I could see that she was about my own age, midthirties. She looked Hispanic, with light mocha skin and dark auburn hair spattered with blood. There was a stillness about her I didn't like, and her lipstick had dried on bluish lips. Around her neck, she wore a silver cross with a tiny diamond chip in it. I slipped my arm under her back. "I hope I don't totally mess you up," I said.

But just then, I heard the siren, and looking behind me, bright lights flashed. A cop jumped out of a police cruiser with a fire extinguisher, pulled me away from the car, and headed to the hood, where he doused the flame. Behind the cruiser were a fire truck and an ambulance. Two firefighters and an EMT rushed out, following the cop to the car. Within minutes, they'd extracted the woman from the car and secured her on a backboard.

"Is she going to be all right?" I asked.

No one answered.

As the ambulance pulled away, the cop, extinguisher still in hand, guided me back to my own car. He was a tall, stocky man in his midthirties, whose eyes looked swollen, either from exhaustion, or maybe the fumes.

He asked me a laundry list of questions, about what time I'd gotten there and if I'd seen any other cars. Then he asked for my driver's license and registration, which I handed over.

"You live on the East Side, huh?" He squinted at the address on my license. "What you doing in West Kent at this hour?"

I explained about the assignment in Connecticut and how I was looking for a rest room. "I work for the *Chronicle.*"

His groan suggested that he wasn't pleased with this development.

"I'm going to need to get her name. And your best guess as to what happened," I said.

"You're gonna have to call the station in the morning. The captain has to clear any release to the press."

Given the hour, this seemed reasonable. It was past deadline anyway, and with the adrenaline subsiding, the pressure in my bladder was back. I wanted to get the hell out of there and find some place to pee. I may have forgotten to tell the cop about the driver's door being open, but I did suggest that he go up to the farmhouse and talk to the old lady.

He denied it later, of course.

2

Providence Woman Dies in Early Morning Crash

BY HALLIE AHERN

Chronicle Staff Reporter

WEST KENT—Lizette Diaz-Salazar, a 33-year-old Providence woman, died early yesterday in a car crash, despite rescue efforts by West Kent police and fire departments.

Her Ford Taurus hit a tree shortly before midnight on the west end of Smith Ave., a dirt road extension, and caught fire. Police extinguished the flame, and firefighters pulled her from the wreck and transported her to the Kent County Hospital, where she was pronounced dead, officials said.

Salazar had apparently gotten lost on her way home from her sister's new apartment in West Warwick, according to police. Her car careened out of control on the narrow, dark road and hit a tree.

Police said that the rain may have affected visibility, and that alcohol was not a factor in the accident.

A wife and mother of three young boys, Salazar worked as a bookkeeper for the Centro de Hispanio in South Providence.

"She was such a dedicated mother," said Marah Antieviech, one of her Prairie Ave. neighbors. "Such a nice person, it's a shame."

See Fatal, page B-19

In the news business, timing is everything. Because the tragedy happened too late to make Saturday's paper, it was considered old news by Sunday, buried inside and continued on the obit page. And since television had missed the opportunity for a gruesome shot, it offered only offhand coverage of the accident. The bottom line? Poor Lizette Salazar's death was given terribly short shrift.

Even I had tried to avoid the task of reporting it. Sitting in my kitchen with the paper spread across the bar, I felt bad about that now. In how many ways could this poor woman be shortchanged? Images began flashing through my head, the violence of the cracked windshield and bent tree, the fresh lipstick on the bluish lips.

She had been two years younger than me, and now she was gone. A mother of three boys. That part seemed amazing to me. She had raised three sons, the oldest almost seventeen years old, while I was barely grown up enough to take care of myself. I ran a hand through my hair, which I'd let get too long and was full of split ends. I like to think that most reporters are perennial teenagers, single-minded and immature, but I'm starting to suspect that it might just be me.

I snapped the paper shut, folding it back to the front page. But this was even worse. Because now I was confronted by Jonathan Frizell's byline on a story that led the paper, Page One. Above the fold.

We'd been promoted together to the *Chronicle*'s investigative team in December and were both on an extended probation, which meant we still had to prove ourselves. Beset by a bevy of smaller, daily story assignments, I had authored only one major investigative piece since the Mazursky murder, and yesterday my only source on a mortgage loan exposé I was trying to develop had begun to backtrack.

Frizell, on the other hand, was prolific. Assigned to the political fund-raising corruption in the state assembly, he had a never-ending source of material.

Of course I knew Frizell's story was coming, had contributed to some of the research, but above the fold? What the hell was earth-shattering about politicians selling their votes to lobbyists? Wasn't this a way of life?

But there was something else bothering me, something I'd heard from one of the Rhode Island bureaucrats I'd interviewed at the political banquet in New Haven—a rumor going around the statehouse that the *Providence Morning Chronicle* was for *sale* and that a national chain was interested.

I sucked down the last of my cranberry juice. I was dressed for my morning run. My sneakers felt tight and the waistband of my running shorts newly irritating.

I threw the paper on the leaning-tower-of-recyclables next to the door, locked the door behind me, and stuck the key in my running bra. I have an addictive personality, and after my brother Sean died almost six years ago, I'd developed problems with insomnia and a sleeping pill dependency. Now, even though I've been off pills for more than five years, I still run every day as part of my recovery, using compulsive physical exhaustion in the morning to stave off anxious thought at night.

Outside, it was another raw spring morning. But there was plenty of fuel in my furnace, and by the time I got to the boulevard, I'd pulled off the sweatshirt and was running with it wrapped around my waist. My legs felt strong on the damp cinders, my body lean and light. If I ran fast enough or long enough, I could obliterate all thoughts of Jonathan Frizell from my brain.

My mother used to say that I was black Irish, but being German herself, she got it wrong. The black Irish have dark hair, dark eyes, and at least a hint of their supposedly Spanish Moor heritage in their complexion. I'm more your everyday Irish, not a real colleen, because my hair is nearly black, but I've got the typical blue eyes and standard-issue skin that sears in sunlight.

So, technically, this was *my* kind of weather. But I'd had enough of the gray sky and constant mist that my mother says is best for the lawn and the garden. After my run, I felt like curling up on the couch with a cup of tea and the rest of the Sunday paper.

The last thing I wanted to do was drive to Foxboro, which is about halfway between Providence and Boston, but I'd promised Walter, my former sponsor, that I'd go to a meeting with him. Not a substance-abuse meeting, like where I'd first met him six years ago. No. For the last few months, he'd been dragging me to a support group for compulsive gamblers. Even though I hadn't bought so much as a scratch ticket since October.

It was noon when I pulled my Honda into the church lot and the last of the Sunday worshippers had left. There was a screech of static from the radio, which turned on and off at whim. I needed to get it fixed. But given the age of my car, a 1995 Civic, it seemed like a foolish investment.

I parked beside a lone minivan with one of those PRECIOUS CARGO bumper stickers on the back and a car seat inside to wait for Walter. He owned three cabs in Boston; but he personally drove one of the oldest of the fleet, a boxy yellow Checker cab. Knowing Walter, he'd probably picked up a last-minute fare. His work ethic was always making him late.

Maybe he wouldn't show and I could forget the meeting entirely. It occurred to me that I should review that mortgage loan data again to see for myself if there was evidence of favoritism. Why was I even here?

But I knew why. I have sort of an all-or-nothing personality, and I got carried away with some research into gambling last fall. Nothing like my sleeping pill problem, which was *real.* And certainly no worse than what happens to most people on a weekend vacation in Las Vegas. But Walter was a twelve-step reformer, a zealot who still went to substance-abuse meetings nearly every day when he hadn't tasted cocaine or alcohol for more than five years. He had stepped in to bail me out, had lent me $2,000 so I could pay my rent and get out of debt. He didn't charge interest, and I owed him this, his private usury fee.

A Mercedes SUV pulled into the lot, a door slammed, and three overweight women got out and headed toward the church. There must be a new Sunday Binge Eaters meeting inside. It was comforting how many different kinds of personal problems could fill a church parking lot.

Somewhere a traffic light changed, and the flow of cars began moving on the street. A white cab with a modern, sleek look and odd blue trim pulled in and parked beside me.

Walter got out of the cab. He was an average-size guy who always wore cowboy boots to give him a couple more inches. Sometimes, like when he was playing guitar or singing at a coffeehouse, he added the cowboy hat to conceal his slightly thinning hair. This, along with an Easy Rider mustache. But he was from New York, not Texas. You knew that the minute he opened his mouth.

"New cab?" I asked, gesturing at the taxi.

He smiled, not bothering to conceal his pride. Ever since he'd gotten engaged, Walter had talked about expanding his enterprise. He was a natural businessman, smart about money, and as successful running his own cab company as he had been as a drug dealer. "Take a good look at it," he said.

I stared at it awhile, trying to figure out what it was I should notice. It was a nice-looking American car that appeared vaguely European. Some kind of Chrysler maybe. "Nice color trim," I finally said.

"Look at the plates," he said.

The plates were from Rhode Island.

"I bought five new medallions in Providence. Unbelievably cheap. The guy was under pressure from some lawsuit and was in a hurry to get out of the business."

I gave him a congratulatory hug. "Why don't we go somewhere for lunch and you can tell me all about your new Rhode Island empire?"

"Nice try," he said, without smiling. Reluctantly, I followed him downstairs to the church basement and the cafeteria-like room where the meetings were held. We sat at one of six rectangular tables and waited for the room to fill. Although mostly male, and mostly middle-aged, there were an increasing number of teenage boys who had developed problems with online poker—and at least a half-dozen women. Soon there were no empty seats at the tables, and newcomers dragged chairs in from other rooms. But at least we weren't in Rhode Island, where I was sure to run into someone I knew.

I was doing okay at the meeting, feeling that I was coming through unscathed, when a new guy, an older man I hadn't met yet, decided to share. Tall and spindly, he wore a tight T-shirt that clung to his ribs, and his fingers were stained yellow from cigarettes. Full of nervous energy, he introduced himself as Al and launched into a story about losing $50,000 in one night of craps.

Under the guise of admitting his faults, Al began to relive good times. He had made six passes in a row and was up $5,000. The crowd was getting loud, attracting the attention of the pit boss. The air smelled of perspiration and perfume. He placed his whole rack on the pass line and everyone's breathing halted as they waited for the rolling of the dice.

And suddenly I was right there, back at the casino, right in the moment before the blackjack dealer turned the final card, the moment of fear and possibility. I knew I should have identified with Al's weakness, seen my own failings in his, but instead I felt an emptiness behind my chest. A yearning for something I wasn't allowed to have. It had been five long months since I'd had that moment, different from any other, when I felt completely and totally alive.

"Are you all right?" Walter asked later, as we walked toward the cars.

I didn't want to talk about it, didn't want to think about the restless feeling I couldn't shake. So I blamed it on the weather. "I wish it would just get it over with and pour."

"May flowers," he said.

"What?"

"We'll have great May flowers. You like all that gardening shit, right?"

I shrugged. My mother was the insane gardener, planting so many gardens at our family home in Worcester that there was virtually no lawn. For years, I'd resisted this impulse to plant things and watch them grow, but this winter I broke down and ordered some English bluebell bulbs from a catalog. Walter seemed to think this was significant.

My gaze landed on Walter's Rhode Island license plate, and I changed the subject, affecting a careless, chipper tone. "So why was that Providence guy so eager to unload the cabs?"

"The guy was Dominican, and apparently he insulted somebody. Laid off someone with connections. Anyway, he says these people found out he had a good policy on his cabs and started targeting them. His rates went through the roof."

I stepped over a puddle in the pavement and stopped dead. "Targeting them?"

"According to this guy, there's this whole underworld of people who smash up cars for the insurance money."

Suddenly the day no longer seemed like such a waste. "You mean like up in Lawrence?" At my last newspaper, the *Ledger* in Boston, I'd written about the flourishing industry of insurance fraud, and about a grandmother who had wound up dying in an accident that had been staged for the claim.

"Yeah. I guess they got their own ring in Providence, only here they go after innocent cars on the street, too. Especially anyone with a commercial policy, a deep pocket like a truck company or cabbie."

We'd reached his cab, which I now realized had been newly washed and waxed. "So if it's so bad, why do you want to do business here?"

"Hey, *I* haven't insulted anyone in the criminal community here." He opened the door to his cab, sat behind the wheel, and grinned. "At least not yet."

And then, as if those constant gray clouds had finally parted and a shaft of sunlight beamed straight down, I saw it all clearly. Innocent motorists at risk of accident or even death. Big payouts to scam artists. The rising insurance rates that force a guy to sell his cab business. It was a perfect subject for a Sunday centerpiece—an in-depth look at insurance fraud in Rhode Island. By Hallie Ahern. Headline above the fold.

"Walter, this cabdriver guy who sold you his fleet, you think he'd talk to me?"

"I don't know. Maybe, but he might not want to piss off this Dominican who runs this shit in his neighborhood."

"He mention this guy's name? The Dominican?"

Walter thought a moment, delving into his neatly cross-filed brain. A switch flicked in his eye, a folder produced. "I think it might have been Manuel—you know, like Ramirez." Walter was a die-hard Red Sox fan. The connection had been made to the Red Sox's star hitter.

Manuel? I got a flutter of something. Lizette Salazar had been Dominican, and her husband's name had been Manuel.

Of course, that was likely a common name in the community. Like John or Jim. But the flutter stirred something else, a memory. When I'd interviewed Lizette's neighbor to get some background about her, she'd mentioned that the husband had worked for an auto body shop. And there had been an odd tone in her voice, as if that meant something more. A long shot, but I had to ask, "He didn't happen to mention the last name of this guy, Manuel, did he?"

Walter shook his head and put the key in the ignition. "Sorry, pal. You're on your own on that one."

3

On Sunday afternoon the newsroom was oddly absent of sound. All the televisions were off and the fax machines mute. There was only a skeletal crew on the Rim, a semicircle of copyeditors' desks where the news gets honed and polished. Two bored reporters sat a good distance apart in the large open room, the Sunday paper spread across their desks.

The *Chronicle,* which was one of the last independently owned metropolitan newspapers in the country, was an enormously profitable corporation, with all sorts of media holdings and nice decor. The carpet was lush, the furniture ergonomic, and the Palladian windows frequently Windexed so that when it wasn't raining, downtown Providence sparkled below.

Someone had sprung for a box of donuts on the morning's coffee run, and I stopped at the copy desk and helped myself to a vanilla-glazed that was already going stale. Because I was originally hired to work in a small bureau in South County and was still new both to the investigative team and the city staff, my desk was a definite afterthought. Stolen from the financial department, it was in the far back corner of the newsroom, closer to the business editor and the sports desk than to the action going on in city.

There was a stack of printouts from Friday's research into state-backed mortgage loans still on my chair. I picked them up, dropped them on the only uncluttered surface, the floor, and sat down to wait as I warmed up the computer. My cell phone battery was screwy, newly recharged, yet drained again, so I checked my phone, hopeful that Matt Cavanaugh had left a message at work. I'd been seeing him for about four months now. He was away at a prosecutors' conference in South Carolina, and I hadn't heard from him in almost a week. The worst part was that I couldn't even complain about it; there were no promises between us, no implicit agreements. Every time we started to get close, he managed to get himself assigned to some huge case that sucked up every waking hour for weeks.

There was no message from him. I turned to the donut for solace, finishing every last crumb.

Finally, the computer was ready. I called up the database and typed "Manuel Salazar" into the search line. The first entry was the fatal accident story I'd written in today's paper. The obituary and funeral announcement also came up. The next two entries yielded more interesting results.

A Manuel Salazar Jr. of Providence had been in a car accident with four other people three months ago and suffered a "serious back injury" according to a ten-inch story out of Cranston that did not have a byline. This Manuel Salazar, however, was sixteen years old at the time. I'm guessing Lizette's oldest son. When I'd first called the neighbor about Lizette's accident, she'd exclaimed, *"After the year she's had, now this!"* But she had refused to elaborate. Maybe this was what she'd meant.

Then, from a Superior Court roundup two years ago, I found that Manuel Salazar, thirty-two, of Prairie Ave., Providence, had been charged with insurance fraud, but the case was dismissed. This one mentioned that he'd been convicted of car theft the year before and worked for the Big T Body Shop in Providence.

The Big T Body Shop was not just any auto body shop. It was known as one of the most corrupt body shops in the state. Its owner, a reputed mob guy named Tito Manaforte, had just gotten out of prison. He'd served time for fencing stolen automobile parts and trying to intimidate a government witness, but word was that these were the least of his transgressions.

It seemed too much of a coincidence that the wife of a professional insurance scammer would die accidentally in a fatal car crash. And yet I knew from my research in Lawrence that insurance scammers rarely staged one-passenger collisions. The point was to get as many claims as possible out of one accident. And they were after the legal fees and phony medical treatment profits. A fatal would have been a mistake.

Unless there were marital problems or real serious money woes.

What was it the old lady had said? *"Looked like that car had it out for that tree."*

At the time, I'd thought it was just another weird Rhode Island expression, but now I wondered: Had she meant that the car had deliberately aimed for the tree? Could she tell that from her porch?

If you were depressed and going to kill yourself anyway, why not do it for cash? Especially if you had three children to provide for.

It was far-fetched, I knew, but most good stories were. I went ahead and typed the key words "insurance fraud" into the search engine. The computer revved up and stalled, making me realize that the category was too broad. I added "motor vehicle" and got half a dozen stories from the early nineties that involved the owner of Johnstown auto body shop taking a sledgehammer to several Lincoln Town Cars. He'd hoped to avoid any kind of rigorous insurance investigation by cutting a local insurance appraiser in on the deal. Caught by his boss, the appraiser flipped and began providing information to the police. Soon afterward, his body was found stuffed in the trunk of a Cadillac Seville.

I was reminded that Rhode Island was a tough place filled with tough people who didn't shy away from killing anyone who got in the way of making good money. I hit the end key and the screen dissolved. Did I really want to do this?

But the tension in my stomach felt as much like excitement as fear.

It was five thirty when I pulled into the parking space in front of my apartment. It was nearly dusk, and across the street Wayland Square was pretty much shut down. It's in a nice neighborhood in the city's East Side, and the shops all speak to affluence: the Books on the Square bookstore, a Starbucks, and some sort of designer dress shop that's way out of my league. A father and his young daughter headed into the pharmacy, but otherwise the wide sidewalks were empty. I considered walking over to the Your Corner Market to pick up a pasta salad for dinner, but decided to save my money. It would be grilled cheese and tomato soup for me.

I turned away from the square and peered in the other direction, across Elmgrove, a thoroughfare of small apartment buildings and renovated Victorian homes. Matt lived in a condo in my favorite Victorian, the one with the turret, about a half block down on the other side of the street. He was supposed to be back today. But then, how would I know for sure, since six and a half days had passed without a word?

I turned back to the entrance to my building. In a neighborhood of varied architecture, of Greek revival mansions and authentic Federalist homes, it was a featureless three-story brick building with reasonable rent and no particular charm. Who cared whether Matt was home or not? Who cared that I had to spend Sunday night alone? I was used to being alone. I was tough. Independent.

I marched through the lobby and up three floors, becoming determinedly more independent as I climbed. By the time I reached the first landing, I'd sworn off Matt, by the second landing, it was all men, and by my third-floor apartment door, it was people in general.

Inside, my apartment seemed especially lonely. I'd moved to Providence from Boston almost a year ago but hadn't exactly settled in. The one-bedroom apartment had good light and hardwood floors and could be a warm, cozy, welcoming abode, but only if someone else lived here. Someone who bought drapes for the picture window that looked out on Elmgrove and the square, someone who actually unpacked their boxes, finished the unfinished furniture, and knew how to arrange scatter rugs and pillows.

I like to pride myself in being low-fuss. I don't waste a lot of time on decorating or makeup or fashion, although at the urging of my friend Carolyn I now own a pair of three-inch high heels I never wear, and a Revlon lid duo in blue.

But I just can't see the point of those small square pillows with special trim. And scatter rugs cause accidents. I'd read that in a story in our paper's special section on senior health.

My idea of warming up a home was to leave the radio turned on all day, always on a talk-radio station. It fools me into thinking I'm not alone, that I have an unlimited number of experts and gurus living under the Formica and inside the cabinets.

At the moment, Joe D'Anzana, one of those squat, bellicose lawyers who run cheesy ads on daytime television, was offering his legal advice. People called in from all over the state with problems, ranging from getting ripped off by a car dealer to finding the best way to finagle an extension of their workmen's comp. Joe, who promoted himself as "the pit bull," had a deep bass with resonance—as if volume alone could win a lawsuit—and a real Rhode Island accent, hard on *a*'s, ignorant of *r*'s and full of extra *w*'s. His advice was always the same. "You gotta protect your rights, even if you gotta bite someone on the buttocks."

Now Ted from Johnstown was saying, "My wife bought a sofa from a real decent department store and the first night I fell asleep on it, I woke up with hives. I blew up like the Michelin guy and practically had to be rushed to the hospital, I looked so freaky."

"You were rushed to the hospital?" D'Anzana asked, trying to contain his excitement about the potential damages.

"I shoulda gone, but I wound up not going. My wife gave me a Benedryl which seemed to take care of it. But I coulda died, if we hadn't had the Benedryl in the house, I coulda died."

I headed for the refrigerator and peered in. A gallon of milk, a half bottle of white wine, a foil-wrapped block of cheddar cheese, and a bag that contained both heels of a loaf of rye bread. Too depressing for Sunday dinner. Maybe I should go for the Pop Tarts. Frosted Cinnamon. My arm froze midway as I reached for the cereal cabinet.

There was a Post-it note stuck on it.

Turn on your phone. I've been trying for two days.

I'll make you dinner if you come over.

Matt

"Your apartment door was unlocked, *again,*" Matt said, by way of a greeting. He was standing in the doorway of his condo with his arms folded across his chest. "And it wasn't too hard to get someone to let me in the lobby."

Matt is good-looking, but in an offhand way. In sweats, he is appealingly rumpled, and on weekends his hair, a quarter inch past his haircut, is never completely combed. He is tall enough to play center in his basketball league, but would be snapped in half on a football field. His nose has been broken at least twice in pickup games, and he would never consider having it fixed, even though the bend of his left nostril suggests a deviated septum that had to make any cold twice as bad.

"Sorry," I said.

He sighed and reached for me with a long arm. The kiss was warmer than usual, as if maybe he'd actually missed me. When he released me, his eyes held mine, searching for something. A response? What?

And then we heard the sizzle of water boiling over on the stove, and we both ran for the kitchen.

His kitchen, which was a good size, was in the back of the condo. He had the entire third floor of the Victorian, which was renovated so that the kitchen was almost brand-new, with light cabinets and Corian countertops and appliances that have all the latest gizmos. For instance, the boiling potato water was spilling onto one of those stovetops with invisible heating elements.

"Shit!" he said, turning off the heat and pushing the pot onto the counter.

He was making mashed potatoes and a roast, which I'm guessing was something his mother used to make on Sundays. I'm guessing this because it's something my mother used to make on Sundays, and because Matt and I share an intense love of mashed potatoes that must stem from these early roots.

Although he's been to Worcester with me twice to meet my mother, I haven't met his family yet. But I've learned a little, mostly in the newsroom. Before his retirement, Matt's father had been involved in ward politics in Providence, and his mother, who is half Italian, was a Pastore, distantly related to the state's first Italian governor. He's got five siblings who are all somehow connected to politics, and the two older brothers overshadow him, according to my friend Carolyn, who has analyzed Matt ad nauseum. I once asked Matt about meeting his family, but seeing the red alert light in his eyes, immediately backed off. I figure they will hate me anyway—for *something* the *Chronicle* has run.

Matt warmed the milk for the potatoes in the microwave before mashing, a nice touch I thought, and within minutes, we were digging in. Because his dining room table is always covered with law books and files, we ate in the kitchen, on a small butcher-block table shoved against the wall. He kept leaning over the table, as if he couldn't get close enough. He wanted to know if the roast beef was rare, if I'd been up to Worcester to see my mother, and then if I'd missed him while he was gone.

"Of course," I said, pleased at the question. I piled a second helping of potatoes onto my plate.

A few minutes of silent chewing passed, and then, in an offhand tone, he asked, "So why did you shut your phone off?"

I was about to tell him that I hadn't shut it off, had recharged it even, hoping for his call, but that the battery kept fading. His expression stopped me. His eyes, a dark, glittering shade of brown, gleamed with something. What was it, suspicion?

And then I realized what was going on. The competitive male ego was at work, fueling his imagination. This was why he was suddenly so attentive. Matt was concerned that in his extended, and I might add noncommunicative, absence, a rival had emerged. Why else had I shut off my phone for the entire weekend?

Maybe I should have soothed his fears. But maybe he shouldn't need a rival to be attentive. "It ran out of juice on Friday and I just forgot," I said, in a stiff way that was not particularly convincing.

"You forgot? For two days?" He made this sound like a curiosity, not an accusation. But I was on to him now.

I didn't tell him that the battery needed to be replaced. Or ask why he never called before the weekend. I merely shrugged. "Sorry." And then, as if I were a guilty party, changed the subject. "You wouldn't believe what happened to me Friday night."

I told him about the accident, about stumbling upon Lizette Salazar in a burning car, and about her husband's record of insurance fraud. "You ever heard of Manuel Salazar?" I asked.

As a prosecutor with the attorney general's office, Matt would never reveal anything involved in a current investigation, but if he shut me down abruptly, I'd guess I was in warm territory. But now his expression looked genuinely blank. The name wasn't ringing any bells. "Our office is too busy for small-time insurance fraud."

I didn't want to share my leads with the law enforcement community, so I didn't explain about the Providence cab company Walter had bought and the tip about Manuel. Instead, I stuck to the general topic. "Is there much of a problem with insurance fraud in Rhode Island?"

"Not like in Massachusetts or New York. There you've got the Russian mobs in the game." He explained that, unlike the other two states, Rhode Island did not mandate no-fault insurance, which meant that, in any car accident in this state, there had to be someone to blame. In a one-car collision like Lizette Salazar's, the family would have to prove that somebody ran her off the road. It would not be an easy claim.

So it really was the most unlikely of staged accidents, and maybe I would have let it go, but I kept hearing that old lady's voice in my head. *"Looked like that car had it out for that tree."*

Back when I was at the *Ledger,* researching the staged accident in Lawrence, a cop had told me that he considered suicide a possibility every time a car had to be scraped off a tree. If you *wanted* to do yourself in, and insurance fraud was practically a way of life in the family, anyway . . . "Maybe I should go to the funeral," I said, as the thought popped into my head.

Going to the funeral would give me a chance to meet the

family in an entirely suitable, entirely safe setting. I could establish a connection and get a lead on a potential source inside the insurance fraud underworld.

Matt must have seen the journalistic gears turning. "Why?"

It could be a powerful story, a tale of the desperation and the economic realities confronting the state's growing immigrant population. "Because I need the closure?" I tried.

He laughed aloud at my utter transparency, then, rising to clear the dishes from the table, he leaned over and kissed the top of my head with this new, surprising, affection. "Closure. Yeah, right."

The *Ledger* in Boston employed a lot of photographers, and in the early years when I worked there, I seemed to go out with every one of them. As a rule, this breed of male was uniformly commitment-phobic, and I'd learned that the fastest way to freak one out was to leave a hairbrush or a Chap Stick behind in the bathroom. So I never showed up at Matt's with an overnight bag filled with cosmetics and a blow-dryer. Instead, I brought a gym bag full of my running clothes, so I could head straight to the boulevard in the morning. After my run, I went back to my own apartment to shower and change.

I thought it was the best thing about living across the street. I mean, how convenient could I possibly be? But for some reason, this arrangement seemed to bother Matt the next morning.

It was still dark, and he'd just turned over to find me sitting on the edge of the bed, pulling on my running shorts. He sat up on his elbows and frowned at me. "Don't you ever just say screw it and go back to sleep?"

This was a man who clearly didn't understand compulsive behavior. I shook my head.

"God," he said, falling back into the pillows again. "You are so disciplined."

Since I wasn't about to explain the difference between compulsion and discipline at six in the morning, I just pulled on my socks and shrugged.

"Sometimes it seems like you just can't get out of here fast enough." He was back up on his elbows again, fully awake.

I turned to him, a little surprised. Didn't he realize that the proper response to men who assert their independence was to guard independence in return? "I run for mental health reasons," I said. "It keeps me sane."

He reached forward to pull me toward him. "So come back afterward," he said. I allowed myself to relax into the warmth of his arms, to feel his body tucked into mine, and his lips nuzzling my neck. His lips were his best feature, generous and gentle. They had done good work last night.

The memory produced a pleasant tingling that began to travel down my spine, and for a moment I imagined myself coming back here after my run, jumping into the shower with him, upending his morning commute, but then reality intervened. "It'll be seven o'clock by then, and you'll hold it against me for making you late for work."

"No, I won't," he said.

"Yes, you will."

He sighed and took another tack. "See me Wednesday night then?"

This was new, this urgency. Usually he just said, "See you soon." How soon was anybody's guess. "If you're not busy," he added.

Okay, I admit it. There is some evil in me. Some part of me that seized this first sign of any leverage and chose to capitalize on it. I pulled just slightly away from him, establishing the distance one needs for extortion. "Can we go out somewhere and *do* something for a change?"

Now it was his turn to look at me with surprise. He had not realized this was an issue with me. That I'd noticed that we only got together at his place or at mine. That we ordered takeout, rented movies, watched college basketball, or played crazy eights, but that we never ever went *out* to a restaurant or a movie or to a show of any kind. The truth was, I hadn't realized it was that much of an issue with me until now, when I'd found myself wielding just the tiniest bit of power.

"Where do you want to go?" he asked, in a tone that suggested that it was no big deal. He'd just never thought of it before.

"I don't care. We don't have to go anywhere expensive." As if I didn't know full well that his real concern wasn't money, but being seen with a *Chronicle* reporter. That he didn't want anybody in the AG's office to worry he might be a source of a leak.

"Hey, how about we really go out on the town? I have a friend who can get us a reservation at L'Espalier," he offered.

L'Espalier was expensive. It was romantic. It was Boston.

I didn't want him to see my face, so I leaned over the bed to grab the running shoes from my bag. I realized that I might be a career liability, and that going out with a *Chronicle* reporter might raise eyebrows in his office. But I couldn't help thinking that our relationship would never have a real chance until it was out in the open. And it bothered me that in Providence, where cheating politicians brandished their mistresses all over town, Matt wasn't willing to risk being seen with me.

I sat up with both shoes in my hands. "I've lived in Providence almost a year and I've never seen a play at Trinity, gone to a concert at PPAC, or eaten at Al Forno."

There was a hint of guilt in his expression. After four erratic months of hiding in our apartments, maybe he was wondering why it had taken me so long to complain. "Okay. Okay, Al Forno for dinner," he said, looking sheepish, "but can we go early before the crowds get there?"

Before anyone he knew was likely to see us? He was a man with ambition, I cut him a break. "Yeah, early is good."

Blackstone Boulevard was a couple-miles-long strip of stately homes with a wide, landscaped mall between the two lanes of traffic. It was a swath of green through the rich part of the city, clipped and trimmed on a regular basis. Because of all the rain, the lawn was unusually lush and green. Today, the mist didn't bother me. Instead, the smell of the sweet, wet grass gave me momentum. I raced along the cinder path, underneath the budding oaks and elms, building up speed.

The boulevard was a popular spot. And even though it was both early and damp, a decent crowd of runners was already out of bed, women in packs together, men alone, taking the path at their own varying paces. I caught up to two women runners in their forties, who were weighed down by water bottles attached to their hips. Ahead of them was a man in Lycra who I saw every morning. He was the kind of guy I'd thought existed only on television and in magazines, tall, with strong, even features and that perfectly cultivated shadow that never materialized into a beard. His aerodynamic running garb outlined every muscle in his legs and backside, and I held my breath in sheer awe every time he passed by. I'd never exchanged a word with him, but in my head I'd named him Mr. Nike. No matter how fast I ran, he ran faster.

Guys like Mr. Nike went out with statuesque Swedish models and never looked twice at women like me, with girlish freckles and boyish frames. Not to mention my T-shirt and running tights didn't match.

As I settled into an even pace, my attention drifted from Mr. Nike's fabulous glutes to more practical matters—the achy feeling developing in both knees. My running shoes were way beyond their road mileage, worn down on the outer soles and frayed at the laces. To save money, I kept putting off buying new ones.

A quick calculation of the debt I still owed Walter led to worry about my job and the possible newspaper merger. The West Coast chain whispered to be the likely acquirer of the *Chronicle* was big on improving "efficiencies," notorious for slashing the news staff. As one of the last hires at the paper, I was vulnerable.

The path came to an end, and Mr. Nike turned around. Without even nodding an acknowledgment of my existence, he set off in a sprint, kicking up the cinders. I smiled as if I didn't care, but last week, the thought of Mr. Nike had inspired me to sign up for a free four-week speed clinic offered by one of the running clubs at the Brown University running track. I was going to beat that guy's running time if it killed me.

4

St. Michael's was in South Providence, a poorer section of the city where much of the growing Hispanic population of the state lived. The exterior was an industrial red brick with a front door in need of paint. But inside, the church was an imposing Gothic revival structure, a cathedral of mahogany and marble, with lofty arcades that separated the main part of the church into three sections and offered two side aisles of egress.

Nonetheless, the mob of mourners clogged the center aisle after the funeral mass. They formed a single line to go through the small lobby, where the Salazar family members had stopped and created an ad hoc receiving line.

As I stood waiting in the pew, I felt as if the entire parish was checking me out. I was dressed appropriately in black pants and muted blue top, and had yet to whip out a notebook, but I suspected that I had "reporter" written all over me. Clearly, I stuck out in a crowd of mostly Latin-based ethnicities.

I was a good thirty feet from the altar, but I still felt overpowered by flowers. Dozens of standing arrangements on either end of the communion rail produced the thick, sorrowful scent of lily and gladiola. Finally, my pew began to empty, and I began to make my way into the center aisle, where I could now see the grieving family in the vestibule. The two sisters, their husbands, and a woman the right age to be Lizette's mother stood together near what looked like a side altar to the Virgin Mary. Clustered around the font of holy water were a teenage boy about seventeen years old, and a man I picked out as Manuel Salazar standing between two identical ten-year-old boys.

Manuel was a large, thickset man, but oddly bookish, with studious wire-rimmed glasses and a tweedy gray sports coat. He had an arm around one of the twins, who wore the stunned expression of a child who wouldn't be able to comprehend the finality of death for some time. The seventeen-year-old son was several inches shorter than his father and stooped, with his forehead tilted to the floor as if he couldn't bring himself to meet anyone's eyes and hear how sorry they were about his mother.

The line moved slowly, and I wondered if I should have ducked out after communion. I was incredibly late for work and hadn't been able to pick up enough useful information to justify my absence. Although women all around me bent their heads together and whispered in knowing tones, the few years of Spanish I'd had in high school and college had not given me the necessary language skills to eavesdrop. I barely could follow the mass, and I knew that by heart.

When a woman I guessed to be Lizette's sister had given the eulogy, I had caught the word *triste*. But I couldn't tell if she was saying Lizette's life had been sad, or life was going to be sad without Lizette. And now, as I stood among friends and neighbors red-eyed with grief, I felt like an intruder.

As the line wound its way into the lobby, I spotted three men standing together at the end of one of the side aisles, watching as the line progressed toward the vestibule. Two of them were large and imposing, and the third one was shorter and had an ugly purple burn that started just under his cheekbone and continued down his neck into his shirt collar. You wanted to wince and turn away.

They were Italian, not Latino. I'm not sure how I could tell, except that they held themselves apart from the crowd, and you could feel a line drawn around them. As people filed past them on their way into the lobby, several nodded respectfully at the man with the burn. The men, in particular, acknowledged him with an air of deference usually reserved for the priest. I'd realized then, that the man must be Tito Manaforte.

Of course. The burn was famous, mentioned every time Tito's name was in newsprint. There were conflicting stories about the burn, but the more enduring was that he had gotten it while in elementary school and still sloppy about the use of accelerants. He had caught his own collar alight while trying to set fire to a schoolmate. The child in question had tried to steal Tito's lunch money.

The three men exuded a contained testosterone, a feral energy. Tito had large, unblinking eyes, and he did not appear to worry whether it was rude to stare. I felt his gaze stake me out as an outsider, follow me as I inched forward in the line of mourners reaching the receiving line. I had the same wary feeling I get as I approach unleashed dogs.

At last, it was my turn to offer my hand and sympathies to Manuel Salazar. Using my limited Spanish, I was able to come up with this. "Te acompano en tu sentimento," I am sorry for your loss. He looked up quizzically, examining my Celtic coloring and foreign face as he accepted my hand. But when I introduced myself, the light changed in his eye. He turned to the teenage son and said, "She was the one who found your mother in the car."

Manuel said something more complicated in Spanish that I couldn't translate and instantly the receiving line closed in around me, and I was surrounded by the family. The woman who had given the eulogy put her arm on mine. She looked a few years younger than Lizette, but had the same birdlike frame. Her mascara had run, so that she had black splotches under her eyes, and she gazed at me with such gratitude that it was embarrassing, as if I were a saint who'd stepped down from one of the statues.

"I am so happy you come," she said, hugging me with force. "So happy you . . ." She pulled away and tears filled her eyes. "So happy you take the time."

I was acutely aware of everyone in the church staring at me, including Tito and his circle of cohorts. The sister, who introduced herself as Marcella Lopez, was pulled away by a man I guessed to be her husband, but she asked him to give her a minute and stepped closer to me. "I have to go. Find the car for the cemetery," she explained. And then, lowering her voice so only I could hear, she added, "But I must thank you again, some other time."

I looked up to see Tito watching the exchange. His gaze followed Marcella as she walked out of the church, and shifted back to me.

"Did she say anything, my mother. Was she awake?" asked the seventeen-year-old, walking toward me with a decided limp.

There was so much hope in his tone that I felt the real loss of this poor woman's life. She was a person, not just a story. A mother who left behind three young sons. I shook my head sadly.

His eyes looked so disappointed that I didn't want to tell him that by the time I got there, she was already dead. Instead, I heard myself elaborating. "I don't think she suffered. She didn't seem to be in any pain."

He thought about this, as if he were trying to picture his mother in peace. Then he looked at me directly in the eye to nod his thanks. Like I'd actually given him something.

A man from the funeral parlor announced that the car to the cemetery was ready. Manuel told his sons to go ahead and tell the driver to wait for him. He turned to me, with a more businesslike tone. "The cops say you did not see any other cars, is this true?" he asked.

I nodded.

"It is no matter," Manuel said, as if to forgive me for this omission. "The old lady saw everything."

"The old lady who called 911?"

"She see the headlights. She see the other car coming over the hill, toward my wife . . ." He shuddered at the image, as if unable to speak, but when I met his eyes, I did not see horror in them.

The same old lady who had implied that Lizette's car was actually aiming for the tree? She'd said nothing about another car forcing her off the road. And no mention of this in the police report the next day.

Manuel saw my surprise. "The old lady is confused first day because of medicine she takes," he explained. "Yesterday, she remember everything and call the police."

Two days after the accident, and suddenly the required witness remembers seeing another car? I tried not to let suspicion into my eyes. "So could she give police a decent identification of the other car, then?"

Was it my imagination or did Manuel glance over at Tito Manaforte before he answered. "Too dark that time of night," he said, shaking his head. "She see only the headlights. But now the police believe me when I tell them, my Lizette, she does not drive this way. She does not drive herself into trees."

5

The intersection looked completely different in the day. The road seemed wider, the trees farther apart. At night it had been a cavern, but in daylight it seemed like an innocent country road, a good place for a lemonade stand.

West Kent was not exactly on the way back to the newsroom. A ten-minute detour, I'd told myself, but it was really more like twenty, and not a prudent move, given how late it was getting. But I wanted to talk to the old lady myself. See what her story was today.

I parked my car right near where Lizette had hit the tree and walked back toward the old lady's house, which was across the intersection and up a slight slope. The garage, which was actually an old barn, listed badly, with wormy clapboards that looked like they were going to fall right into the road. But the farmhouse, which sat behind the garage and angled toward the intersection, was in better repair. The old lady had two clay pots of yellow pansies on either side of the porch stairs. In a neat pile in the far corner were carpentry tools, a coiling of extension cords, and an empty takeout coffee cup. It looked as if a construction crew had just left for the day.

The windows were open and there was an Oldsmobile parked on the road, so I gathered the old lady was home. I climbed up to the porch and knocked on the door.

She appeared wearing the same bathrobe that I'd seen her in the night of the accident. She must have thrown the long black wig on when she heard me knocking on the door because it was slightly askew. "You want something?"

I identified myself as a *Chronicle* reporter and told her I'd like to ask her a few questions about the fatal car accident.

Despite her disheveled appearance, the old woman had not been sleeping. And she didn't seem medicated, either. She was alert enough to recognize me immediately. "What do you need me for? You were there."

"I wanted to ask you about the car you saw. Before I got there. The one you told police about."

She began to shut the door.

"Please," I shouted. "Please, it's important."

"Important to you maybe. Not to me." But she didn't slam the door; instead, she reopened it, seizing the opportunity to scold me. "All you reporters do is try to ruin people's lives. Poor Billy, after all he did for the city, in prison. And the likes of you breaking that poor man's heart, destroying his life by turning him into some kind of criminal—day after day."

She was talking about the former mayor of Providence, Billy Lopresti. The corruption in his administration had provided Jonathan Frizell with many a front-page byline. He'd covered the federal probe as well as the jury trial that had sent the mayor to prison for extortion. It drove nearly everyone in the media crazy that Billy remained a favorite with many Rhode Islanders—especially women of a certain age.

"I have nothing to do with any of those stories." On impulse, I added, "And I don't like the guy who writes them much either."

"Really?" She pulled the door back, and I caught a glimpse of three or four cats lying on floors and armchairs.

"He's very condescending," I said in all honesty.

Despite the raw wind, she did not invite me inside, but stepped out onto the porch, tightening the belt of her bathrobe. "Terrible that poor woman died." Her eyes met mine. I saw real sadness in them.

"I just came from the funeral."

"Three motherless boys."

I nodded solemnly. There would be nothing to gain by challenging her story right away. She'd only become defensive and kick me out. I had to pretend to believe her.

"You see the accident from up there?" I pointed toward the far end of the porch.

"That's right."

I took a couple of steps in that direction, glanced back to make sure she didn't think I was trespassing. But she had no problem with me wanting to see for myself.

"Those bright headlights, you can see 'em good from up here." She let the door slam behind her and followed me to the edge of the porch, pointing in the direction of the accident site. She had a decent view between the scrub and trees.

"I saw a car come down from thataway." She pointed toward the woods. "Veering this way and that. Right at that poor woman in the car," she said.

She looked straight into my eyes as she said this, as if completely unaware she'd told me something different that night. "And then I heard that crash. That crash was just awful." She put her hands to her ears. "This way and that. That car was weaving. Poor woman was left with no choice but to run off the damn road."

I pulled my notebook out of my purse and flipped open a page. "All right if I use this in the paper?"

"Anna Theresa Plummer," she said. "Not like the guy who fixes your sink, either." She spelled out Plummer for me. "You're not going to take my picture, now, are you?" She touched her wig. "I don't want no picture of me in my damn bathrobe in the *Chronicle*."

I tried to reassure her by showing her that I didn't have a camera with me, but I'd missed her meaning.

"Because I'd have to change my clothes and fix my hair if you were going to take a picture," she continued. "And that would take me an hour or so. You going to come back in an hour or so?"

Anna Theresa Plummer had made a complete conversion. In fact, I was getting the impression that I'd get better information out of her if I promised her the front page. "It's getting kind of late. Why don't we talk now, and I'll send the photographer back when you're dressed?" I asked.

"What time?" she asked.

"I'll send someone in the afternoon." I started wracking my brain for a photographer who owed me a favor. "Or maybe tomorrow. Sometimes it takes awhile for the assignment to be processed."

The wind began kicking up. I had to hold each page of my notebook down, but the old woman seemed not to mind. She tugged on a strand of hair, as if to keep her wig in place, and gestured for me to take a seat in the plastic molded chair. She took the wicker settee.

"You remember anything else?" I wanted her to keep talking because the more lies she made up, the easier it would be to catch her in one of them later, in print.

"Like I told you, I saw mostly just lights, but let me see . . ." She closed her eyes, as if trying to conjure the memory. "I was sitting here on the porch, and I think maybe the car was a pretty big one because the engine was so damn loud. Maybe a Caddy with the muffler gone." She screwed her eyes even tighter as if this would help her elaborate, and then opened them in excitement. "Oh yes, now I remember. There was some kind of flashy hood ornament or such. And the driver didn't stop or nothing to see if anyone had been hurt. And one of its back taillights was out, I could see that when it took off. Just kept going in that direction." She pointed to where the road continued beyond the accident site.

She was watching carefully as I took all this down, which I did diligently.

"If you ask me, they oughta go after the driver of that car. Lock him up in jail and throw away the key. Poor woman. Mother of three boys." The sadness of this struck her, and she looked off. "I had three boys myself. All grown and gone now, though."

I let a moment of silence pass. And then: "Mrs. Plummer, the night of the accident you told me that it looked like the Salazar woman's car was actually aiming for the tree."

She did not miss a beat. "I never said such a thing."

"You said that it looked like the car had it out for the tree."

She hesitated only a second. "That's just an expression."

"That means?"

"That means?" She seemed confused at first, but quickly recovered. "It means the car was going real fast—had to swerve real fast to get out of the way of that oncoming car."

"Did it hit the tree twice?"

She blinked. "Why?"

"You said that night that it hit the tree twice."

"Oh," she looked confused again. "I gotta think back. Maybe it did. Maybe it did hit that tree twice. Kinda a richochet effect."

"Did you tell that to police?" I asked.

She sighed with exasperation. "I told most everything to that Officer Harrington, on Sunday, but he doesn't listen so good. He's one of those people who's always in a damn rush. Doesn't seem at all interested in helping that poor man. Don't know which end is up. So broken up about his wife."

I lifted my head from the notebook. "You met Lizette Salazar's husband?"

She looked startled for a moment. Caught herself. Swallowed. "No. No. Not really." And then, "Well, just once. He came the day after the accident, with a lawyer, to take pictures of the area. You know, the tree she smashed into. I walked over to give him my condolences."

I didn't want to unnerve her by writing this down, but I was memorizing it all for the moment I got back in my car. Manuel Salazar stakes out the territory for an insurance claim *the day after* his wife died.

"Did you get the name of the lawyer?" I asked casually.

"Let me see, what was it again? That guy everyone knows. Tip of my tongue. Oh you know who I mean, that guy you hear on the radio. The one who thinks he's some kind of dog."

The state's number-one ambulance chaser and Sunday afternoon talk show host. The pit bull. No editor would question the likelihood of a bribe coming from this corner. "Joe D'Anzana?" I asked helpfully.

"That's right," she answered. "That's his name."

It was just after noon when I got back to the newsroom. I'd left a message this morning on Dorothy's voice mail that I was going to be late, but I hadn't meant *this* late.

"Was it the pope's funeral or what?" Dorothy asked, as I walked over to the city desk to explain.

Electrified by the bits of information I could now string together, I practically glowed, but Dorothy Sacks, city editor, didn't notice. Sitting in front of her computer, with her legs crossed and revealing one sockless foot in a Birkenstock sandal, she'd already shifted her attention back to her computer screen.

"Yesterday's fatal," I said by way of explanation. I was not referring to when it happened, but when it ran in the paper.

"Oh, that's right, West Kent," she said, as she continued to frown at the screen. In her midforties, Dorothy was from the Berkshires in an obvious way—serious, earthy, and opposed to makeup and fashion as part of her personal politics. She was single and childless and never talked about her personal life, which led to all sorts of outrageous gossip that she never, ever, acknowledged.

I was bursting with information, desperate to line up Dorothy's support, which I'd need to convince the team that this story was worthy of investigative team attention. We were to decide a new subject for a series today, and everyone would be pushing his own idea. Although the other four members of the team were more secure in their jobs than I was, everyone worried that the merger would mean a cutback in the team. We were all keenly aware of the need to strut our stuff.

"I got a great story here. You remember that grandmother who died in the staged accident a few years back in Lawrence?" I asked.

"Lawrence?" She looked up from her computer screen, blinking. "What happened to that tip you were working on about the state-backed mortgage loans?"

"Source wimped out on me. Said the loan in question went through the proper channels, after all, but this fatal . . ."

She waved me off. Her gaze had shifted past me, and I turned and saw Marcy, the state editor in charge of regional news, returning from lunch. "You better get ahold of Stepenhauser and make sure he can cover that historical preservation conference," Dorothy called across the room. "It's getting national attention."

Marching to the desk, Marcy would have mowed me down if I hadn't moved. "You have got to be kidding me," she said. "I need him in Newport for the Holstein trial."

"Corey, then?" Dorothy said.

"I've got three bureau reporters out on maternity leave, Arlan in chemo, and you want me to cover a historical preservation conference? Forget it. Have Lifestyle do it." Marcy walked off in a huff, without giving Dorothy a chance to argue.

Dorothy looked at me then, but it was only so that I would acknowledge Marcy's rude behavior. Accordingly, I rolled my eyes. And since I had her attention, tried again. "This fatal in West Kent—"

"But no teenagers were involved, right? And no drinking?"

"No, but—"

Dorothy had already picked up the phone, presumably to call the Lifestyle editor. "Save it for the meeting."

"You're definitely coming?" I asked. Although Dorothy was the editorial liaison and mentor to the investigative team, she'd been missing a lot of our meetings because of the staffing problems. Although technically we voted among ourselves to decide our next big project, her support always swayed the outcome.

"Of course," Dorothy said, as if she hadn't missed the last three meetings, allowing Jonathan Frizell to rule the roost. And then, "Jonathan's got a good lead on another no-show political appointment."

This wasn't good news.

Dorothy had already shifted her attention to her phone call. "You gotta help me out, Terrence, please, I'm begging you. I'm completely out of staff."

I grabbed a legal pad and headed into the Fishbowl, where all but the most top-secret meetings with editors were held. On slow days, reporters watched from their desks to see who got called into the Fishbowl, carefully reading the hand gestures between editors and reporters. Last month, after one of the staff artists was reamed out by the managing editor in the Fishbowl, he'd retaliated by drawing oversized and colorful tropical fish that he pasted at different heights on the outside of the glass walls. No one had taken them down yet.

Inside the Fishbowl, Bennett Castiglia, our computer database expert, sat at the far end of the conference table, licking his thumb as he read through a file. He was skinny, with pimples on his forehead and chin, and he always carried a laptop. He looked about fifteen years old, but was actually in his midtwenties and incredibly diligent. He was more thoughtful than the typical shoot-from-the-hip reporter, and we'd formed an unspoken alliance.

He sat with Ryan Skendarian, who also looked underage but was thirty years old and had already won a Pulitzer. Unlike most reporters, Ryan didn't shout his every opinion at the top of his lungs, so he was difficult to read.

To their right was Jonathan Frizell, who nodded a silent greeting, and to Bennett's left sat Ellen Felty, the only other woman on the investigative team. In her late forties, she was very fair, with thick blond hair that hadn't aged and a smooth forehead. She was married to one of the editorial writers, but didn't wield it as a source of power. She tended to be brisk. "I've got a phone interview at one o'clock that I can't miss," she said, glancing at Dorothy, who was just walking into the room. "Can we get started?"

Dorothy took a seat at the table, and several reporters announced they had hot new tips. Ellen had a source inside the state Department of Public Works who thought there had been contract award favoritism in a sewer expansion project; Bennett wanted to evaluate the data on child custody awards in Family Court for discrimination against fathers; and Jonathan, as expected, had a tip about a no-show appointment of the governor.

"Call me crazy, but just for once, I think we should write about something other than political corruption," Bennett commented.

Dorothy dispensed with Ellen's tip by announcing it was already under investigation by a city reporter and said *Parade* had recently done something too similar to Bennett's idea.

"I've got something," I said.

But she held up a hand. "Let's hear Jonathan out first."

Jonathan, in his late thirties, was short and barrel-chested. He was the product of too much elite education, from prep school on through to his graduate degrees. Originally, I'd assumed this meant he came from old Yankee money, but I'd been corrected. Frizell was what was known as swamp Yankee, a rural descendant of the early settlers in Connecticut and Rhode Island who never quite made it. As it turned out, Frizell's father had been a drinker, and Jonathan had to fend for himself with financial aid and scholarships. Maybe that would have impressed me, if that had made him more a man of the people. Instead, he seemed to deliberately cultivate an air of disinterest.

"It's simple," he said, as if this might be the only way we'd understand it.

But in fact, it was. The plan called for eight to ten hours a day of reporter surveillance of Albert Riordan, who had been a hefty contributor to the governor's campaign fund, as he went about his new job as the state's director of business regulation. Apparently, Riordan spent all day lunching, shopping, or gambling at the dog track. All the investigative team needed to do was take turns hanging out in cars and alleys to record Riordan's every movement, so that we could document his day-to-day avoidance of anything having to do with work.

"You're kidding us, right?" Bennett asked.

Frizell appeared not to have heard his question. "My source says that Riordan hasn't been in the office more than four hours a week since the day he was appointed." Jonathan had a tendency to pause with this infuriating little half smile on his face. It was as if we all needed time to grasp the import of what he'd just said. Ellen and I exchanged a look, waiting for him to continue. "It would take us, what? Two weeks' worth of surveillance to verify this story? It would prove all that bullshit about cleaning up state government was all just for the cameras."

Although demanding of man-hours, it was a decent story, and as Jonathan had pointed out, simple to execute. Compared to other investigative projects, which are all labor-intensive, this was a big bang for our newspaper's buck. If it wasn't yet another story of Jonathan's, we all might be agreeing to do it.

"What's Hallie's idea?" Ellen asked.

I started by explaining the fatal accident that I'd stumbled upon on my way home Friday night. I told them about the husband's history of insurance fraud, and about the little old lady who changed her story, remembering new details two days after the accident. "After meeting with Joe D'Anzana."

There was a universal groan at this mention of the personal injury lawyer's name, but no one seemed bowled over by the story idea.

"I don't get it." Bennett asked, "Why do they need to make up another car?"

I explained how Rhode Islands no-fault insurance worked. "Someone else has to be at fault to make the big claim. It doesn't matter if they can ever *find* that someone else, they can still claim against the portion of the insurance for uninsured motorists. But they need a witness to testify about the imaginary car."

"So okay. Say this is all true. Big deal. Some guy is trying to get the big payout on his wife's accident. It's a daily story. Why do we care?" Jonathan asked.

"Because it isn't just this one guy. According to my sources, there's a ring operating in Providence. It's like a way of life, a living, for a whole underworld of people. And it exploits immigrants."

Dorothy looked up with new interest. Immigration was a

major issue in Rhode Island. In the country's smallest state, the Hispanic population had doubled in the last decade. And despite the city's much touted renaissance, the Hispanic community was poorer here than anywhere else in the country.

"And if this woman was so desperate for money that she sacrificed herself on the altar of an insurance claim, isn't this the ultimate story of a staged accident? Doesn't this encapsulate the financial desperation of the immigrant population in one killer lead?"

"If you could prove it," Dorothy said, in a tone that suggested the difficulty in that premise. And then, "By the way, do we know if this woman was a legal immigrant?"

"She was," I said. "Her family came here from New York. But you've got to believe it's a lot of undocumented workers who are willing to slam themselves into another car for a couple hundred bucks."

There was a long pause as the team seemed to weigh the news value of the always contentious immigration issue. "What makes you think that the people at the funeral are the same ones involved in this staged accident ring?" Ellen finally asked.

"The husband works at the Big T Body Shop." And then, after pausing the way Frizell always did, for impact, I let it drop. "And Tito Manaforte was at the funeral."

At the mention of Tito Manaforte, all eyes lifted to mine.

"Christ," Dorothy said. "How long has he been out of jail?"

"Three weeks." Bennett knew everything.

"Did you see that ugly burn on his neck?" Ryan asked.

I nodded.

The four other reporters began a lively debate about how exactly Tito Manaforte had gotten that burn. Ellen had heard about a fight with battery acid. Ryan believed that Tito had been caught in one of his father's buildings that had been torched. Bennett said he'd seen a piece on a Web site that insisted that Tito's burn had been self-inflicted.

Dorothy interrupted. "So you're saying that Tito Manaforte is somehow involved in yesterday's fatal?"

"He *owns* an auto body shop," Bennett pointed out. In Rhode Island, "auto body shop" was practically synonymous with fraud and corruption.

"*Somebody* bribed that old lady," I said.

"The cops are saying there was a bribe?" Dorothy asked.

"Well, not yet, but—"

"Have they said the accident was at all suspicious?" Ellen asked.

"I haven't talked to the cops yet," I had to admit.

"You're basically talking about a hunch, then," Jonathan said.

"Hey, Tito Manaforte is involved," Bennett said. "That's enough for me. Shall we vote?" He raised his hand for my story idea. I shot him a look of gratitude.

But Dorothy was shaking her head. "Tito makes it more interesting, but he also makes it more dangerous. There might be something in this predatory car ring, but it'll take more resources than we have right now to investigate. This Riordan thing is timely. A hell of a lot easier to research."

Bennett lowered his hand and sighed in resignation to another Frizell-run project. The other reporters stared out the glass wall, between the more brightly colored fish cutouts, as if searching the newsroom for an escape. Ellen opened her mouth, but shut it without saying anything.

"Just give me a couple of days to run this down," I begged. "To see if I can find an inside source on this insurance ring. If it's too complicated, I'll give up."

Dorothy pursed her lips, looking stern in thought. But this was her usual expression when she was wrestling with herself about what was fair. She was trying to come up with a compromise.

"Since we're short-staffed in the bureaus anyway, Hallie, you can do the follow on the West Kent fatal for daily," she said. "If the cops come up with any kind of tie to Tito Manaforte, then we can talk about doing a larger investigative piece for sometime later." And then, so as not to offer any false encouragement, she added, "But right now, leave that investigation to police. I want all our energy, all our effort, concentrated on Jonathan's story."

6

"But you don't have any *real* evidence to prove this old lady is lying or that she has a reason to make this up?" Officer Harrington said.

We were at the West Kent police station, the next day, in a gray-looking back office with a wooden table and a computer terminal. I was sitting at the table, opposite Harrington who had grabbed a chair and sat on it backwards.

"I don't have surveillance tape of her *taking* the bribe, if that's what you mean."

His eyes met mine to convey that he didn't find this comment amusing. In the daylight, I realized he was older than he'd looked under the streetlights, probably early forties, with that same weary air of exhaustion.

He was stubbornly unimpressed by Manuel Salazar's criminal history or his employment at the Big T Auto Body Shop.

"That doesn't change the fact that the man lost his wife," he said.

"I know, but don't you think it's weird the old lady switched her story? That she only remembered seeing another car—after she met with Salazar and his lawyer. Joe D'Anzana, by the way."

He sighed. For about the third time. "Look, maybe if you had told me what she said that night, I coulda confirmed some of this."

Like it was my fault? "I *told* you to go talk to her."

"You ran off as fast as you could."

"But I *told* you to talk to her."

He shook his head, unwilling to yield. I could challenge his honesty, but we both knew that wasn't going to help me.

"Look, my little department just lost two officers," he finally said. "The rest of us are working double shifts. If you bring me proof that she's lying, that the husband and his lawyer bribed her, I'll listen to you, but otherwise I'm going to leave it to the insurance companies. It's their money at stake, let *them* pay for the forensic investigation."

According to his Web site, Lester Wilson was a mechanical engineer with a degree from Worcester Polytechnic and a specialist in "accident reconstruction" who had consulted for several major insurance companies, as well as for personal injury lawyers. In other words, he played both sides of the fence. And not just in Rhode Island; apparently his expertise was sought nationwide. He cited several cases in New Jersey and California, but the most interesting thing about him was his list of published papers on various reconstruction topics. One of them was titled: "The Effect of Driver Performance on Accident Avoidance."

I didn't know if that meant he could tell whether a driver deliberately drove herself into a tree or not, but I figured that calling an industry expert might be worth a shot.

I did this from my newly purchased cell phone the next morning as I sat in my car on Richmond Street. I was doing my surveillance duty on Frizell's story, waiting for the state's new business regulation head to skip out of his office. Like a good doobie, I'd arrived early enough to notice that Riordan did not show up for work until 9:15. A real scandal.

Like the radio, the heater in the car was faulty. After fifteen minutes of the Sahara, I'd turned it off, and was now so completely frozen the Sahara was looking good again.

Anyway, I figured that now that he'd arrived at the office, Albert Riordan would at least stay for coffee, so I dialed Lester Wilson's office from the car. Experts like Lester were more willing to talk generally about the science of their work, which was always good for business, than to offer their expertise for free on specific cases. So I told him I was doing a story about the growing problem of accident fraud and needed a "backgrounder" on automobile crash reconstruction. He'd had another appointment cancel on him that afternoon and said he could give me an hour. "This for the Sunday paper?" he asked.

"Yes." This was not a lie. If I actually ever got this story off the ground, it would start on a Sunday. We agreed on two o'clock, and Lester Wilson didn't object when I suggested we meet at the impound lot in East Providence, which was one of the largest impound lots in the state. It was also where Lizette's wreck had been towed.

"Oh yeah," Lester said, gaining enthusiasm, "they've got some really cool destruction down there. This could be fun," he said. "You pick out the car, and I'll tell you if I can figure out what happened to it."

"Okay," I said, trying not to reveal elation. This was a gift from God, and if I were still a practicing Catholic, I might have made the sign of a cross—right there at the steering wheel. Instead, I snapped my phone shut and silently prayed that Lester was every bit of the miracle man described on his Web site. That maybe he could gaze into Lizette Salazar's car wreck today and know what had happened last weekend.

On the sidewalk, two women in business suits split to get around a homeless man who was asking for spare change. I decided to get out of the car and stretch, take a walk up and down the street just to circulate the blood. Watched pots never boil and watched doorways never open. Contrary to reports, Riordan appeared to be working a full morning.

Back in my car, the rest of the morning passed tediously, and it seemed like forever until Ellen Felty pulled up behind me in her canary yellow Miata to relieve my surveillance duties at one o'clock.

"Not exactly incognito," I said.

"We're not CIA for god's sake."

I suggested that she park in the garage, and stay nearby on foot. She made a face, before finally shrugging her assent. I thought I might have been picking up on a lack of support for Frizell's project, which improved my mood considerably.

"Riordan hasn't even left for lunch yet," I told her.

"Some exposé," she said, as she pulled away from the curb.

The impound lot was in an industrial section of East Providence, on a road marked as a dead end, but with no clear end in sight. I drove through an outer gate and an eight-foot-tall fence of chain link and barbed wire into what looked like a visitors' parking lot. Lester was waiting for me outside the office, carrying a folder.

He was a small, sinewy man, in his late forties, with faded red hair, and a pale, almost invisible mustache. He wore a salesman's suit and a pair of silver aviator glasses.

I got out of my car and we exchanged greetings. Lester pulled out a résumé and brochure from his folder, and I stuffed it into my backpack. He wanted to begin by showing me one of his "test cars," so I let him lead the way.

We passed through a second gate—this time the fencing was at least ten feet tall and looked electrified—into the main part of the yard, and I had to stop and catch my breath. There were acres of car wrecks, organized in neat but endless rows, with numbered signs. Like a state fair, only all drivers had been rip-roaring drunk.

"How many *are* there?" I asked, trying not to sound dejected as I followed Lester down a row of smashed windshields, missing doors, and crinkled bodies pulled away from flattened tires.

"I don't know, maybe a thousand. Sad bunch, aren't they?" Lester said, stepping over a crumpled piece of metal that had once been a car door, and headed toward the back row. The asphalt was all broken or pitted with little wells of yesterday's rain trapped in the cracks.

Wilson was a fast talker, trying to educate me about both the history and science of automotive forensics in five minutes flat. I followed behind him, struggling to keep up, making notations about tires and road surfaces. But my eyes were scanning the rows of amputated cars, knowing the odds were overwhelming that I'd never find what was left of Lizette Salazar's scorched Taurus.

Wilson came to sudden stop. My pen jerked down the page, trailing ink and stabbing through the paper. We were standing in front of an ancient Oldsmobile with its front crushed in and its windshield cracked. "This car here," he pointed to the Oldsmobile, "was a donation to the cause. I smashed this sucker up just last month."

Something in his tone told me that he wasn't revealing a screwup, so I waited, and he pulled up his pants leg to show me a three-inch scar just under his knee. "I lost my shin pad on this one and my leg hit the dashboard," he said. "But it was worth it. Got some good data out of this one, all right."

He went on to explain that he worked with a team recreating accidents, deliberately smashing vehicles into each other to see exactly what happened during a collision at varying speeds. The reports were used nationwide. "This one here"—he pointed again—"I hit at about forty miles per hour. Must have skidded about ten feet, helluva a mark."

"You mean you have to be inside, driving it, when it crashes?" I said in disbelief.

"Certain things you can't tell about the effect of speed on a crash unless you outfit the car with an accelerometer and have a human actually driving the car." He could not quite extinguish a boyish enthusiasm.

"We attract quite an audience. Cops, insurance agents, and lawyers mostly. Those lawyers love a good collision." He got a chuckle out of this.

"Couldn't you get killed?"

"If you don't know what you're doing, sure. But I'm protected. I wear a crash helmet, a neck roll, knee pads, shin guards, and sometimes body Kevlar to redistribute the impact. I make out okay." He gestured to his leg scar. "A few stitches. No big deal. You should see my helmet though, got a crack right here." He pointed to a spot on his receding hairline, "That's where I hit the windshield one time."

"Someone pay you to do that?"

"People pay for my expertise. This kind of field research gives me the expertise."

I flipped the notebook to a fresh page and wrote this down in a manner that could actually be read back. Because now I realized this wasn't just fluff for my pretend background feature, but an important indicator of the money that must be involved in the accident fraud business. It had spawned an industry of experts willing to personally smash up cars so they could tell who was lying.

In the back of the lot, the asphalt crumbled away, and the cars were parked on the damp, soggy grass that was squashed under the tires. Limbs from trees on the other side of the security fence bowed over the barbed wire to provide shade. Lester had dragged me here, to what appeared to be the old-age home of car wrecks, to illustrate something from a rather ancient accident. I scanned the vehicles dutifully, but they all looked like they were from *That '70s Show*. I was not hopeful about finding Lizette's recently devastated Taurus anywhere near.

From somewhere on the other side of the fence, dogs began

barking. "A couple of shepherds, penned up all day. Freaking warehouse keeps them for security," Lester said. "People who own 'em should be shot."

We stopped before a rusted Toyota. The trunk had been crushed so badly that the back tires were gone and what was left of the rear quarters lay directly on the grass. The driver's seat had been pushed all the way back toward the trunk. "That there was a real interesting case," Lester said, raising his voice to be heard above the barking dogs.

"A bakery truck rammed into this Toyota about two o'clock in the morning. Young kid, eighteen years old, was leaving a bar. Prosecutors wanted to charge the bakery truck with vehicular homicide, but the driver kept insisting that the Toyota bolted out of a side street with all his lights off."

I made notes, as if this was important, but my mind was still on finding Lizette's wreck. There must be some sort of system of organizing these cars. Maybe a last-in, first-out formation?

"Like some sort of death wish," Lester was saying.

This jerked me back to attention. "You think that happens?" I tried to sound casual. "You think people use their cars to kill themselves?"

The lenses in his sunglasses were the kind that got darker in the sunlight and now I could barely see his eyes. "I wonder about every single teenager who dies hitting a tree, because, let's face it, they have more and more mental problems today."

"Is there any way to tell, for example, whether a driver of a one-car accident could have done it deliberately?"

"There are a few things," he said, "like whether they were wearing a seat belt. People with a death wish usually don't wear a seat belt."

I felt a minor shiver of excitement. Lizette had not been

wearing a seat belt. "But that's not exactly conclusive, right?"

"Of course not, but we can also take prints from the victim's shoes, check to see if the driver was hitting the gas pedal or the brakes on impact."

I had a vague memory of high heels on Lizette's feet. Did they go with her to the hospital? I wondered.

"But in this case here, that wasn't really the issue. I was hired by the lawyer for the bakery truck. All we cared about was the vehicular homicide charge. An analysis of the lamp filaments showed that the lights were definitely off during impact. The vehicular homicide charges were dropped."

I copied down the part about the lamp filaments, then asked, "Can you tell by the filament of the brake light whether the driver was using the brakes?"

"Sometimes," he said.

"So you think the kid wanted to kill himself?"

He shrugged. "You gotta wonder, but the parents didn't want to believe it. It's natural when you lose a loved one. You want someone else to blame."

I nodded, but the notion of finding someone to blame brought my thoughts back to Lizette's crash. "Is there a section where the new wrecks come in?" I asked.

"Sure," he said, and began marching back toward the entrance and into the section that we had bypassed on our march to the Oldsmobile.

And then, at the end of the first row, I spotted it on the left, a bluish Taurus, the hood completely buckled and charred. Could it possibly be Lizette's? I took a step closer and saw that the front fender on the passenger side was indented in a cylindrical shape, the perfect form of the trunk of the tree. Lester noticed, followed my gaze.

"That one, with the hood all charred up . . ." I adopted a light tone, trying to make my interest sound theoretical. Please, God, let this be Lizette's wreck, I prayed silently. And then, "What could you tell me about that one?"

He tilted his head and smiled as if to accept the challenge, then slid between the cars to get to the Taurus. He surveyed the car from the outside first, walking slowly around it, front to back, and ending up standing beside the driver's door, which he opened. I scanned the inside of the car, trying to see if it looked familiar. Then a remnant of that acrid burning smell wafted from the car, finding its way to the back of my throat. There was no mistaking it. Then I spotted the Happy Meal figurines still in the back seat and was overwhelmed by a wave of elation and nausea.

Lester was standing beside the open door, holding the driver's seat belt in his hand and studying the cloth. He gestured for me to come to his side and then showed me the underside of the cloth part of the belt, running his thumb across what looked like ridges. "This is what we call loaded. This here is where the belt stretched on impact. One thing I can tell you, the driver was wearing a seat belt."

Looking at the belt closely, I could see where the material had stretched and thinned. But I could also still see Lizette lying across the console, nothing tying her to the driver's seat.

Then he ducked his head, studying something under the driver seat carriage. "Big driver. I'm guessing a man."

So much for forensics, I thought.

He wanted me to crouch beside him so I could see his reasoning. He showed me a black lever. "See how the seat is set in the furthest position to accommodate long legs. Driver was a big person. Guy probably. And . . ." His eyes lit on the windshield and he stood up suddenly, practically knocking me backward. I rose to my feet. He pointed excitedly to the centerline of the windshield crack, which started high, above the rearview mirror and was left of center. "Had to have a passenger with him. Even if the driver wasn't belted, he couldn't make this crack. There had to be a passenger, unbelted." He leaned across the console and grabbed the seat belt, turned it over. "Just as I thought. No signs of use during the impact."

He insisted that I switch places with him, so that I could see the difference in a seat belt that hadn't been worn. The difference was distinct. This belt was completely smooth, all around, no ridges, no thinning. For a minute, I wondered if this could be the wrong car. But the smell of petroleum was too familiar, and suddenly I remembered finding the driver's door ajar.

I got out of the car and took a moment to try to steady myself.

"You okay?" Lester asked.

"Would you be able to tell me if this car hit the tree twice?"

He walked around the front of the car, to the passenger side, and crouched down, examining the point of impact. When he stood up, his tone was cold. "How did you know that?"

"I know a little bit about this accident."

He waited.

I decided to come clean. I explained how I'd come upon Lizette's burning car and how the old lady had lied to police. About Lizette's husband's history of insurance fraud and my certainty that there'd been a bribe.

"I *thought* you were doing a general piece on fraud." He took off his sunglasses and put them in his pocket, so that I would have to look him right in the eye.

"It is a general piece on fraud, but . . . Well, I got the idea from a specific case."

He stiffened. "Look, my time is my livelihood. I can't afford to get involved in a criminal case. Especially when I've been tricked."

I apologized profusely, promised I wouldn't use his name on anything he told me about the forensics on the Taurus.

"Because once you put my name in the paper, the AG can start subpoenaing me and I got to show up for court for free. It goes on forever, and time is all I got, lady. It's all I got." He continued, "They have their own experts. You call the state police. They have forensic guys that can come here and tell you the same thing."

I apologized again and repeated my promise not to use his name. Not to even mention his name to the police.

This seemed to appease him. He put his sunglasses back on, at least. An awkward moment passed. I wanted only to get the hell out of the impound lot. Then a thought struck him. "This husband of hers, tell me more about him. He a freelancer in this fraud thing?"

"He works for Tito Manaforte at the Big T," I said.

The blood drained from his face. "Oh shit," he said. "You know how he got that burn, right?"

"I've heard a few variations."

"Who investigated this, West Kent Police?"

I nodded again.

"Off the record, I'll deny I ever said this. That I ever fucking met you."

I reached into my backpack and handed him back his brochure. "I will forget I ever knew your name."

"Because I do *not* want to be called as any kind of a witness in any kind a case involving Tito Manaforte. He owns people at every level. Appraisers. Lawyers, insurance investigators. The kind of people who hire me. I want nothing to do with this case."

"He owns people *at every level?*"

He gave me a look that suggested I was a babe in the woods to even register surprise. "Are you kidding? You have to ask why the cops won't investigate or why they didn't pick up on this in the first place? I mean, there's no way this woman was driving this car. Someone at least five feet ten, and given these stretch marks, probably weighing over one eighty. Maybe the driver panicked and took off, or more likely . . ."

"More likely what?"

"These people know what they're doing. If they were involved in this, I'm guessing this woman was dead before she even got in the car. Tito's operation is pretty sophisticated. All they had to do was put a driver in protective gear, the chest pad and a helmet, and have 'em drive the car real soft into the tree, make it look like an accident. Must have been too soft the first time. That's why they rammed the tree a second time.

Then he had another thought. "You said the car was burning when you got there?"

"Yeah."

He stepped around to the front of the car and examined the charred engine underneath the buckled hood. "Easiest thing in the world to ignite a car engine. All you need is a bag of potato chips and a lighter. And all the evidence goes up in flames."

7

The lobby of the *Providence Morning Chronicle* was a universe of granite—silver-flecked granite pillars holding up the ceiling, granite tile halfway up the wall, and a slick granite floor. Flipping my badge at a man at the security desk, I practically slid into Dorothy when she burst out of the elevator.

"I've got to talk to you," I said.

"Can't stop." Dressed more formally than usual, Dorothy was wearing a white button-down shirt, horribly wrinkled linen pants, and tinted nylon socks underneath her Birkenstocks. She was also carrying what looked like someone's father's briefcase. "United Way meeting," she said with a grimace. The *Chronicle* required its top editors to take turns giving back to the community, which meant board meetings and fund-raisers among the favored local charities.

"Can I walk with you?" I asked.

"If you can keep up," Dorothy said, without slowing her pace. "I'm already ten minutes late."

I made a quick pivot and followed her onto the street. Outside, the late afternoon was a little grayer and a little colder, but, luckily, no rain. The rush hour was just beginning and several lanes of cars sped down Fountain Street as if they were racing each other to the finish line. You couldn't even think about crossing until the red light at the corner forced them to halt. "A development on the Salazar story," I said.

Dorothy switched the square-topped briefcase from one hand to the other. "The fatal?"

I told her about the "loaded" seat belt Lizette had not been wearing, about the position of the driver's seat, and about how easy it was to light a bag of chips and ignite an engine.

"You got the cops saying the fire was arson?" Her voice lifted and she looked up, her eyes darting back at the *Chronicle* building: a breaking news development could be just the excuse she needed to ditch the United Way meeting.

"Not the cops." Here I had to explain that I'd found a forensic expert on the Web. That he had met me at the impound lot and examined the car. But when I'd gone back to Harrington afterward, he'd remained defensive, rejecting these findings as any kind of proof. "He'd called it 'someone's theory' and refused to comment unless I told him where it came from."

The light in Dorothy's eyes faded. Her tone became steely. "Didn't I tell you to let the cops take the lead on this one?"

I told her what my source had said about Tito owning "people at every level."

"Did he name specific people?"

I shook my head.

"Then that accusation is a little broad, wouldn't you say?" She began threading her way through the cars that had stopped at the red light, her eyes ahead of her, staking out the curb.

I strove to catch up, reiterating the important points: the old lady who'd been bribed, the husband's speedy hiring of the personal injury lawyer, the connection to Tito Manaforte at the Big T.

I had to raise my voice above someone in a Suburu lying on his horn. I wasn't sure Dorothy had heard me. Certainly, my argument made no great headway across the street. On the opposite sidewalk, she continued her march, her bottom lip curled in, as if she were biting back a week's worth of irritation. The heavy briefcase swung dangerously at her side.

"Dorothy, please. I've *got* something here. I know I do." Following behind her, I was still making my plea to her back. "This woman was *murdered* and no one cares."

Finally, she slowed a little. I gave the briefcase wide berth as I caught up and walked at her side. "And this forensic expert you dug up. Is he willing to go on the record?" she asked.

"He doesn't want to get involved in a criminal case, plus I think he's scared of Tito Manaforte."

She raised her brow in mock surprise. "Ever wonder why?"

"This is an important story," I countered.

The irritation flashed in her eyes now. "This is *no* story. You've got *no* police. *No* official source. Christ, you don't even have anyone in this poor woman's family calling for an investigation."

"The husband isn't going to call for an investigation. He's the one who probably did it."

"You got anybody in law enforcement saying he's a suspect?"

Dorothy interrupted. "A person of interest? Or for that matter, anyone other than your off-the-record expert-for-hire who thinks that there's even been a crime committed here?"

"No, and I'm not saying I have enough for a story, just enough to nose around some more."

She stopped in the middle of the sidewalk, forcing two businessmen who were walking toward us, into the street. "You're supposed to be working on the Riordan story. With Jonathan. Remember?"

"I am. I am. I did my surveillance this morning. Followed Riordan to his office, where he worked a full morning, by the way. Not even a coffee break. And I can do both, I promise."

Had I worn her down? Maybe. She swung the briefcase in front of her, the burden of it requiring both hands. "Then unless you can interest state police, you'd better find someone credible, a family member, a social worker, someone other than you who thinks this is murder and calls for an investigation. Otherwise, you are just wasting company time."

I'd agreed to meet Matt at six for dinner, and by the time I left Dorothy in the street, I was late. Carolyn, who now worked in Lifestyle as the food editor, had brought in a short black dress of her teenage daughter's that she insisted I borrow. I changed into the dress and a pair of heels in the *Chronicle* lobby bathroom and headed out, managing to remain determinedly nonresentful as I drove to the restaurant. I refused to feel like a senior citizen at an early-bird special. This was an important compromise on Matt's part. Our first date out in the open. Baby steps, I told myself. Baby steps.

I found a spot on the street and parked. I didn't see his Audi as I walked through the lot, and had a vain hope that I'd beaten him here even though I was fifteen minutes late.

Al Forno was inside a renovated mill building, made more inviting with a brick path through a terraced garden. Matt, who had had a friend drop him off, was sitting outside on a stone bench behind the lattice waiting for me. He wasn't even annoyed. As he rose from the bench, he offered a wide grin and an appreciative nod to show he liked the short black dress I'd borrowed.

I don't know what it is about suits that transform men so completely, but even in your basic Brooks Brothers knockoff, Matt looked more of everything I liked about him, taller, sturdier, and just a little more grown-up. He smelled good, too, a lime scent that made me suspect he'd actually taken the time to apply aftershave in the men's room of the attorney general's office.

Although the bar was already full at this early hour, we got an excellent table by the window in the downstairs dining room. It was a long and narrow room, with the exposed brick painted a clean white. Strands of small lights around the large windows made the industrial view of the Narragansett River seem oddly intimate. The other two couples at the tables were too involved in each other to notice that we'd arrived.

"You like champagne?" Matt asked, reaching for the wine list.

I shook my head.

"Me, either. You think it's okay to celebrate with beer?"

"As long as it's got a lime in it. What are we celebrating?"

His hand slid underneath the table onto my thigh, where it radiated heat. I felt the ripples, as if he'd skipped a stone across my flesh.

"Off the record?" he asked, but without the usual caution. He hadn't even let go of my skirt.

"Of course."

"I got word that I'm going to be promoted."

"Deputy?"

"In charge of the Criminal Division."

I couldn't reach across the table and kiss him as I wanted to, so I clasped my hand over his, still on my thigh. "Congratulations."

Not until the waitress delivered our Coronas did his hand leave my leg. Although I'd been hungry when I got there, now I was famished. We ordered clams Al Forno and crispy oysters, and fancy grilled steaks. And because the restaurant makes you order dessert at the beginning of the meal, we decided to share a root beer float made with hand-churned ice cream.

He clinked his beer bottle against mine and we both took long swigs. We were halfway through the steaks when Matt asked me how the funeral went.

"Can I ask you a question?" I returned.

More buoyant than usual, he was in the mood to indulge. "Okay," he said.

"I was wondering how often you think some of these small, rural police departments miss things."

A wave of caution crossed his eyes. "Like insurance fraud?"

"Sort of," I lowered my voice. "But I mean a bigger crime. Like murder."

He answered cautiously. "Theoretically, anyone can miss evidence."

"I'm not asking about theory."

"Is this about that fatal accident?"

I nodded. "I think she might have been murdered."

"They talked about this at the funeral?"

"No. I went back to check out the car today, at the impound lot."

"You usually need to be with a cop or an insurance investigator to get into an impound lot."

I ignored this observation. "I think you should get the state police lab to take a look at the car. I don't think Lizette Salazar was driving it." I explained about the seat belts. How she wasn't wearing one, that it was stretched from impact.

"You got a source on this?" he asked.

I gave him a blank look.

"Yeah, right. Someone's gotta be feeding you this tip, that she was murdered. This seat belt stuff. Where are you getting this?"

Matt wasn't the only one who was cautious. I wasn't going to give him any information that he could try to subpoena later if a police investigation developed.

He scanned my face and realized I wasn't going to answer him. Finally, he said, "Okay, look, I'm guessing your source isn't that ironclad or you wouldn't need a police investigation to sell it to your editor. But here's the deal. The state police have their hands full with the carjackings in Newport and those two dead prostitutes who turned up in the river. They aren't on the lookout for new assignments, especially in a case where the local PD doesn't want help."

"Even if someone was murdered?"

"You are talking about a Dominican immigrant, who you say has a petty criminal for a husband—"

"Because she's an immigrant, her life doesn't matter?"

"It would matter more to the West Kent police if she was *from* West Kent," Matt said. "Just a fact of life. The real problem is that there isn't anyone, not her husband, not her parents, not her kids, absolutely no one but our crusading *Chronicle* reporter here who thinks it's murder. Right?"

No one I could admit to. I did not reply.

The waitress arrived, trying to refill our water glasses. Matt waved her off and waited until she left. He put his hand over mine. "I'm sorry, babe. This is just a really tough sell right now. Maybe if you can get me a family member, someone who calls the office and demands an investigation, then I can lean on someone to do something."

By the time we'd devoured the steaks, Lizette Salazar had been pushed to a far corner of my mind. Then the float arrived. It came with two straws, and even though the restaurant was beginning to fill up, Matt forgot to worry about us being seen together. As I took a sip, he leaned forward to grab his straw between his lips, his face near mine. He pretended to be protecting his share of the float, he let his hand drift back to the edge of my skirt. I kicked off my shoe and rubbed his ankle with my toes.

"You want to come back to my place tonight to help me celebrate?" he asked.

There was no need to answer. Our eyes were saying what was going to happen next. "And maybe even stay awhile in the morning?"

"Maybe," I replied.

"I feel like I've probably been an asshole the last couple of weeks," he said.

I raised my eyebrows as if I didn't understand.

"Okay. Last couple of months. I know. I got wind that this

promotion was in the works and I've been totally wrapped up in it. That's all I've been thinking about. Like every minute of every day. How to nail this down. How not to screw up in front of Aidan." Aidan Carpenter was Rhode Island's attorney general.

His expression was turned inward, as if he were reviewing the weeks, seeing his mistakes. "You know, I've had so many setbacks I probably went overboard."

Before I moved to Providence, one of Matt's witnesses, a young woman whose brother had been killed in a gang war, had been shot to death on her doorstep. On both its front page and its editorial page, the *Chronicle* had assigned most of the blame to the AG's office for not providing adequate police protection. Matt had to weather both the political fallout and the emotional guilt, with the latter being the more profound. He'd just been coming out of a six-month tailspin when I met him in the fall.

He lifted his eyes to mine. "I was a little paranoid, I guess. You okay with that?"

Because Matt came from such a political family, an awful lot was expected from him. Not just from his parents, but from his grandparents on both sides and even, because Rhode Island was such a small state, from the press. This promotion would not just be noted in the *Chronicle,* it would likely elicit an entire column from our political writer, who would reiterate the witness-shooting controversy and speculate about Matt's future success.

Matt was asking me to understand this. And I, of all people, was able to empathize with the pressures and excesses of ambition. God knows I've trespassed on a few relationships for a good story.

I raised the root beer float in the air. "To assholes like us."

He sought my eyes, looking at me a long time with this expression that I've only seen a couple of times. It's a mixture of gratitude and disbelief, as if he'd never really expected someone like me. A rare moment when I think, Hey, maybe this guy won't totally take me for granted. And then he laughed, which made me think I'd handled the almost apology with just the right levity.

"Want to get out of here?" I asked, pushing the root beer away.

He nodded and grabbed the waitress as she passed to get the check, and because it was his promotion insisted on paying it. He'd slung his arm across my waist, and my heart began pumping as if I was running a 10K race. How fast could we get back to his apartment? But as we headed toward the lobby, he became aware of the line of people forming in front of the hostess. His arm dropped to his side and his posture stiffened.

The parking lot, completely empty when I arrived, was now crammed with all sorts of yuppie cars, BMWs, Mercedes, and Volvos. As we began down the center row, toward the street where I'd left my Honda, we passed a man getting off of a Harley-Davidson.

"Cavanaugh," the man called out. It was dark now. The man was in a shadow and had a motorcycle helmet on. He was about as tall as Matt, but with broader shoulders, and wore a leather jacket with a lot of padding and mesh, and over his blue jeans, a pair of leather boots that looked sport specific. Something about the way he held himself, his straight shoulders, struck a familiar chord.

"Piedmont," Matt replied with a wave. He did not slow his pace.

But Piedmont was a friendly guy. He caught up to Matt, put himself square in front of him, and took off his helmet. Instantly, I recognized the strong angle of jaw beneath the perfect five o'clock shadow. It was Mr. Nike, the guy I ogled on the boulevard. Apparently, he color-coordinated in all sports.

"Hey, where were you last month?" Piedmont asked. "You missed the game."

"Where else?" Matt said.

"The White Cross case? Aidan told me a little about it." Piedmont knew Matt's boss, the attorney general, well enough to make small talk. "When's that going to trial?"

"Next week." Matt took a step to his left, so that he was a foot of pavement away from me.

Piedmont saw the movement, glanced toward me. He studied me with intensity, as if he wanted to glean everything from this one moment. Matt said nothing. Piedmont's eyes moved from me to Matt, waiting for the introduction. None came.

"You still thinking about joining the league at the health club?" Piedmont asked. "We could use you under the boards."

"I'll call you." Matt made a step to go.

Piedmont turned back to me. His eyes, a remarkably fierce blue, were exacting. "You know, I know you from somewhere."

"The boulevard, maybe. I think I've seen you running there."

"Really?" he asked, in a tone that suggested that all the time I'd ogled him, tried to catch up to him, failed to beat him, all that had gone unnoticed. But he removed a pair of leather gloves, and offered his hand. The man had some sort of chemical voltage. I felt the heat of his palm up into my elbow.

"Dane Piedmont," he said. "Matt and I go way back. Law school."

A lawyer biker? He still had my hand, waiting for my name.

"Hallie Ahern." I almost forgot that Matt was still standing beside me until I noticed Dane looking at him, silently nudging for an elaboration.

Silence. Did I have head lice, or what? Dropping my hand, Dane Piedmont looked at me harder, still trying to piece something together. "I know you from somewhere else, too."

Matt was shifting his weight between his feet, growing restless. I knew I should stiffen, back up, and signal that this conversation was nearing its end, but Mr. Nike had a strange gravitational pull on me.

He was still staring at me, as if the world depended on his understanding our connection. It was flattering. And then the blue eyes lit. "I know what it is. I saw you on television, right after the referendum campaign. You're a reporter, right? You work for the *Chronicle*?"

I nodded.

"And you wrote the story about the Mazursky murder, right? The convenience store guy." His voice grew excited at the recollection. "You were even there when it happened, right?" And then to Matt. "Is that how you two met?"

Matt had a frozen expression on his face that was really pissing me off.

"Yes," I answered. I'd quoted Matt on the follow-up stories. It was public information. On the record. His boss, the attorney general, already knew about it.

"That was a helluva story," Dane said warmly. "I read that whole series."

It was at this moment that Matt finally found his voice. "Yeah. She had a real rough time of it, if you remember the story. Still a little wary, I guess." He tossed a look of sympathy my way. "I was walking her back to her car." He managed to feign an expression of professional detachment. As if he'd just run into me at the bar and was performing a service for the promotion of public safety.

Dane Piedmont had no difficulty interpreting Matt's code. I was just a conversation in a bar, not a date. "Does that mean you're going back inside? I'm meeting Rosenberg at the bar. You want to have a drink with us?" he asked Matt.

There was an awkward silence and I was seized with the need to bolt, to leave Matt to try to explain my reaction. "Don't worry about me," I heard myself say, "Go ahead."

"No. Another time," Matt said to Dane. "I'll call you."

But now anger was rising from my chest to my throat. I spoke quickly. "Really, I'm fine." I pointed vaguely through the lot. "My car is right there. Please, don't bother. Nice to see you again, Matt." I gestured to Dane. "Nice to meet you."

I hurried away, turning sideways to fit between two parked cars to get to the next row. I didn't slow my pace or look back until I'd made it through the parking lot onto the street. As I was unlocking my car door, I saw Matt racing through the parking lot toward me.

"Hallie! Wait!"

I jumped inside my Honda and slammed the door shut. He ran up to the driver's side, his voice slightly muffled through the closed window. "Hallie—"

"Get away from the car," I shouted through the glass.

"Please, Hallie." His hand made a move for the door handle.

I hit the lock button and turned the key in the ignition. The radio suddenly blared a Cardi's Furniture ad. I had to shout above it. "Get your hand away from the door."

He didn't move and I wasn't sure he heard me. I opened the

window a crack and continued to shout, "Get away from the car, Matt, because this relationship is so *over.*"

"Hallie, please, don't do this," he said, but he took a step back, and that was all I needed. My foot hit the gas pedal and I peeled out of the parking spot, fully in gear.

8

At about five o'clock in the morning, I gave up on the idea of sleep. My covers were thrown on the floor and the top sheet was pulled from the bed, twisted around one leg. I had cried throughout the night, overpowered by humiliation. At the moment, I absolutely hated him.

Hate gives you energy. Even at five A.M. I got up, got a glass of cranberry juice from the fridge, and sat at the bar in my kitchen and fumed. I'd turned my cell phone off so Matt couldn't call. For once, the outer door to my building had been locked, and last night, right after I'd gotten home, he had been reduced to standing in the downstairs lobby and leaning on my buzzer for about ten minutes. He'd given up too easily, I'd thought.

I had prided myself on being a low-maintenance girlfriend, but now I could see that had been a terrible mistake. I had asked for too little, and thus had gotten it. I felt abused, not just by last night, but by every minute I'd put into an obviously lopsided relationship.

Now, at this early hour, I could see from my picture window that the lights of his condominium were still out. He had *no* problem sleeping. The asshole.

When I was in Boston, I'd wasted too many years hung up on a boyfriend from college. It had led me to a lot of bad decisions, both personally and professionally. I'd be damned if I ever let myself make the mistake of hanging on again.

The newspaper's cafeteria had not yet opened, so I sat alone in an empty newsroom without coffee, in desperate need of an alternate fuel to boost my spirits. Fury had abated, and there was now a hole in my stomach where all that hate for Matt had been.

Plus, Ellen Felty had called in sick, so I had to cover for her. This meant I would have an entire eight-hour day to think about Matt as I sat in my car outside the Department of Business Regulation offices trying to document the unremarkable comings and goings of Albert Riordan.

I plugged Lizette Salazar's name into my computer and waited for it to sift through our database for her obituary. To distract myself, I was trying to look up Lizette's sister Marcella to see if I could find her address. I'd never in a million years go back to Matt for help now, but it occurred to me that if I could get a family member to call for an investigation, I could pressure state police myself.

Finally, the text appeared.

She is survived by her husband, Manuel, three sons, Manuel Jr., Enrico, and Robert, of Providence, two sisters, Ana Pena of West Warwick and Marcella Lopez of Providence.

I grabbed the most current phone book from one of the sports reporter's desks and looked up Lopez. There were about a thousand in Providence. I returned to the database archive and typed in "Marcella Lopez," in the hopes that she appeared in print some other way. That maybe, like her sister, Lizette, she worked for a social service agency. But the only story that came up was the obituary I'd just been reading.

It occurred to me that my best bet might be to make a visit to the social service agency where Lizette Salazar had worked. I looked up the address and phone number of the Centro de Hispanio in South Providence and wrote it on the back of the notebook I kept in my bag. Maybe I could find someone there who had concerns about Lizette's alleged accident. And if not, at least there might be a coworker who knew how I could reach her sister.

Two business reporters walked past me with coffee in their hands, which alerted me to the fact that time was passing, and that the cafeteria was now open. Plus, I had to stop by the photo desk to see if a photographer had been assigned to waste all morning with me following Riordan.

But as I turned to go, the phone rang. It was Walter. He had the cell phone number of the guy who had sold him the cabs, a man named Caspar Vasquez, who had said he *might* be willing to talk to me. "But I'd call him right away, before he changes his mind again."

For a moment, the cloudy, sad feeling weighting my body

lifted. Walter had delivered my cabbie! The newsroom was waking up. All at once the Rim and city desk were filled with editors. The business reporters, always the first to arrive, were already clicking away at their keyboards. The sound level began to rise with their jabs and parries.

Coffee could wait. I tried Caspar Vasquez's cell phone number and got his voice mail, which told me in both Spanish and English to leave a short message. I left a long one that included my name, cell phone number, and how eager I was to talk to him, any time, at his convenience. I repeated my cell phone number again, and told him that I'd be waiting by it all day, but that he could call me at night, too. Any hour, night or day.

Luckily I got to Richmond Street early, because Riordan arrived twenty minutes before the start of the workday. Although I scribbled this into my notebook, the photographer, Susan Tulanowski, one of my favorites, did not bother to capture this on camera. We thought we were going to have excitement at about two o'clock, when the chief of the state's business regulation office snuck out, his head tipped low, on his brisk walk to his car. As we followed a safe distance behind his sharp new BMW, both Susan and I prayed to the journalism gods that he was off to the dog track, and that we might catch him in line at the betting counter. But Riordan headed in the opposite direction and got off the highway onto Gano Street.

Following him to the East Side in my Honda, we parked a block back on Waterman Street. Susan snapped him with her telephoto lens as he continued at that same brisk pace into an office building. Unfortunately, the building turned out to be doctors' offices. And judging by the directory in the lobby,

Riordan had apparently left his state duties for an appointment with his internist.

The next morning, I awoke feeling restless. After leaving one more feeble message on my work phone, Matt had given up trying to reach me. Worse, I could see from my window that he hadn't returned to his condo last night, and his car still wasn't there this morning.

The relationship had never had a chance. Not with Matt's political ambitions and his high-pressure family. I'd been deluding myself to think I'd ever be anything more than someone to fill the gap, the occasional hours he'd had between important cases. I pulled myself away from the window, feeling empty and alone.

Normally, I felt better after I ran, but this morning the agitation would not abate, not after five miles at top speed, not after deep breathing and stretches, and not after an extra glass of milk with breakfast.

Caspar Vasquez hadn't called back, either. Nor had he answered any one of a dozen calls I'd placed to his cell phone. My best shot at this story was to find someone who would pressure the police to investigate the accident. Since I was off Riordan duty until noon, I decided to drive to the Centro de Hispanio de Providence first thing in the morning.

The Southside of Providence was full of social service agencies, industrial-age two-family homes, and slapped-together town houses. But the main thoroughfare, Broad Street, was vibrant, with busy storefronts promising easy credit in both English and Spanish, and a Burger King with the largest parking lot I'd ever seen.

There was construction at a gas station, with a big hole dug around the pumps and several men with shovels and hard hats standing nearby. They peered into my car when I stopped at the intersection. I clicked my car locks and waited impatiently for the light to turn.

The community center was in the storefront between an Asian nail salon and a bodega. There was one sign above the door, handcrafted with carved wooden letters identifying this as the Centro de Hispanio de Providence.

Inside, there was one big reception area with three tweedy-looking couches pushed against the walls and several wing chairs. The walls looked newly painted in municipal beige, but colorful hooked rugs had been thrown over a muted wall-to-wall carpet.

The receptionist, a young man in his twenties who wore a three-carat zirconium stud in each ear, spoke perfect English, took my name, and didn't seem overly alarmed when I admitted that I didn't have an appointment with the director. He smiled pleasantly and told me to help myself to some coffee. "She likes to make time for the *Chronicle*."

The coffee was set up on a table in the corner, between two bulletin boards and plastic wall pockets filled with informational pamphlets that ran the gamut from mental health to legal services. I poured myself a coffee, and then, for lack of anything else to do, started to scan the bulletin boards. One was crammed with press clips. In a genuine, but still weak, attempt to offset all the negative coverage of Hispanic gangs, the *Chronicle* had devoted several front-page stories to the increases in the Latino population, a profile of Providence's newest Dominican state representative in the General Assembly, and a feature about an expanding Colombian Food Market that had broken ground on a third location.

On the other bulletin board, there were half a dozen photos taken at the Hispanic center's Christmas party. These photos featured a host of Anglo bureaucrats: the new mayor, one of the U.S. senators, a couple of businessmen in stiff-looking suits, and several men and women who probably worked in social service agencies.

Then, in the very corner of the last photo, I saw a familiar face—Dane Piedmont. He looked lawyerly in pinstripes, as he stood between two men, one with a perfectly formed and shaved head, and the other, whom I recognized as the Dominican lawyer who'd made headlines as the first Latino appointed to the bench. Perhaps Dane was toasting to this. His plastic cup was raised. It wasn't a very good photo of him, his nose looked longer in profile, but he still managed to stir a distracting redirection of blood flow. What was it about this guy?

"Señorita Ahern?" a voice intruded.

I turned to see a robust woman about my own height. She had auburn hair piled high on her head and wore a flowered dress with a short linen jacket that gave it authority. Introducing herself as the director, Vergen Jiminez stepped beside me to see what I had been looking at.

"I met him a couple of days ago at a restaurant," I said. "Does he represent the community center?"

Her eyes lit up in a way that suggested she, too, responded to Dane Piedmont's gravitational pull. "He does good work for many of the nonprofits, but has been especially good to us here."

"What is he? A public defender?"

She shook her head. "For us he handles tenants' rights. Right now he donates his time to help one of our community members whose landlord is trying to evict him."

"Pro bono?"

"Always," she said. Her auburn brows curved in a "can you believe it?" shape for only a moment. "He has a private practice, too, but there is wealth in his family, I've heard. He says he likes to give back." It occurred to me that Dane Piedmont might have known Lizette. I made a mental note to look him up in the Rhode Island lawyer's directory.

Vergen Jimenez's attention had shifted to the coffee cup in my other hand. "Is it strong enough?" she asked, and without waiting for an answer, continued, "Because Rico, yesterday he added too much water. He's a tea drinker. He knows nothing about making coffee." She dropped my hand to lean over and inspect the color of my coffee. "Looks too milky to me."

It tasted stronger than an ambulance chaser with its double espresso shots. "Delicious," I said, forcing myself to take a sip. I had to tell her twice more that the coffee was strong enough before she would believe me. Then, as if in an afterthought, she asked what had brought me to the Hispanic Community Center.

"Lizette Salazar," I said.

The enthusiasm did not fade from her eyes. "You are writing a story about her? A tribute to the wonderful job she did here at the Community Center?"

A perfect cover, but Vergen Jiminez's warmth was disconcerting. It made me not want to lie. "I am interested in what you can tell me about her work here, but my real focus is the car accident that took her life."

Now she looked at me more carefully, calculating something. "I don't know how much I can help you, but we will go to my office, where we can sit down in private."

I followed her upstairs to the second floor, which was broken up into several small offices. The director's office, which looked down on Broad Street, was modest, with the same beige walls and carpeting, but there was a nubby yellow and red weaving framed on one wall and a collage of stained glass parrots on another. Vergen Jiminez proudly pointed to a third piece, a forest of trees painted on bark, and explained that it was real bark from Brazil. "This is all by local Latino artists. Perhaps you'd want to write about them sometime?" she asked.

I nodded noncommittally and took a seat on a slatted chair opposite the desk, where Vergen was already seated. There was an oversize papier-mâché vase filled with red paper roses between us. I moved my chair to the right, so I could see her face. The warmth in her eyes had been replaced by wariness.

The first rule of an interview is this: Before you ask the tough questions, the ones that might get you thrown out of the office, get the easy stuff out of the way. "I'm trying to reach Lizette's sister, Marcella Lopez. Do you have a phone number for her by any chance?"

People are always relieved by the simple questions. And they like to be able to offer you something. Vergen Jiminez walked across the room, picked up a large cardboard box that was in the corner, and dropped it on the desk between us. "Lizette's things," she explained, pulling out a Rolodex and flipping through it. After a minute, she shook her head at her own miscalculation. "Of course, she does not have a card for her sisters. She knew those numbers by heart." Then her eyes met mine. "But if I remember correctly, Marcella lives in Lower South. She owns a lunch counter—with her husband."

"In Providence?"

She seemed uncertain a moment, and then it came to her. "No, in Lincoln. At the dog track, I believe. Is there some reason you need to reach her?"

"I'm hoping she'll pressure police for a more thorough investigation."

Vergen did not register surprise. She seemed to be choosing her words deliberately. "Lizette worked so hard in life, I would hate to see her torn apart in death for the sake of a news story."

Why would she say this unless she knew Lizette's husband's sideline in the fraud business? Unless she had suspicions of her own. The window in the office was open, raindrops had collected on the sill, and the breeze blew an envelope off the desk and onto the floor. "I have no intention of tearing Lizette apart," I said.

Vergen Jiminez glanced at the envelope, decided to leave it on the floor. "Because there is always something in the paper about this gang member or that drive-by or some new drug deal that went bad in Central Falls, but there is so little written about the hardworking Latino families who live here."

"I don't want to tear Lizette apart," I repeated. "I'm trying to understand why she died."

"She died because her car hit a tree," Vergen said flatly.

"Did you know that her husband hired a personal injury lawyer the very next day?"

A wave of sadness traveled across her face. "Young girls make poor choices when they marry. Why must this be a news story?"

I was getting frustrated. Did she really think I was operating out of some perverse desire to malign the victim and somehow denigrate the Dominican community? "Police would only be too happy if I dropped this. They want to write this accident off. The truth is, they don't care about Lizette because she isn't from *their* community."

I tried to get a read on her response. But her expressive face was now thoroughly guarded. She sat very, very still, waiting for me to continue.

The thing about off-the-record information was that even if you could never verify it to use it in print, you could still use it as kindling. But just like lighting a fire, you had to be careful, because the flames could take off. Still, if you were going to get anywhere on a story, you had to take risks about who you could trust. And Vergen Jimenez seemed a rather stalwart member of the community.

"I have a source who has examined Lizette's car. An expert who raised serious questions about whether she was alone in the car," I confided. "Whether she was even driving. And whether the car accident was used as a cover."

For a moment there was shock. "The police are saying this?" she asked.

"This is an independent expert. Police aren't interested. Maybe it's because she's a Dominican immigrant. Maybe they are just lazy. But what if she was killed? It would be an insult to just let her killer get away."

"It bothers you?" Her tone was dubious.

Suddenly, I felt defensive. "I was the one who found her in that burning car. That's how I first got involved with this story. And yes, it bothers me that her husband stands to make half a million and police are so quick to ignore that as a motive."

Vergen's phone rang, but she didn't answer it. "Half a million," she said softly, as if processing the number.

I waited for the ringing to stop. "Look, I'm not going to pretend I'm not motivated by my own needs. I'm after a front-page story. But I think that somebody, and clearly it's not going to be Lizette's husband, has to pressure the cops to do their job. To make sure this really was an accident."

Vergen reached into the carton on the desk and pulled out a framed photo. It was one of those posed shots, a Sears photo that must have been several years old. Lizette looked even smaller and thinner than I remembered from the night of the accident, but she was a beautiful woman, with wide-set eyes and a narrow point of a chin set determinedly at the camera. She didn't smile in the photo, but gazed forward steadily, sitting between her twin boys, toddlers, her arms reeling them in. Behind her stood her eldest son, who must have been in elementary school. He didn't smile, either, but had one hand protectively on his mother's shoulder. The husband, Manuel, was not in the family picture.

"This is a woman who cared for her sons, for her family," Vergen said. "The husband? He isn't in this photo because he was cheating on her. Or because he was drinking in a bar. He isn't in the photo because he worked all the time. And yes, he does things, plenty of things Lizette does not like, but do you understand how hard it is for our people here?"

"I know it's not easy—," I began, but she cut me off.

"You have *heard,* maybe. But you don't *know*. You don't understand how it is to live here, lucky to get eight dollars an hour to clean an office at night or maybe nine dollars an hour to make jewelry. Everyone, the husband, the wife, they both have to work two, three jobs to pay the rent. Even a dump is sky-high. There is no way to get ahead, to make something for your family, unless someone takes a risk."

Was she condoning insurance fraud? I wondered.

She reached back into the box and pulled out several catalogs and a stack of forms to show me. Avon cosmetic products. "We had to clear out Lizette's office, and look what we find. She never rested, this woman. She worked here, a bookkeeper, she had a head for numbers. But also her English was so good, she took on extra work as an interpreter for some of the local attorneys. But that is not enough. She sells makeup on the side.

"Every minute she tries to earn just a little more for those boys. So badly, she wanted Manny, the eldest, to go to the university. She was determined he wouldn't end up . . ." Vergen caught herself, stopped, revised. "She wanted something better for him than work in a garage."

I was scribbling like crazy, trying to get every word down in my notebook, trying to catch up, but I looked up and our eyes met on this last statement. There was such fervor in her tone that I wondered who, exactly, wanted these things for young Manny. Lizette or Vergen Jiminez?

"Dominicans, they are entrepreneurs by nature," she went on. "They are the first to open their own shops. Their own businesses. And there are no banks giving them loans for this. They have to find the money somewhere."

I stared at her. Insurance fraud as a source of capital? "So you are saying that Manuel Salazar was merely an innovative provider?"

"I'm saying that nothing I know about him, nothing you have told me, makes me believe that he would kill Lizette."

"But what if someone else did? Why *not* go to the cops? Why *not* ask police to investigate?"

She turned from me to gaze at the framed photo of Lizette and her sons, now propped up on the desk. Her voice was distant. "I must think about this. I must think about what Lizette would have wanted."

And then her eyes met mine, and I understood why she had shown me the Avon catalog, why this was such a struggle.

I should never have mentioned the half million dollars. Because what Lizette Salazar would have wanted was the cash to send her sons to college, and Vergen Jiminez was a shrewd woman. She knew that auto insurance didn't pay out on murder.

9

According to the online directory, Dane R. Piedmont, Esq., specialized in real estate law. Since he did so much legal work for the center and Lizette had freelanced as an interpreter, it made sense that they would have worked together. I liked to think I called him exclusively to get more information about that connection, but I have a feeling I may have been motivated by the fact that he was so good-looking.

In any event, it was Friday afternoon by the time I finally got a chance to call him, and neither he nor his secretary answered the phone. I left both my office and my cell phone number, but had no real hopes of hearing from him until Monday.

With absolutely nothing to do on a Friday night, I headed up to Worcester to spend the evening with my mother. Anything was better than staying alone in Providence, staring out my window at Matt's empty driveway across the street.

There were a lot of places I wanted to visit in Rhode Island on my days off. The vineyards in Sakonnet. The mansions in Newport. The beaches on Block Island.

The dog track in Lincoln had not been tops on my list.

For one thing, I wasn't supposed to go any place where there was gambling. For another, I'd been taken in by those animal rights advertisements, showing the nearly starving greyhounds, homeless after their prime years, hollow-eyed and yearning for a good home. I expected a depression-era aura, with lots of men in felt fedoras hanging around the track looking tired and jobless.

But the tip from Vergen Jiminez was the best lead I had to find Marcella Lopez, so I had no choice but to drive out to Lincoln Saturday afternoon. I was surprised to find the dog track a rather upbeat place. There was a very nice security guy at the information booth who gave me one of those have-a-nice-day smiles when I asked where I could find the lunch counter. He pointed toward a short hallway to glass doors with a sign that said *BOARDWALK*.

On the other side of the doors, in a glitzy ballroom of blinking lights and blaring merry-go-round music, I found a frenzy of leisure-bound senior citizens, mostly women, and young couples clustered around slot machines. Of course, I had known that the dog track featured state lottery–owned slots here, but I'd pictured a couple dozen. There were thousands of machines on either side of a tiled aisle with fancy chandeliers overhead. Wherever the greyhounds and their betting fans were, they were secondary to what really was a casino.

I started to feel lightheaded. The carnival-like music and clinking coins sent a shiver of excitement to my fingers. I told myself that the slots were stupid, requiring absolutely no skill. If I wanted to get anywhere on this story, I had to stay focused. Had to keep walking, placing one foot ahead of another.

Soon I was halfway down the hall, but the yearning didn't go away. And as I scoured the concession stands that flanked the left side of the hall, I grew impatient. There was a Dunkin' Donuts, an ATM machine, and a busy sub shop on the right, but there was no sign of Marcella or anyone who looked like he could be her husband. Behind the sub shop counter, two older women wearing red aprons and folded paper hats struggled to keep up with the crowd. A man in line told me there were more lunch counters upstairs.

I backtracked through the casino and climbed the staircase to another enormous hall. Here the lighting was dim and the floor gritty. Men sat quietly at cubicles staring into computer screens or in front of television monitors broadcasting the latest simulcast results.

The men, and they were almost all men, didn't wear fedoras, but they still managed that jobless look, with sweaty baseball caps and clouded reading glasses, as they sipped draft beer. There were no-smoking signs everywhere, and yet everyone was lighting up. Smoke streamed from the top of TV monitors and rose up toward the dim lights. It was hard to see and even harder to breathe.

I glanced to my left and saw the only evidence of an alternate world filled with natural light—arched entrances to what had to be the dog track. These entrances were separated by rows of concession stands. There was another Dunkin' Donuts and, next to it, a stand that looked like a deli or hot dog grill.

As I got closer, I spotted the man who had been with Marcella at the funeral. He was wearing a Sunny Day T-shirt and blue jeans, waiting on a line of at least three people.

I remained at a safe distance, in a new section of computer cubicles and television screens broadcasting a half dozen races. I stood, pretending to be transfixed by a Taunton dog race, while watching the deli counter out of the corner of my eye.

I stood there maybe fifteen minutes, watching the customers lining up for hot dogs and Diet Cokes. Marcella's husband worked feverishly, managing both the cash register and the grill, handling the crowd alone.

"Busted Eye is back in today's race," a woman beside me said. She was in her late twenties, with shoulder-length hair that was orange blond, and a tarantula tattooed in the gap between her T-shirt and her blue jeans.

I looked to my left to see if she was talking to me, or someone beside me.

"Busted Eye," she explained. "The dog that was in the paper all last year. The one that got suspended for the cocaine."

I had no idea what she was talking about, but I nodded anyway.

"I don't know what they got him on now, Creatine or some shit, supposed to still be in the game." A buzzer at the betting booth sounded. "Gotta go. That's last call for the two o'clock race," she said, heading across the room, toward the betting booth.

I glanced back at the deli counter. Still no sign of Marcella. The buzzer was high-pitched; I felt it in my teeth, and it made me even more restless. I'd held up my end of the bargain, passing up the slot machines. And what had it gotten me? No progress on the story whatsoever.

I'd received a race tip from a woman who looked like she spent a lot of time here. I thought of the money in my wallet. I had fifty dollars because my mother hadn't let me take her out to dinner last night, but insisted we eat the leftover Swiss steak in her refrigerator. Fifty dollars I would have spent anyway.

I ran to catch up to the woman with the tattoo in the betting line. Her name was Tricia, and she explained that because Busted Eye had had such a long layoff, what with his drug suspension and everything, there were long odds against him, making it a higher paying bet. But since it was such long odds, she suggested I only bet on him to place. "And not the whole paycheck," she added.

I went to the two-dollar window, placed five bets, and headed toward the track with a surge of mostly older men, leaving their monitors and simulcast races for the real thing.

We filtered into a grandstand area with descending rows of red, white, and blue bleachers that must have harked back to a more patriotic era of dog racing. Even on a Saturday afternoon, the number of people sliding into their seats would fill less than a quarter of the arena.

The grandstand viewed the outdoor track through floor-to-ceiling glass, and at first the abundance of sunlight came as a shock. I squinted at the paddocks, where a team of people readied the dogs for the race. Settling into an aisle seat in an empty row, I studied my race form, refusing to allow my mind to drift in any direction, refusing to think about Walter or the look of disappointment that would be on his face.

And then the gun went off, and the greyhounds bounded out of the gate in their yellow vests. I found my dog by his number as they galloped around the first leg. From my seat on the high-rise bleachers, I peered down on the race and my whole body felt the swirl of the action below. Instantly, I was carried away, caught up in the thrill of suspended time, when the adrenaline surged, when the only thing that mattered was whether Busted Eye could keep his lead.

He neared the finish line, and I stood, screaming his name, chanting along with a hundred other people, also at their feet, shouting for their dogs. Busted Eye skidded into first place. The odds had been 10 to 1 for a victory. I'd won one hundred dollars, plus my ten dollars back.

On the advice of Joe, a silver-haired man who wore a scally cap and a warm-up suit, I watched the tote board, which recalculated the odds based on the betting, and waited until the very last minute before running up to bet a quinella.

My feet were light as I took the stairs, headed back to the betting windows to place the next few bets, but they grew heavy after about six or seven races, after I'd managed to lose my winnings and the $50 I'd come with.

See, this is where Walter is all wrong about me having a gambling addiction. After a fifteen-minute conversation with myself, and a fatherly look of concern from Joe, I was able to exert an admirable display of self-restraint. Instead of getting in line with everyone else at the ATM machine, I decided to go home before I got myself in any serious trouble.

On my way out, I happened to glance at the lunch counter. The same man was working the register, but standing near him beside the grill with a rag in her hand was Marcella. She was wearing a bright green apron over a T-shirt and pair of jeans. Her hair was tied up, making her small features look more severe.

She headed toward the far end of the counter, cleaning off

a spill with the rag. As I approached, she looked up. Instantly, her gaze darted to someone behind me. I turned and saw a man. He was about thirty years old, with puffy eyes and thin brown hair in a ponytail. He wore baggy blue jeans and a Monster Truck T-shirt.

I followed her to the other end of the counter, where she was scrubbing the Formica surface in short, tight circles. "I need to talk to you," I said in a low tone. "About your sister."

Without lifting her gaze from her countertop scrubbing, she whispered, "Not here."

"Where?"

She didn't answer.

"I can wait around."

She met my eyes, saw my plea. Maybe she still felt grateful I'd come to the funeral, because she leaned forward as if to scrub the outer edge of the counter and whispered: "Meet me in the toilet." She craned her neck to check the Coca-Cola clock on the wall. "Twenty minutes. Now, go back to the track. Don't bet anymore." And then, with a glance back at the man with the Monster Truck T-shirt, who was now paying for a hot dog at the register, she added, "Act normal. You are being followed."

The twenty minutes that I spent waiting in the grandstand were the creepiest twenty minutes of my life. The man with the Monster Truck T-shirt kept his distance, sitting four rows behind me. I felt his eyes boring into my back the entire time. If I shifted to the right, I imagined his eyes shifting behind me. When I stood up to shout at the dogs, I could almost feel his weight rise from the bleachers.

A shiver chased me as I climbed the stairs to the exit, and I found myself taking the stairs two at a time. At the top, I checked over my shoulder, expecting to see him beating a path behind me, but he was still in his bleacher seat. He turned and our eyes met. He gave me a long, cold glare and then, a weird, even more frightening smile. The sunlight caught something silver in his tongue.

I took off and practically ran through the long hall to the ladies' room, taking a moment to catch my breath before I opened the door.

Inside, I found Marcella already there, checking under the stalls to make sure they weren't occupied. Satisfied that we were alone, she turned and leaned against the sink.

"How did you know I was being followed?"

"Norman. He works for Tito."

"He follows reporters?"

She blinked rapidly, as if my English stumped her. After a minute. "Reporter for paper, yes. Maybe that's why." Then another thought struck her. "Unless . . . how much you lose?"

"Fifty dollars." I was standing opposite the mirror and could see my own guilty expression.

"Is not enough."

"Enough for what?"

"A couple thousand, you lose, then he follow you."

"Is he a loan shark?"

She shook her head.

"Then why else is he following me if I lose big?"

She must have heard the excitement in my voice, because she shook her head more adamantly this time. "No. Is not loan shark. He *gives* you the money."

"Gives?"

"You take a seat in one of the cars," she said.

I was horrified on my own and every other gambler's behalf. "You mean like he's a recruiter?"

But Marcella waved away my outrage. "Lots of these people, they are grateful. But you did not lose enough. Norman, he did not see you come in here?"

"He stayed in the bleachers."

She exhaled relief. "Good. Someone else gets his interest. But he works for Tito. So he cannot see us together."

I was torn here, wanting to know more about Norman and his recruitment of losing gamblers for car crashes, but Marcella was obviously growing anxious. I had to be careful, get the most important questions answered first. "It's about your sister's car accident."

She tilted her head, prompting me to go on.

I knew nothing about Marcella Lopez, except that she seemed distraught by her sister's death and that she owned a lunch counter with her husband. I wanted to assume this made her honest and hardworking, but her dismissive attitude toward Norman's recruiting practices made me aware that I had no idea whose corner she was in. I had to be careful, had to feel her out before I tried to enlist her help. I began slowly. "You probably already know that your brother-in-law has hired Joe D'Anzana, the lawyer, to sue for a claim."

Her eyes absorbed the information; it appeared to be news to her. She took an extra moment, then probed for information. "He has found a witness?"

The question told me two things. First, that she knew Manuel needed a witness to sue, which meant Marcella knew a thing or two about how car insurance worked in Rhode Island.

And second, that if she had to get the information from me, Manuel was not keeping her up-to-date.

"The woman who lived in the farmhouse across the street from where it happened," I offered. "She *claims* that she saw another car run your sister off the road." I waited to see if Marcella would become defensive of her brother-in-law.

"This woman, she calls the police to tell this? You know when?" There was a hint of urgency in her tone.

I had enough to push on. "She didn't call police for a couple of days. Not until after Manuel went to her house on *Saturday* with his lawyer."

Her eyes flickered in a back-and-forth movement, which I hoped meant she was processing the significance of the timing. Before her sister's body had even made it to the funeral parlor.

I plunged on. "Your sister wasn't wearing her seat belt when I found her."

She looked up, but there was no surprise. I guessed that the cops or the hospital had already told her that. I was at a crossroads here. I had to tell her enough to get her to talk to me, and yet I was wary of giving information to the enemy camp.

"I might be a little crazy here," I tried to make it sound hypothetical, "but do you think there's any chance that the car wreck was *not* an accident?"

Her expression froze.

"Your sister have any enemies?"

She began blinking rapidly. The fact that she didn't deny it, or say that I was out of my mind, told me all I wanted to know. Because she was a family member, it was even riskier sharing information with her than it was with Vergen Jiminez. Still, I decided to go for broke. "I went to the wreck with a guy who reconstructs accidents, an expert. He showed me how the driver's seat belt was loaded, stretched, in a distinct manner." I used my hands to illustrate a pretend seat belt and its thinning. "It means someone *was* wearing the seat belt at the time of the accident. He seemed to think there was a possibility that someone else was driving that car."

The blinking continued. Again, no signs of disbelief.

"In fact, he seemed to think it was impossible that she could have been driving that car. And because the hood was on fire, he actually thought . . ." I paused to try to gauge the eyes. Behind them, I saw anger, not tears.

"What?" she demanded.

"He thought that she might have been dead before she got in the car. That the whole thing could be a cover-up for . . ." I stopped again, as if it were difficult for me to even say it out loud. "For murder. He actually said that. Is that crazy, or is there someone who might have wanted to kill your sister?"

She remained silent, an absolute silence that filled the room. I became aware of a faucet dripping. "Outside of your brother-in-law, and the insurance claim, there isn't anybody who would benefit from your sister's death, right?"

She pulled herself off of the sink. "I must go."

I stood in her path to the door. "Because if there is anybody who would benefit from your sister's murder, it would be a terrible thing to let them get away with it."

Marcella's eyes flitted from me to the door and back. "These people, they kill you for five dollars," she said.

"Don't worry. I won't put your name in the paper. Ever. I just want you to go to police. Demand a forensic investigation on the car. They won't release your name to anyone in the media if you tell them you're afraid for your life."

Her expression tightened, and she began to panic. "Cops? No. They would not believe me. And Roman, he leave me if I go to the cops."

"Okay, okay." Roman must be her husband. Either he had a criminal record or he was an illegal immigrant.

"Lizette. She was supposed to be at my sister Ana's that night. But she never show up. We do not know where she was before that accident. Or where she was going. Manuel does not know. But this, this he does not tell police."

"You think he might have—"

But she shook her head. "No. Manuel loves my sister. But he owes money to Tito, and he is practical man. He does nothing that hurts his insurance claim." Her eyes focused on my backpack. "You work for the paper. You write a story to tell the police to do their job."

"I can't," I said. "I don't have proof of anything."

The bathroom door opened and a younger woman helped an older woman with a cane into one of the stalls. I was surprised Marcella didn't use their arrival as an excuse to flee, but instead she turned and pretended to be washing her hands. I reached into my backpack to search for the pink lipstick I always forgot to wear.

It seemed forever until the two women left, but when they did, Marcella turned to me. "So you go out and get some proof, no?"

I looked at her levelly. "I need help."

She didn't reply.

"I need *your* help."

Behind Marcella the faucet dripped. She turned to shut it off, but I could see her expression in the mirror, her dark eyes mired in conflict.

"I will never even hint at who you are. Not even as an unidentified family member. If I put anything you tell me in the paper, I identify you as a 'background source.' "

"And you don't tell Manuel I speak to you?"

"Promise. I won't do anything that puts you in danger."

"My life is already in danger. Cause he knows I know."

"Manuel?"

She turned back to face me, and I saw the amusement in her eyes. She made a dismissive gesture with her hand, suggesting Manuel was no one to fear. "He is moneygrubbing, but he does not do this to my sister. It is Tito. That's why he come to the funeral. To try to scare me, keep me quiet, but I'm not going to let him. Manuel. Roman. Yeah, big men all right. That's why he gets away with it. That's why he makes the money. Because they are such cowards. But he's not going to get away with it this time."

"You think Tito drove the car into the tree?"

She shrugged off this level of detail. "He has people who work for him. They know how to smash a car into a tree and walk away. Make it pay for Manuel, so he does not ask too many questions."

"But why? Why would Tito Manaforte want your sister dead?" I asked again.

She started to say something and stopped. Her eyes filled with tears. In my backpack, I found a wadded-up tissue. It was unused, but a corner of it was stained blue from an exploded pen. I offered it tentatively. She took it from me, but after a closer look, walked into a stall and grabbed some toilet paper instead.

"Why?" I repeated. "For the accident money? Wouldn't that go to Manuel?"

She shook her head, dabbed at her eyes, then checked the mirror to make sure she didn't look like she was crying. After a moment, she turned around. Something in her mind settled, a new decision made. Her voice dropped another couple of decibels, and she gripped my arm. "You will put him in jail, yes?" The pressure of her fingers was insistent. She was exacting an agreement.

"I'll try. I'll try my best, but police don't seem to be interested in your sister's death. The best way to put Tito behind bars is for me to get proof about that car ring."

"That's why she is dead," she said softly. "The car ring."

I was afraid any question I asked would remind her that I was a reporter, so I remained silent and waited.

"You never tell anyone I told you this?"

I nodded vigorously.

"Tito, he use my nephew, Manny, in two accidents. The last one, Manny got real hurt. His back." She put her hand to her vertebrae. "But he gets only a couple hundred. Lizette, she is sick of Manuel doing whatever Tito tells him. She does not think straight anymore. When Tito gives Manuel some money to buy car for new accident, Lizette, she takes the money. She gives it to the doctor for tests on Manny's back. And to do surgery."

Vaguely, I remembered the eldest son limping toward me in the church vestibule "She stole Tito's money? How much?"

"Ten thousand dollars," she answered. "Tito finds out. A week later, Lizette is dead."

10

"You can't sit around forever and mourn that asshole," Carolyn said.

"I'm not mourning." I was sitting at her breakfast table and had stared a little too long into my coffee.

"Then go out with Eddy." Eddy was one of Carolyn's ex-husbands. She had two. He was the father of her youngest.

"Too weird," I replied. Carolyn had been my boss when I worked in the bureau and was my only real friend at the paper. I'd driven down to her house in South Kingstown from the dog track to babysit the girls so that she could go out with some guy from Newport. I'd spent the night in case Carolyn got lucky, which she almost always did, but the date had not gone well, and she'd come home early. I'd stayed over anyway, on the promise of pancakes.

A well-endowed woman, Carolyn believed that casual clothing made everyone look fat, and shunned it accordingly. Thus, she was an odd-looking short-order cook standing at the stove in her satin bathrobe and kitten-heeled slippers that could pass for footwear at a disco. But clearly she knew pancakes, which she made in almost uniform, silver-dollar size.

As usual, she'd been reading my mood correctly. I'd slept fitfully on the trundle bed in the girls' room and was feeling desperate. But, for once, it wasn't because of Matt. I was more troubled by Marcella—or more accurately—my inability to do anything with such an explosive tip. Lizette Salazar may have been murdered for ten grand—the price of a used car, for god's sake. It was a story that touched on poverty, crime, and a way of life for desperate immigrants. A freaking Pulitzer. And I'd never be allowed to write it.

I'd promised Marcella that I wouldn't identify her. And once the excitement of the tip itself had worn off, I knew that Dorothy never would give me the green light on a story that accused Tito of murder based solely on a single background source. And who else would be willing to risk Tito's wrath to talk to the press? Even off the record?

"You know, Eddy's really good-looking," Carolyn was saying. When I didn't respond, she called to the living room, where her daughters were ensconced in front of the television set. "Katie, come here, tell Hallie that your father is good-looking."

"He's not bald!" Katie called from the couch, without budging from the television. She was only eleven, but had hit puberty early and only half-listened to anything her mother said. Either that or Carolyn had tried to fix up her father before.

The kitchen was small, but sunny, and stuffed with many signs of Carolyn's new job as food editor. A rack of gourmet baking spices, sent to her by one of the catalog companies, was on the countertop. A zester, some sort of long, silver kitchen implement she was writing about, lay in the sink, and several dozen cookbooks, all of them brand-new, took up three shelves of the painted cupboard, with the overflow stacked on the floor.

"Eddy needs somebody. And so do you," Carolyn said, snapping off the flame and transferring the pancakes to a serving dish. Eight years older than me, she tended to be maternal, but not just to me or her daughters or other reporters who worked for her. To everyone. This sometimes pissed people off. But she was a generous person, and sincere in this offering of her former husband. Apparently, she'd forgotten that when I'd first started at the *Chronicle,* she'd filled our slow news days with tales of her two ex-husbands' shortcomings. I was pretty sure that Eddy was the one who had the flash temper.

What I needed was another background source. Someone who would corroborate Marcella's information. Certainly, Manuel Salazar wasn't about to jeopardize his half-million-dollar insurance suit to avenge his wife's murder. But could there be anyone else inside Tito's organization who had a motive to talk to me?

Carolyn placed the pancakes and a plate of bacon on the table and called the girls for breakfast. "And he's making real good money these days at the shop, too," she added.

This explained why they were friendly; he must be making his child-support payments on time. Then another thought occurred to me. "The auto body shop? The one in Providence? That's Eddy?"

"It's not like that," Carolyn said, defensively. "He's totally on the up-and-up."

"No, it's not that." I was thinking that Eddy might know Tito Manaforte or someone who used to work for him. But I was also thinking about one of Dorothy's latest edicts, that we not discuss our leads outside of the team. This seemed sort of pretentious and unnecessary to me—what were we, federal agents?—but it made some sense with Carolyn, who wasn't the most tight-lipped person in the world.

But Carolyn misinterpreted my hesitation. "It's that useless excuse of a boyfriend stopping you," she said. "Look, I've heard about his brothers. If he's anything like they are, he's already screwing at least three other women."

"He's nothing like his brothers," I objected. Matt frowned on his two older brothers, especially the eldest, who'd been divorced twice. At least I didn't *think* Matt was anything like his brothers. But I now remembered his space in the driveway that was empty so early in the morning. Sitting beside me, Deirdre, the fourteen-year-old, pushed the plate of pancakes my way, but suddenly I wasn't feeling so hungry.

"It doesn't matter," Carolyn said. "It's time to move on."

"Not with your *husband*." I looked to Katie for confirmation, but she merely shrugged and passed the bacon to her mother. "Besides, I've got to focus on the job. Frizell's been getting all the headlines."

"No shit." Carolyn took a piece of bacon, examined its underside, and dropped it back on the plate. "You'd think there wasn't anyone else working on that investigative team."

"Really?"

She sensed my alarm. Softened it up a little. "Well . . . the last month or so."

I groaned. Not just the last month. Last few months. And rumor was that the sale of the paper was going to be announced this week.

"You working on anything?" she asked.

I hesitated again, thinking of Dorothy's edict. But Carolyn

had an ex-husband who ran a body shop. Telling her wouldn't be idle newsroom gossip. She was a freaking source. "Has Eddy ever said anything to you about insurance fraud?" I asked Carolyn.

"You mean, other than it's a way of life for half the body shops out there?"

"He said that?"

She gave me a duh look. "How long you been living in Little Rhody, now? A year almost? You didn't know that?"

"Everybody knows that." This came from Deirdre.

"You working on a story about insurance fraud?" Carolyn asked. "Haven't we done that to death?"

"This is different." I put my finger to my lips to indicate it was top-secret. She silently crossed her heart and hoped to die. I explained about the predator car ring targeting innocent drivers on the road. And about Tito Manaforte at the helm.

Carolyn had put down her fork and folded her arms under her breasts, listening intently. I was reminded that despite her questionable judgment in husbands, she'd been a good bureau chief. When I was finished, she stood, grabbed a pen and pad from the counter, and wrote down a phone number. "Here, call Eddy. He'll talk your ear off, but he gets the inside on a lot of body shop gossip. He's totally obsessed with Tito and how the hell a convicted felon gets a city towing contract. Eddy should be able to give you *something* worthwhile." Then she stopped, folded her arms again across her satiny robe, and looked thoughtful. "But what you really need here is a victim. Somebody with a sob story who could bring the story to life."

I offered to clear the table so the girls could go back to their television program. In between trips to the sink and dishwasher, I told Carolyn the whole story of Lizette Salazar.

Sitting at the table, this time with the slippers up on a chair, Carolyn was quiet, pensive even, as she sipped what was now cold coffee. I'd revealed everything from the car crash to the old lady on the porch to the dog track. But she offered no aha at the climax—the ten-thousand-dollar theft from Tito Manaforte and the motive for murder. Instead she said, "You'll never prove murder. And even if you did, Dorothy wouldn't run the story without an indictment. Not in a million years. Your best shot at this story is proving there's a predator car ring."

I was wiping around Carolyn's coffee with the sponge and stopped. First things first. How many times did I have to relearn that essential point? You start every investigation at the beginning, not at the end. Prove there was an insurance fraud ring in Providence *before* trying to link it to Lizette's murder.

Carolyn lifted her coffee so that I could get at the crumbs near her cup. Then she grabbed the sponge out of my hand, sniffed it, and tossed it into the trash. "Plus, the whole thing's too complicated," she continued. "This Lizette person was too wrapped up with these people to make a good victim. You need someone else. Someone alive for starters. And with no ties. A real *innocent* victim everyone can feel sorry for."

My first thought was of Lizette's son, Manuel, who'd injured his back so badly in a staged accident that he'd needed surgery. But as a willing participant, he wasn't completely innocent. Then I remembered Vasquez, the cabdriver.

Driving home from Carolyn's, I called Walter from my cell phone and begged him to intervene on my behalf. I promised to go back to Gamblers Anonymous meetings as soon as this assignment was over, if he could just get Caspar to return my phone call.

I don't know if it was Walter's persuasive powers, or simply that Caspar had nothing better to do on a Sunday. But two hours later, when I was home and stepping out of my shower, my cell phone rang. Finally, Caspar Vasquez had returned my call.

The bakery was on Broad Street, across from a used-car dealership with lots of tinsel-like garland that was going limp from the rain. It was quiet on a Sunday, and I was able to park right on the street.

Outside, tall, clouded windows with shaky calligraphy advertised everything from corn bread to hot sandwiches to CAKES FOR EVERY OCCASION. Inside, it was painted a fresh yellow with an old tile floor that had been scrubbed so hard that several tiles were completely bleached of color.

After a quick introduction, Caspar and I sat at one of the small tables opposite the long counter. We were in front of the window and I could see there was no one on the street except for a gray-haired woman sweeping the entrance to the produce market and a man in his twenties walking alone with his ear to a cell phone.

The coffee was strong and came in small white porcelain cups with matching saucers. Before I'd even taken a sip, Caspar ordered the woman behind the counter to bring me some special Dominican cake.

The cake had a lot of whipped meringue and thin slices of peach. I was still stuffed from Carolyn's pancakes. Plus, I have a thing about peaches. When my frugal German mother was feeling especially frugal, she used to serve canned peaches with Cool Whip to my brother, Sean, and me and insist it was dessert. We were not allowed to leave uneaten food on a plate. "Tiene buena pinta," I said. *That looks good.*

Caspar Vasquez was a wiry man in his early sixties, with graying hair, and salt-and-pepper eyebrows that grew long and wild, like a field in the wind. But he had a warm smile. "¿Hablas español?"

"Un poquito." A little.

He pointed to the cake. "Taste it. It's going to be on every restaurant menu in Rhode Island before I'm through."

I dug the fork into a corner of the cake and took a nibble of the whipped meringue. "Delicious," I said, in English this time. Then I put down the fork and picked up my pen. "As Walter probably told you, I'm interested in your accident."

"The cabs," Caspar said with a good-natured groan. "Your friend practically stole them from me, but . . . this"—he pointed to the cake again—"this was too good an opportunity to pass up. I've owned this place only two weeks now, and already we got orders for our Tres Leches in five restaurants."

I noticed that he had excellent English, with only the slightest accent, as if he'd lived here a long time or had made his way up here from New York. "Congratulations," I said.

He did not reply, but watched to see if I wrote any of this down. His bushy eyebrow hairs seemed to have shifted, as if a hurricane had come through. I made a feeble note on my pad. Cake. I wrote, and added a question mark. Cake?

Caspar glanced at my largely untouched cake with a sad expression. "Don't tell me you're watching your weight. You have a beautiful figure. You girls"—Caspar immediately corrected himself—"women, are always on some crazy new diet. No butter. No bread. No nothing. You should enjoy the little bit of dessert that life has to offer."

God, I wished I could get past this peach thing. "Tres Leches," I said. "Three-milk cake?" I asked to distract him.

He seemed pleased at my translation. "You want to know the ingredients?"

I nodded and he began to rattle off a list that I diligently copied into my notebook. When he was finished, I allowed a moment to pass before I redirected the conversation. "Now, tell me about this accident you had. About why you felt you had to get out of the cab business?"

A blood rush to his face practically perked through his cheeks. "Insurance! It's through the roof." He pointed upward with an emphatic gesture. "And who pays? The little guy. The guy trying to make the honest living. Those of us out killing ourselves to feed our families, we pay for the fat cats in the big office towers and the scum who make money the easy way." He shook his head sadly. "My wife and I have worked too hard to put up with this . . . this . . . nonsense."

I took down the quote in my notebook. "Walter tells me that you fired someone? And this is retaliation. That you and your cabs were targeted?"

"It's my business, I fire whoever I want," he said, but his anger had dissipated, and his tone changed. "But you know, there are not so many good-paying jobs. This is why they turn to this. There are no choices when you don't know the language—and worse, when you don't have papers."

"Illegal immigrants. They do this?"

"If they can't find other jobs, it's like finding gold to them. But these people, they are, how you say, in the backseat. They do not run these rings. They take a ride, risk their lives, for a couple hundred. The real money goes to the criminals. And to the lawyers and the doctors who have their hands out for little pockets of cash."

He shook his head at the state of things. "It goes on

everywhere. Worse up in Boston and down in New York, I hear, where the Russian gangs run everything."

For a national perspective, I could go to the Internet, or get someone from the insurance industry. What I needed from Caspar were the gritty details of what happened to him in Providence. "Who did you fire?"

"It's more than that. . . . Some in the community, they are jealous of my business success. They do not like that I speak my mind. But if honest businessmen don't speak their minds . . ." He broke off, letting me imagine those consequences. And then, "But that part is not important."

It was an evasion. I decided to shift gears. "Tell me about your accident," I prodded.

He threw back his coffee as if it were a shot of tequila and stared off into Broad Street a moment. After what looked like a painful swallow, he began. "I was driving on 195, when these two cars, a Chevy Malibu and a Plymouth, I think, they played some kind of game on the highway. They stop. They start. I move slow in the middle lane. But then, one of the cars pulls just ahead of me, and the other, it is in the right lane. Then the one in front of me stops dead on the highway. I have nowhere to go. I try to stop, but I smash right into the Chevy in front of me, crushing the trunk. I hit here." He touched his forehead. "It all goes dark. They take me to hospital. Say I have a concussion. At first I can't remember what happened. The insurance says it is *my* fault. Then it starts to come back to me, in bits. That ever happen to you?"

I shook my head. "I've never been in a car accident."

"You are lucky. Because when you start to remember, no one believes you. But my cousin, he tells me, he finds out. They go after me because I had a good policy."

I was writing frantically, trying to keep up. "Who is 'they'?"

"These cars. The one to my right, it just disappears. The other, it has four passengers. They all claim they are injured, but none of them go to hospital, I heard. They go to a back doctor a day later."

"Is all this, what you just told me, in the police report?" A public document would be very handy here. It would be something Dorothy could hold in her hand, something I could point to as the proof she'd insisted would be so hard to find.

But he shook his head. "I can't tell this to police. Because I am Dominican, they don't trust me. They think we are all crooks."

I shook my head at the injustice, and wondered how whoever targeted his cab would feel about his talking to a newspaper reporter. But he hadn't asked me to withhold his name from the story. Not yet, anyway.

"How about your insurance agent? Will he or she talk to me?"

Caspar shook his head. "We are not, how you say, settled yet."

"Your lawyer?"

"I'm not going to pay one of those crooks." Caspar Vasquez was planning to represent himself in court. That would go over real big with Dorothy. To try to cover my exasperation, I forced a bite of the cake.

This returned Caspar to his original train of thought. "You know, this cake," he said, eyes glittering with purpose, "this cake is my future."

I swallowed without tasting. "How about the date of your accident. When did it happen?" It had occurred to me that if a carload of scammers were trying to put in an insurance claim, someone somewhere had to have filed a police report, and I could get it from headquarters.

He gave me the date, and watched me as I wrote it into my notebook. "It would make a subject for that column on your business pages. What's the name of that column that runs on Mondays?"

It took me a moment to realize that we'd left the accident again and were back to the cake. " 'Your Business'?"

"Exactly. My business." He swallowed and licked a bit of meringue from his fingertip.

Although "Your Business" featured a lot of small companies with big plans, they were mostly of a high-tech nature. The local bakery was not a prime subject. "I'm not a business reporter," I apologized. "I work for a completely different department."

"Yet you are interested in my cab business. And my insurance."

I opened my mouth to explain that I was an investigative reporter and interested in his insurance because it was part of a bigger story, but I shut my mouth again. Caspar Vasquez did not care why I was interested in his accident. I also sensed that he did not especially care about the jurisdictional issues of newspaper politics. "Do you have any proof that you were targeted, set up?"

"I have word from someone inside the business. Someone who knows."

"Someone who is planning to testify for you in court?" I asked.

He shook his head. "He get killed if he does such a thing."

So Caspar had no proof. *Someone who told someone* would not make it with Dorothy Sacks. To the investigative team, he would just sound like some bitter old cabbie trying to explain away a poor driving record. "The truth is that I'm not allowed to write stories for the business section," I said.

"Too bad," he said, eyes veering to my uneaten cake. "Because this guy I know, who tells me, he knows a lot about how these crooks work. He says they keep accounts. Records of the claims. The settlements. Who gets paid. Even a book, like recipes."

"Like recipes? What are you talking about?" I tried to sound skeptical, but my heart had started twirling inside my chest, as if there were an internal propeller that could lift me from my chair. Records. Could they really keep records?

"Plans, how you say . . ." He began drawing in the air with his finger.

"Pictures?" I asked.

He shook his head. Kept drawing in the air. "Like directions for each kind of accident."

"Diagrams?"

He nodded. "Yes. How to hit cars for the most damage and not get too hurt. And many instructions on what to say to the police, what to put in the report, what to say to the doctors. They call it . . . a *screep* book."

This took me a minute to translate. Script book? As in the accident completely scripted, laid out in detail on a page? I hovered somewhere over the table a moment, then forced myself down. This was too good to be true. Unlikely. Far-fetched. "And this guy can get his hands on this book?"

Caspar's eyes met mine. Had the brows shifted direction again, or was I imagining that? "Not this book. The top guys keep that. Tito or the other guy who runs operation—"

"Tito?" I interrupted him. "Your guy worked for Tito?"

He made a palm-upward gesture that translated as "who else?" Then he continued, "My cousin's cousin, he used to be what they call a runner. Set up the accidents. He knows a lot of things. The locations. Even some of the doctors, the lawyers, they use."

Had he already guessed that this was exactly the kind of break I needed and that I'd be willing to do anything to get it? "Why would this guy be willing to talk to me?"

"Because he's family and knows we Dominicans get no breaks we don't make for ourselves." He frowned. "He has saved enough money to go back home, but he knows if my bakery takes off, his family, his sisters, his aunts who stay here have jobs. The future is there." He pointed at the cake.

A moment passed. Tentatively, I reached for the plate. The untouched slice scolded me for my lack of diplomacy. I began to scrape off a peach.

"You don't like peaches?" he asked.

"Allergic." I lied.

"If I was some fancy new shop in the mall, you reporters would be all over me, trying my cake," he said.

I thought about that. If they served this cake in some cool café on Thayer Street, we might do a feature. Interview the college kids who claimed it was their newest, latest, obsession. I scraped off the remainder of the peach and took a large forkful of the cake. It was surprisingly moist. The flavors were mostly vanilla and orange; it tasted nothing of peach.

Caspar Vasquez was an honest, hardworking man taking on the long odds of launching a new business. It seemed to me that the paper loved these recipes for ethnic specialties. Italian cookies at Christmas, charoset during Passover, a Cape Verdean corn-and-bean stew for special celebrations. Why not a Dominican cake? I thought of Carolyn. The newly appointed food editor. I took another bite of the cream icing.

"And how often does your paper write positive stories about the Dominican community?" Caspar pressed.

He had a point. Outside of our annual Hispanic Month, the *Chronicle* tended to cover its newest immigrant populations only when they suffered disease outbreaks or committed horrendous crimes. I told myself that the paper had a legitimate interest in broadening its Hispanic readership in Rhode Island, a responsibility to educate the parochial majority about the richness of minority culture, instead of just the problems of poverty.

God, I was insightful. More noble than the rest. And being brand-new in the job, Carolyn might need story ideas. "I can mention this as a possible feature in the food section."

"That runs on Wednesdays?" Caspar Vasquez must have done an exhaustive review of each day's *Chronicle*, cover to cover.

"I can't promise; I can only ask. It's up to the food editor."

His world-weary smile suggested that his years in America had taught him to give nothing away for free. "Likewise. I can only ask. It's up to my cousin to decide if it's worth his time to talk to a reporter."

11

Tres Leches

BY CAROLYN RIZZUTO

Chronicle Food Editor

It translates as Three Milk Cake, a Dominican delicacy with a dense sweet cake lightened by a froth of meringue that will melt in your mouth.

Actually, the origin of this rich dessert is a subject of debate. Some say that it came from Sinaloa, Mexico. Others argue Guatemala or Nicaragua. Wherever the source, the cake is popular with Rhode Island's Dominican community and a top seller at Caspar's, a new bakery in Providence that also supplies several downtown restaurants with the dessert item.

Tres Leches is made by soaking butter cake in three different kinds of milk: regular, sweetened condensed, and evaporated. It is frosted with whipped cream or meringue and decorated with fruit. Caspar Vasquez, the new owner of Caspar's, says the key is in the freshness of the orange juice and zest, as well as the quality of peach slices.

***See* Recipe, page D-4**

I held up the day's food section and mouthed the words to Carolyn as I stood over her desk. "I owe you."

But she didn't see me. I was standing just outside her office, a doorless cubicle in the Lifestyle department upstairs, but she was in the middle of a phone conversation. It was someone she didn't like, I could tell by the way she was sitting, shoulders slumped forward and receiver turned just slightly away from her ear. She rolled her eyes. Not at me, but at something the person on the other end of the phone said.

"Thank you," I tried again, waving the paper to get her attention, but she was now listening in a focused way that suggested a conversation with upper management. She held up her hand, telling me to wait.

Wearing a silk suit of some sort of nubby texture that was soon to be in department stores everywhere, Carolyn picked at one of the nubs on her lapel. "Today? We have to have the meeting *today*?"

By her petulant tone, I suspected that she was talking to Terrence Westhauser, the Lifestyle department editor. Not because Terrence was difficult. In fact, from what I'd heard of him, he was a decent sort, much respected as both creative and fair. But he was Carolyn's boss, and Carolyn hated anyone who was a boss.

"Oh." Now Carolyn was looking up, eyes wide. "Oh no." Her eyes met mine, transmitting alarm. Bad news was at hand.

When she finally hung up, I asked, "You didn't get in trouble for ditching the corn feature, did you?"

"Nah. The paper loves that ethnic shit. Terrence said it reached out to the community." Her tone made it sound like a pretension on the part of upper management, but I breathed a sigh of relief anyway. "It's the one and only thing he's liked that I've done so far," she added.

It was actually only the third or fourth food section she'd put out since she'd taken the job, but there was no point in arguing. Carolyn's distrust of anyone in newspaper authority was deeply engrained. "So what's wrong?"

"The papers were signed this morning."

Our eyes met. Although we'd known the sale of the *Chronicle* was likely, it still hit hard. We shared a moment of mourning for the paper we knew, a moment of fear for the unknown ahead.

"We shouldn't be shocked," I said, although clearly we both were.

"It gets worse." Carolyn stood so she could reach across the desk and put her hand on my shoulder, steeling me. "Terrence says they're gonna make the announcement by the end of the month. I've got to meet with him this afternoon and decide who in my department can go." She sliced her finger across her throat. "They're cutting the news staff by at least fifteen percent. Not just buyouts. We're talking a massive layoff."

Downstairs in the newsroom, the word had gotten out. There was none of the usual banter between reporters, no gathering around the copy machine, and no arguments in the sports department about who was to blame for last night's Red Sox defeat. Voices were low, as if there were a casket in the room, and even the ringing phones seemed muted. People sat at their desks, staring dull-eyed into their screens.

Kira, one of the business reporters, greeted me at my desk by handing me the press release announcing the sale. The Ink and Mirror Media Group, owner of the *Los Angeles Herald* and two dozen other underfunded daily metropolitan newspapers across the country, was a darling among analysts for its "focus on the bottom line." I tried to take some solace from the closing line of the press release, a quote from Ian Clew, the new publisher, promising to "maintain the high quality of reporting for which the *Chronicle* is known." But in my heart, I knew that every big chain that had ever bought and butchered an independent newspaper had said exactly the same thing.

"You're lucky," Kira said. "I hear he *likes* investigative reporting."

"Really?" I tried to sound hopeful. Still, a five-man investigative team would have to be considered unnecessarily lavish in a newspaper our size. If 15 percent of the news staff was going to be laid off, at least one of us would be cut from the team.

I pushed the press release away from me, and stared numbly into the newsroom. At length, I began to focus on a moving body—Jonathan Frizell walking toward the copy machine. His square, sturdy frame was uncharacteristically slouched, and the look of self-satisfaction one came to expect from him was frighteningly absent.

"His wife is having a baby," Kira told me. "Before the announcement, he was telling everybody about it."

Frizell, a father? I'd had a hard enough time believing he'd found a wife. And yet, I could picture him, somehow, on all fours, roughhousing with a toddler. Could see him doting on the junior Frizell in little Lacoste shirts and Baby Gap chinos. I felt something that approximated empathy. As blithely confident as he liked to appear, Frizell was worried, too. Maybe more worried than the rest of us.

Behind me, the murmurs in the financial department were growing louder. Phones began to ring more frenetically, and conversation resumed at a louder decibel. Three of the sports reporters crumpled up their press releases and starting throwing them at the trash basket in a shooting contest. One of them landed next to my foot.

The wall clock that hung in the financial department was sophisticated, resembling a Cartier watch, with its Roman numerals, but it still ticked off the minutes loudly, like in a schoolroom. I only had an hour before I had to relieve Ryan, who was currently stuck on our Riordan surveillance.

I put in another call to Dane Piedmont, who had still not called me back. After making such a big fuss about me being a reporter, he was clearly evading a chance to help the media. But he was a long shot anyway. Even if he knew Lizette, I doubted she'd confided much about her husband's involvement in the car ring.

Then I returned to my notes. Leafing through them, I stopped dead at the shorthand I'd scribbled on the final page: "Records. Diagrams. Top guys keep."

Top guys, not top guy. A definite plural. It occurred to me now that if Lizette had been able to steal ten thousand dollars from Tito, it probably meant that cash had been stored at her home. If Tito trusted Manuel with cash, why not business records?

At the city desk, I saw Dorothy look over her shoulder toward the Fishbowl. Following her gaze, I saw Nathan, the managing editor, sitting with Ellen Felty at the conference table.

I began flipping backward in the notebook to my earlier interview with Marcella and found her cell phone number. Grabbing the phone, I punched it in and caught her in her car, on the way to the dog track.

She sounded amused when I asked her about the script book. "They need a book for directions for how to smash up?"

"That's what this guy says. They have detailed instructions. Like recipes for the accidents—that's the way he explained it."

"I do not believe Manuel has such a thing," Marcella, too, pronounced it *screep book*. "Lizette never talked about *this* book."

"Lizette talked about *other* kinds of books?"

Marcella snorted something in Spanish, presumably at another driver. I heard a horn in the background, and then Marcella began reaming someone out.

Dorothy stood up and began to stride purposefully down the middle aisle toward the Fishbowl. She wore a grim expression similar to the one I'd seen on Carolyn's face earlier today. Were they having the same kind of emergency meeting? Trying to decide just how many and who could be cut from the investigative team?

"My sister was smart," Marcella finally said in English, "smarter than Manuel. Good with the numbers."

Was she saying that Lizette *kept* the books? "What are you trying to tell me?"

There was a significant pause.

"I have not told you this before," Marcella began. "But you must promise it is not in your story. Not anywhere."

I promised.

"Lizette did not like this business. This work of Manuel's, but sometime, he needed her to keep it all straight. The claims they make. The money that comes from the companies. Who gets paid. How much the accident make. She help him sometimes."

"So there *are* financial records at her house?" I asked, excitedly.

There was another long, protracted silence on the other end of the phone.

As Dorothy headed toward the Fishbowl, she ran into two men in business suits whom I'd never seen before. Corporate guys from L.A., or maybe one of them was the new publisher. The three of them stopped outside the conference room. Dorothy was forcing a smile, shaking hands.

"You think you could get inside the house? Look around and see?" I asked.

Marcella did not answer.

The *Chronicle* editors and the corporate guys were all sitting down together now, inside the Fishbowl. The corporate guys were doing all the talking. Dorothy was folding her arms protectively over her chest. With documentation, a running calculation of how much was coming in from the accidents and how much went out to lawyers, I'd have no trouble convincing any of them that this story should go straight to the front page.

"Please?" I pressed.

"I promise Manuel, I clean out Lizette's things for him," she finally replied. "Maybe. I go there tomorrow, when he's at work, but—"

"Thank you!" I said.

"But what if I find these books? It does nothing to prove Tito killed my sister."

"Nothing by itself ever proves anything," I said to Marcella. "It's little bits that add up."

This did not seem to impress her. So I continued, "Tito is out on parole. That means if we get anything, *any* evidence that he was involved in *any* kind of crime, they'll send him back to prison."

There was a painfully long silence as Marcella considered this. And then, "You have to do something for me. An exchange."

Didn't anybody ever do anything just because it was a good idea? Dorothy was reading something from a piece of paper to the corporate guys. Circulation numbers? Feedback on articles? A list of reporters deemed expendable?

"You go to that lawyer," Marcella continued.

"What lawyer?" For a moment, my mind flitted back to Dane.

"The lawyer that helps Manuel. Who wants to make the money on my sister's death. You ask him if he thinks there is a car that ran my sister off the road, why no one looks for it? Why he does not ask the police to do their jobs? You see what he says?"

I was stunned, mostly by what a good idea this was. If Joe D'Anzana wasn't tacitly accepting this case as fraud, *why* wasn't he pushing the cops to investigate? Criminal charges would only benefit his civil suit. I thought about Caspar's claim that his cousin knew the names of the lawyers and doctors involved in the scam. Maybe D'Anzana wasn't just a cheesy, unethical lawyer; maybe he was an integral part of the ring.

I told Marcella. "I'll try to get there today."

I spent another long, fruitless afternoon parked on Richmond Street, waiting for the state's business regulation head to leave his office. When Riordan finally did duck out, at about three o'clock, I followed him to that same medical office on the East Side. This time, I noticed that there were residential apartments on the third floor. When he was safely inside, I got out of my car and walked into the lobby, where I copied the names on the mailboxes into my notebook. I prayed to God that Albert Riordan was, at the very least, having an affair.

Back in the newsroom, Jonathan was unrealistically encouraged. "Do a database search on the names on the mailbox," he said, as if I wouldn't figure this out on my own. And then, "I hear Riordan likes young babes. In their twenties."

I had a hard time picturing Riordan with a twenty-year-old, but then I have a hard time picturing any sixty-year-old man with any young babe, so I nodded along. Then Jonathan went into a story about how Riordan had once been seen leaving the Marriott Hotel with a former Miss Rhode Island. Now that Frizell was going to be a father, this kind of deviant behavior filled him with a new level of outrage.

I pretended to be listening, but I kept eyeing the clock, eager to leave. I was hoping to get to D'Anzana's office just after six o'clock, when even the most dedicated administrative assistants left for the day and the lawyers were forced to answer their own buzzers and telephones.

It was just about a quarter to six when I left the *Chronicle* and headed to my car. I was in full dialogue, mentally rehearsing my opening pitch to D'Anzana. I didn't pay much attention to the man leaning against the building outside on Fountain Street.

It wasn't until I was halfway down the block on Union,

heading to Washington Street where I'd parked my car, that I heard footsteps gaining on me. I turned and saw him a few yards behind me. His head was turned down, so I couldn't see his face, but there was a big blue blob on his biceps that might have been a tattoo.

He was following me; I could feel it. Arteries opened and pumped blood into my legs. I sped down the street at power-walk pace. All extraneous thought, all ferment about Matt and insecurity about my job was completely blown out of my head. I grabbed my keys, splaying them between my fingers as a weapon, ridges out.

Strangely, the fear was invigorating, a rush of electricity that made me feel acutely alive. Then, as I turned right onto Washington Street, I saw another man, standing on the curb at the far end of the block, right near where I'd parked my car. I couldn't make out his face, but he was medium height, with long, straight hair under a blue bandana. And he was wearing a rain poncho, even though it wasn't raining.

As I approached, he lifted something over his head. An ax? Crowbar? He was searching the sidewalk for something, waiting. And then his gaze landed on me. My muscles tightened, and I froze on the street. In an instant, the crowbar came down. Once on the windshield, once on the passenger door window. There was a loud crash and chunks of glass skittered across the sidewalk.

Two women who had just walked out of a nearby restaurant began shouting for police. The man in the rain poncho took off, running in the opposite direction, across the street.

My car.

I began running. A crowd began to gather on the sidewalk,

making it hard to press through. As I got closer, I had to slow down to step across a moat of broken glass. One of the women from the restaurant held up her arm like a safety patrol, warning me away. Twelve years old, with bald tires and in need of a good wash, my Honda looked like the kind of victim that might not recover. The windshield was a mosaic of cracked glass that lay over the car like an ugly curtain. The passenger window was blown out, its safety glass reduced to the strange glass baubles on the seat and on the ground.

A Providence police cruiser pulled up, double-parked in the street, and a cop jumped out. He had young eyes, but hair that was completely silver. The two women from the restaurant immediately began to fill him in on what happened.

"Is that your car?" he asked me.

Mutely, I nodded.

"Did you see who did it?"

I was having a tough time forming words. "I was a block away," I finally answered.

One of the women from the restaurant stepped in. "Damn vandals," I heard her say. She began to give the cop an identification of the guy with the crowbar. "About twenty-five or thirty. Straight blond hair. And wearing some weird poncho."

While the cop was writing all this down, the man who had followed me from the *Chronicle* caught up. He brushed so close to me, he nearly pushed me off the sidewalk. "Too bad about your car," he said.

My foot skidded through the granules of glass as I was forced away from the curb. He stood between me and my car, a pulsating blockade. I backed away.

He tilted his head as if assessing the damage and offered a

low whistle of appreciation. Then he pointed to a tow truck that was making its way up Washington Street. The lettering on the door said "The Big T."

He leaned toward me, so his bare shoulder almost touched mine, and I could see that his tattoo was a serpent, coiled. "You got something you need fixed? You go to Tito. He'll fix it for you."

The cop was not particularly shocked by the vandalism. "Tough break," he said. "But luckily it's mostly glass damage. No deductible. You got Triple A?"

I shook my head.

"Well, you're going to have to get it out of here. Can't leave it on the street."

I glanced at the Big T tow truck that was now double-parked right behind the police cruiser and considered telling the cop about the man with the serpent tattoo. But if I told the cop about Tito's threat, I'd be dragged down to the station for questioning, which would take hours. Plus, the threat would go into an official report, which could easily be picked up by our police reporter. If Dorothy heard about it, she would never let me pursue the story about the fraud ring.

"A friend is coming to pick me up. Can I deal with it later?"

"I wouldn't wait too long. It'll be picked clean. You really need to get it off the street." He gestured to the Big T truck. "They can tow it for you. You want me to tell them to take it?" the cop asked.

I glanced at my watch as Walter's cab turned the corner. We wouldn't get to Joe D'Anzana's office until almost seven o'clock, now. It was too late. I'd just have Walter take me home. Maybe he would know a good tow company I could call.

"I hear they do pretty good work," the cop said.

Tito had gone to great lengths to try to get my car, I thought. What was it he wanted to say to me?

A shiver plunged down my back, sending impulses to my fingertips. *He might not say anything. He might just shoot me in the back of the head.*

But I'd love to get inside that body shop. If Tito wanted to kill me, he'd have done it. He was more interested in sending me a message.

This is crazy, Hallie. What would you possibly gain?

Maybe I could overhear something. Or see something suspicious. Seeing something suspicious wasn't good enough, the voice inside scolded. You need proof. Records. Documents. Photographs.

It was then that I thought about the camera function in my new cell phone.

I felt the same way I had running down Washington Street—fully engaged. No extraneous thoughts, anger, or remorse. I was standing before the mother of all slot machines.

"Or you can call someone else to come tow your car," the cop was saying.

I was stopped in that moment when everything else ceased to exist while you waited for the dealer to turn the card, when the fear of losing was as exciting as the possibility of a big win.

"Well, since the Big T truck is already here," I heard myself tell the cop, "let them take it away."

12

The next morning, I got the call. "Who you got?" a male voice asked, without identifying himself or making any attempts at a preliminary introduction. The bullying undertone and fear in my stomach told me it was Tito Manaforte.

I was sitting at my desk, having just gotten off the phone with Eddy, Carolyn's ex-husband, who told me that he'd seen Tito Manaforte at a PawSox game with "that attack lawyer on TV." He meant Joe D'Anzana. "I think they got a relationship" was Eddy's assessment.

Although it was pretty much just gossip—which couldn't be used in a story—it was still an interesting morsel, and I'd been feeling semivictorious as I sipped an extralarge coffee with too much caffeine. But now I spilled half of it trying to find an empty spot on my desk to put it down.

"You got insurance, right?" Tito asked again.

"Yes. Of course." I feigned ignorance. "Is this the tow company?"

"The tow company. The tow lot. The people who are going to replace your glass, unless you got a problem with that. You got a problem with that?"

"No. No. Of course not. Is this the Big T Body Shop?"

He laughed a raw, humorless laugh that did not provide an answer. But he knew that I knew who he was, I could tell by his short, impatient breathing. The puddle of coffee on my desk quivered toward the floor. I grabbed some tissues from a box on the next desk and threw them on top, waiting, it seemed like forever, for him to say something.

"I need you to call your insurance company and get an okay on this. You got a policy with Whitehouse?" he finally asked.

"Yes." He wasn't psychic or anything. This was New England's largest car insurer. Unless you were in the high-risk pool, there was a better-than-average chance Whitehouse wrote your policy.

"Okay, then. You ask for Marty D'Errico, he's an adjuster, a good buddy of mine. You tell him I sent you. Then everything should go good and you can come get your car at five o'clock." He laughed as if this were the biggest joke in the world and hung up the phone.

The Big T Auto Body Shop was on West Fountain Street, less than a mile from the newsroom, but on the other side of the highway in an industrial neighborhood inhabited mostly by auto body and parts shops. There were vehicles everywhere: cars, trucks, even a couple of boats up in cradles, all wedged together in crowded lots and parked on the crumbling brick-paved street in front of the buildings.

The Big T was the largest of the body shops, with four bays opening onto West Fountain and another two opening onto a side street. It was a one-story brick building with a tall sign mounted to the flat roof that said merely AUTO BODY, as if this were the only auto body shop in the world. On the awning, over the door, lettering identified the place as "The Big T." You got the feeling it didn't need a whole lot of advertising.

This late in the day it was quiet, with most of the garage doors already snapped shut for the day. Walter parked his cab about a block up the street across from Matarese Towing, where an enormous tractor trailer appeared to be in the midst of dissection, and the lot was surrounded by tall fencing, barbed wire, and two signs warning about a dog.

I took a deep breath and tried to remember what the hell I had been thinking by letting the Big T tow my car. That I'd waltz in there and photograph every car that had ever been used to commit insurance fraud in the state of Rhode Island? Or maybe I was thinking I'd find one of those script books lying on the counter?

"Let me go in with you," Walter said.

"No," I said swiftly. To have any chance at getting anything at all, I'd need to blend into the background. With his cowboy boots and alpha-male swagger, Walter did not blend. He competed for dominance without so much as opening his mouth.

He stared at me a moment and frowned. "I'm really starting to wonder about what motivates you."

"Keeping my job."

He shook his head.

"You think I want to *lose* my job?"

"I think there's something else going on."

"I told you about the layoffs."

"I know," he said, "but you're pushing the envelope in a weird way."

I pretended not to understand. "What does that mean?"

Dangling from the ignition was a gray rabbit's-foot key chain his girlfriend, Geralyn, had given him as a joke. He stroked it thoughtfully a moment. "I know you don't want to hear this. But I think it's all about the action, Hallie. About the rush."

"You've gone to too many meetings, Walter. I *could* just be doing my job."

"Or you could be keeping yourself so busy, so highly charged, that you don't have to deal with anything."

I rolled my eyes.

He opened his mouth to say something, but must have decided to chuck it. He must have remembered about the futility of preaching. We'd been to so many twelve-step meetings together, I could actually see by the struggle in his expression that he was trying to detach.

"Okay, okay," he finally said, changing tack. "Anyone tries anything, go right for his eyes." He made a poking gesture with his hands. "If they can't see you, they can't kill you."

I nodded.

Then he reached for my cell phone, double-checked to make sure it was programmed to redial his number, and handed it back to me. "All you do is hit the send key, and I'm coming in after you."

He tilted his left ankle and let his knee fall wide so I could see the gun hidden inside the cowboy boot. After he was robbed a second time at gunpoint, he'd taken to carrying a

.38-caliber handgun in an ankle holster whenever he drove his cab. "And no matter what, if you're not out in twenty minutes, I'm coming in after you."

A shoot-out between a made man and a former drug dealer? Nothing I wanted to be responsible for. I told myself that I'd just go into the body shop like any other customer and pick up my car. If I had a chance to snap photos of a few license plates with my cell phone camera or listen in on a few conversations without taking an unnecessary risk, fine. If not, I'd just get the hell out of there as fast as I could.

I reached for the gray rabbit's foot and stroked it. "You think this works?"

"If you're not stupid, it works okay," Walter replied. "If you're stupid, nothing helps."

With that bit of wisdom, I got out of the car and headed toward the Big T. We'd had a break in the rain. A day of almost sunshine that had even begun to dry up the puddles in the sidewalk before the rain was supposed to start again tomorrow.

There were a dozen cars in various states of disrepair parked around the perimeter of the Big T building, front ends facing the brick. I stopped twenty feet away, bent down as if I were fiddling with my backpack, and copied the three license plate numbers I could read into a notepad.

Through the only open door of a bay, I could see a man in a jumpsuit and safety glasses holding an enormous silver power tool in a pistol grip. He looked up at me briefly, and I dropped the notepad inside the backpack and righted myself. He turned away and began to cut through an Oldsmobile like it was a piece of cake.

Maybe Walter was right about the rush. But that exhilarated feeling I'd been searching for now just felt like fear. Telling myself that Tito couldn't bump me off in his place of business when there was still daylight, I straightened my shoulders and tried not to feel the whining of the electrical tool in my teeth.

I was prepared for greasy floors and dingy cinder block and a lot of bad lighting inside. Instead, I found spotless black and white tile. A clutter-free reception counter with a bell on it, and on the desk beneath, a neatly organized in-box, a dozen Post-its symmetrically arranged on a desk blotter, and keys pinned in neat rows on a bulletin board. Behind the desk was a three-drawer file cabinet, with three loose-leaf binders standing side by side on top. In picture frames on the wall were a photo of a very nice Corvette and a Certificate of Achievement for Heavy-Duty Towing.

There were, however, no other customers in sight, and the counter was unmanned. To the right was a hallway to what I guessed opened to the service area and the bays I'd walked past. Somewhere behind the reception desk, I could hear men arguing. I could see through a window into what looked like a supply or stock room. Three men stood with their backs toward me gesturing to each other with their hands.

I didn't ring the little bell. Instead, I leaned over the counter and tried to see if there were any labels on the loose-leaf binders. Like maybe one that said *Script Book,* or *Ill-Gotten Gains*, or simply *Incriminating Evidence Hallie Could Use*. The first two had nothing on them. A third had something in block print, but I couldn't make it out.

The escalating argument in the inner office checked any notion I might have to lean any farther over the desk. One of the voices definitely had a Spanish accent and could have been Manuel. The other sounded like Tito. The whining of the electrical equipment in the bay suddenly stopped and I caught the words "full of shit" and "moron."

"Oh my Gawd, have you been waiting long?" a woman asked.

I jumped up from the counter and turned to see a tall, thin woman in her late twenties walking out of the service area with a clipboard in her hand. Her hair was bleached completely white and pulled so tightly into a ponytail that it seemed to stretch her forehead. She had on a low-slung pair of blue jeans and a tank top that should have been worn under a blouse and not alone.

"Just a couple minutes," I said.

"I am *so* sorry," she went on. "Tito hates it if we make any customer wait. He goes ripshit. You won't complain, will ya?"

"Don't worry."

She smiled, revealing enormous white teeth that also looked bleached. Skirting around me to get behind the counter, she dropped the clipboard on the desk and with a wince acknowledged the argument going on in the supply room. "Tito is in a mood, today. What's your name?"

I gave her my name and she began searching among the various sheets of Post-its pinned to the half wall. She grabbed one, studied it a moment. "Oh," she said to herself.

She took a moment to check me out more carefully. I was wearing a khaki blazer over a button-down shirt and cargo pants. Obvious reporter clothes. She flashed her smile again, but this time it seemed a little forced. I gathered that she had made some sort of connection.

"How much do I owe you?" I made a move toward the bag over my shoulder, but she shook her head.

"Insurance covers all glass."

"The towing?"

But she shook her head again and glanced over her shoulder at the supply room, where the men were still yelling. A young, wiry man with a nub of beard seemed to be the object of Tito's wrath. "What the fuck are you trying to say?" I heard Tito demand.

The young man began to shout back an explanation.

"Franco, he just doesn't know when to shut up," the receptionist said.

"Is the car ready?" I asked.

"Oh, it's ready." She turned to make a move toward the door, but halted. I could tell she didn't want to go in. "Just a minute." She pushed herself forward and opened the door. I listened to hear if the argument would cease, but it didn't. She'd have to wait while the men inside continued to duke it out.

The door shut behind her, but no one acknowledged her entrance. The men stepped farther into the room and appeared to be huddled around something, with their backs still toward me. I could see someone's arm raised, a fist punching the air. "Don't tell me how to run my fucking business, you nimrod," I heard Tito shout. I told myself to just wait patiently at the reception counter. The object was to get out of here alive—without involving Walter.

But the continued energy of the voices from the supply room suggested the argument was far from over, and I couldn't help thinking that it would only take a minute to walk over to the hallway to see if I could peek into any of the bays and snap a few license plates. It wasn't cordoned off as if it were top-secret or anything. I could pretend to be checking out the garage or looking for my car.

As I headed toward the hallway, my heart began to pump

and the rush of blood produced a tingling sensation in my shoulders and arms. This must be what a heart attack feels like, I thought. Only I liked the feeling. Walter was right about that. Every other concern—even how the hell I was going to pull off this story—disappeared in this circulatory high that made my thinking suddenly clear. But why else had I come here, put myself through this, if I wasn't willing to take a peek?

The hallway was a long corridor with a line of open doorways, each leading to what looked like the four separate bays I'd seen on the street. I hesitated at the threshold and listened. Behind me, I could hear the angry voices still battling.

The first bay appeared dark, closed for the day. I walked farther to the second, which was a larger garage with three separate work areas. With my cell phone, I snapped the license plates of a Mercury Sable with a dented front fender and a Volkswagen Passat on a hydraulic lift. I had to squeeze past the Passat to get the plate of the last car, an old Malibu with the door torn off.

I swiftly retreated to the corridor, where I could hear that the argument had not abated. With another check over my shoulder to make sure no one had turned to peer out of the window into reception, I headed back to the third bay.

This was the bay that I'd seen from the sidewalk, with the man working on the Oldsmobile with the license plate missing. I ducked past it to the last bay, which was glassed in. I saw another man leaning over a car with a paint gun. The entire room seemed to be raining a fine ruby mist.

Suddenly, I became aware of a pause in the men's arguing. As I headed back through the corridor, the lighter strains of a female voice began to murmur. The receptionist must be telling Tito that I was here.

I had just made it to the entrance to the reception area

when I saw Tito begin to turn. I leaned into the door and pretended to be squinting into the nearest bay.

"What are you looking for?" It was the receptionist. She was standing outside the now open door of the supply room.

"I'm just checking out that Oldsmobile." I made scissors with my fingers and pretended to cut through the air. "Pretty cool, the way he's ripping it apart." I said.

Behind her, the young Hispanic man marched out of the supply room and headed through the reception area toward the front door. "And don't come back," Tito called after him.

The door slammed. The receptionist stood completely rigid, as if bracing herself for Tito's reaction.

"And you can all go home," he said to the receptionist and the other man he'd been arguing with. They moved quickly, as if they couldn't wait to get the hell out of there. I shivered and fingered the cell phone in my pocket. The receptionist stopped briefly at the desk to pick up her handbag and without looking at me again, she headed out the front door followed by the two men. The door clicked behind them and there was scratching that might have been a lock.

Tito approached me. Up close, the purple of his scar was darker, as if colored by the anger that seemed to be his normal state. He was wearing a Big T T-shirt with the sleeves cut off, tight-fitting blue jeans, and a pair of souped-up ankle-height basketball sneakers that were red, white, and blue.

"You need to wait in the waiting area," he said, pointing to the row of plastic chairs near the door.

"Sure," I said meekly. It was hard to keep my eyes off the mottled texture of the skin.

"Now." The command reverberated off the tile floor into my knees.

I started toward the chairs, wondering if I should just keep going out the door. How far could I get before I felt his hands around my neck. Inside my pocket, I flipped open the phone and felt for the send key. The phone fell out of my pocket onto the floor.

Tito turned abruptly, headed toward the file cabinet, and swung open the lower drawer. He was reaching for something. Oh Christ, he was going for a gun.

My hand went for the door. I twisted the handle. It was locked.

He spun around. "Where the hell you going?"

I looked back. There was no gun in his hand. He was holding two Ziploc bags. The gallon size.

For the first time, his anger abated. He chuckled to himself. "Come on, scaredy-cat, get over here. We ain't done," he said, plopping the bags on the counter.

Slowly, I picked up my phone and made my way back toward the counter. Inside one of the bags, I could see my shaving razor, with the razor missing, a notebook I'd been looking for, a stapler, a Chap Stick, and a very old and shriveled orange. In the other bag was the end of a sleeve of saltines, and two half-empty water bottles.

"Don't you ever clean your car?" Tito asked.

"Sometimes," I lied.

He shook his head. "You gotta do a better job than this. This"—he pointed to the orange—"this was rotting, for Christ's sake. And this"—he pointed to the water bottles—"how much water do you spill on your floor? You got mold in the carpeting. It smells like an old rag. And your floorboards are rusting through."

I took the baggies and put them under my arm to try to

stop them from offending him. But he was still clearly disturbed.

"A hole in the floorboards—that's a death trap," he said. "A car costs a good chunk a change. Yah gotta take care of it better than that." It was eerily reminiscent of advice my mother had given me. "Those Hondas, they got a good resale value if you take care of them decent."

Had he lured me here to give me a lecture on car hygiene? I uttered some sort of vague promise. He turned and reached behind him underneath the counter to grab something. He handed me a bottle of spray carpet freshener.

"Usually I hand out one of the fresheners you hang from your mirror. But you got real problems with those rugs. I sprayed them once, but I want you to spray them again when you get home."

I nodded obediently.

"And take your car over to Henley and get him to fix your radio. I don't do electronics. But you should come back and let me replace those floorboards. That could be dangerous."

I nodded again, although I had no intention of ever coming back.

Then he dropped an insurance form and a pen on the counter. "Sign here," he ordered. I signed the form, trying not to let my hand shake. All I could think was: Why, why had Tito gone to all that trouble to get me here, if he wasn't going to kill me or threaten me within an inch of my life?

"Your car's out back, all ready to go. You probably want to get the hell out of here, don't ya?" He chuckled again.

Yeah, I wanted to get the hell out of here. Especially before Walter stormed in brandishing a gun. I no longer even cared about the car. But I grabbed my plastic bags and the carpet freshener from the counter and tried to smile as if I were sharing his joke.

"It looks real good, your car. Manny did a real good job. But you know, I want something, too."

He was staring at me, waiting for me to ask what he wanted, what I'd be willing to surrender to get out of the door alive. "What?" I asked, trying to sound calmer than I felt. "What do you want?"

He looked at me, levelly. "I want you to be fair," he said.

"Fair?" Had I heard him right? "Fair?" I repeated.

"I want you to listen to all parties, not just one." His eyes, which were wide-set and a little slitty, actually looked earnest. "Marcella," he said, "she's got her issues."

I wanted to cut this conversation short, get out of here before the time Walter allotted me ran out, so I shrugged, as if to say, I didn't really know much about Marcella, and made a move toward the door. But he stuck his arm out to block my path, and kept staring at me, the slitty eyes narrowing so that they almost seemed to close. "Look, I know you're talking to her."

I got a creepy feeling thinking about Norman following me and reporting back to Tito. But I wasn't about to confirm that I'd been talking to Marcella. I lifted my palms upward and shook my head in confusion, as if I had no idea what he was talking about.

"She hates me." For a moment, Tito sounded almost wounded.

"I don't know what this has to do with me," I tried.

"She's only been married to Roman a year, you know. We used to go out, Marcella and me, years ago. That's how Manuel got the job here. Through Marcella."

I tried not to stare at him in disbelief. I'd so firmly planted

Marcella in the straight, hardworking, law-abiding category, that it was shocking to think she might ever have looped arms with this man. Let alone be his girlfriend.

"She's a head case. Fucked-up, man. Still blames me for the ACI."

For getting sent to the Adult Correctional Institute to serve time? That seemed like good judgment on her part.

His eyes met mine, read my misunderstanding. "Not my sentence." He snorted. "Hers. She thinks I shoulda been able to keep her out. But she fucked up too bad, man. No one could do nothing for her."

This took a moment to process, but I refused to allow him the enjoyment of seeing my shock. I kept my eyes settled on his. "What did she do?" I asked.

He smiled. "Lots of things. Including lying to the judge. Her name was Diaz then. It was in your paper."

Perjury? I got a sick feeling in my stomach.

He put his hand on my shoulder and stood too close. His breath smelled of old coffee. "She's not exactly what you call a stand-up guy, Marcella. She wants to blame somebody for her sister's death. So she picked me. But why the hell would I risk it? Lizette was no one with nothing."

The coldness of this assessment hung in the air, and I was reminded of Marcella's comment about how cheap life was to Tito. I stepped backward, so that his hand dropped from my shoulder. I couldn't challenge his lack of motive without giving Marcella away, so I forced myself to look at him directly in the eye. "I don't know what you're talking about."

He stomped his red, white, and blue sneaker into the floor. "Look, enough with the bullshit. You were seen at the dog track."

Norman had seen me go up to the lunch counter, but I was certain he hadn't followed me to the ladies' room. Settling into my knees to regain balance, I took a breath, and forced myself not to overreact. "I like to bet on the dogs," I said, casually. And then, in case he didn't believe me, "I gamble, and I got the debt to prove it."

He clucked at this confession. "Gambling is for idiots," he said.

I ignored this comment. Instead, I tried to defuse his anger by giving him some bit of conversation he couldn't object to—something that would benefit Manuel's insurance claim. "The only thing Marcella has ever said to me—and it was at the church the day of the funeral—was about the cops. Why the cops aren't doing more to find out who drove her sister off the road."

Either I sounded convincing or this clicked with something else he knew because his eyes, a canine brown, relaxed a little, the ferocity muted. He picked up the forms I had signed from the counter and folded them in half. "That should be her number-one concern. Her nephews." A reference to the insurance claim. "But Marcella is a real cunt."

"I've got someone outside waiting for me. I really gotta go."

"And even if this accident is a gold mine, I had nothing to do with it," he continued. The mix of candor and denial made this sound oddly sincere. A part of me wanted to take this down in a notebook, quote him on this. But the other part knew that would be stupid. I just had to get the hell out of here. I nodded, trying to convince Tito that I'd been persuaded.

He searched my eyes as if he could see through my head if he just glared hard enough. Every organ in my body felt vulnerable, but I stood completely still, refusing to look away. At last, he was either convinced, or he'd had enough, because he turned. Gesturing for me to follow him, he headed toward a back door.

Outside, there was still a late afternoon sun, and I actually had to squint. We were in a parking lot with about two dozen cars in it. Behind the lot, separated by a chain-link fence with barbed wire across the top, was another, larger lot, also crammed with cars. The air smelled of gasoline.

I scanned for the exit as I followed Tito down the first row, so that I almost bumped into his back when he suddenly stopped. It took a minute to regain balance, to take in the transformation of my twelve-year-old Honda. The new windshield and passenger-side window gleamed. The entire car had been washed and polished. Except for a rearview window beach sticker that I'd bought last summer, it didn't even look like my car.

Then I noticed the pane of smoked glass cut into the roof. "I don't have a sunroof," I said.

He smiled and opened the driver's door for me. "You do now."

13

I drove home with the sunroof open, trying not to enjoy the elusive spring sun on my shoulder and the evening air blowing through my hair. But the truth was that I'd always wanted to drive with the feeling of freedom that only wind on a highway can inspire. This wasn't a convertible, but it was damn close.

Walter had said I should just consider myself lucky to be alive and not worry about the sunroof. He'd remarked that he'd never seen my Honda so clean. Then he drove off mumbling something about bringing one of his cabs to Tito with a smashed windshield. But as much as I loved the sunroof, reporters weren't allowed to accept gifts, particularly gifts of value. When I'd offered this objection to Tito, he'd sidestepped it brilliantly, insisting that it wasn't a present from him, but from Manuel. "For trying to save his wife's life. A Good Samaritan reward," he'd said.

It was a lie, I knew. A gift was another way to try to intimidate me. But there was no way to return it without leaving a gaping hole in my roof. And I couldn't help but reach up and touch the crank. It was a nice piece of hardware he'd thrown in.

Once I got back to my apartment, I downloaded the photos from my cell phone onto my laptop and recorded the last few license plates I'd copied as I drove past the front of Tito's on my way home. A total of almost a dozen cars. I had to hope at least one of them was involved in fraud and that I could convince Bennett Castiglia to help me. As the investigative team's computer expert, he had access to all kinds of databases, including Department of Motor Vehicle and Superior Court records, and could look up the names of the car owners, the accident reports, and any charges filed. This would be a tricky favor to ask since, technically, Dorothy had put the kibosh on this story.

I was trying hard to fend off feelings of desperation. But I knew that unless I got a major break, I was coming to the end of the road on this story. Especially since now I had an even bigger problem: If it was true about the perjury, my primary source was a court-certified liar. Wouldn't Dorothy love that?

I spotted my running shoes lying near the bedroom door where they'd landed this morning. My shins ached and I almost never ran twice in one day, but right now it seemed like the only way to settle my nerves.

I needed to get outside before the last of this sun went down, and more important, before Matt got home from work and there was a chance I'd run into him on the boulevard. I didn't want to see that loping gait, or catch him in the Boston College sweatshirt of his that I slept in sometimes. So I changed quickly into a T-shirt and shorts and pulled on my running shoes.

I didn't stop to lace up until I got to the boulevard. I'd been merely jogging until then, but once in the grassy mall, I decided that since I'd already done a long run this morning, I would focus on some speed work. It was the perfect time. At the dinner hour, the park was relatively empty, absent the teams of walking women and kiddie strollers that had clogged the path this morning. I could run hard enough to push myself into a blank exhaustion.

I needed to stretch before this kind of sprinting, and I dropped to an out-of-the-way patch of grass, lying on my back and pulling both knees to my chest. Staring at the sky and trying to release the stiffness of my hips and lower vertebrae, I closed my eyes and exhaled slowly. But I couldn't relax, couldn't lose the creepy feeling that Tito Manaforte had eyes everywhere.

If he had people watching me at the dog track, did he have them watching me leave my apartment? I sat up, looked up and down the path, then on both sides of the street. There was a line of cars parked at an angle on Butler before it broadened into the boulevard, but there didn't appear to be anyone in them. At least no one I could see.

I lay back down, berating myself for my nerves. Tito was probably lying about Marcella, doing his best to discredit her. I closed my eyes to shut out the sky. My exhale became a groan. No amount of deep breathing was going to make this story any easier to prove. Then, suddenly, I felt the ground rumble beneath me. I opened my eyes in time to see an enormous black Rottweiler mix barreling through the bushes, heading right for me.

The dog, about ten feet away, was square, like a prizefighter, with muscular haunches and a head half the size of its body. I sat up, began to search the ground for a stick. I couldn't find one.

As the dog ran toward me, I jumped to my feet. I backed up. It had huge nostrils and a jaw that looked prehistoric, but I knew not to run. The smartest thing was to stay perfectly still. If I ran, I'd be prey.

The dog circled me and snarled. It had a collar, but no apparent owner. I scanned the park searching for someone to come restrain this beast, but no one showed.

Suddenly, I was no longer scared, but angry at whoever owned this stupid dog and let it run free, angry at this aggressive animal, intimidating me. I realized then, that the worst thing I could do was let it know that I was scared, that it had an advantage. Standing my ground, I snarled back. "You're a bad, bad dog," I said in a low, commanding way.

The dog's eyes glittered at the insult. The ruff on its neck rose like a Mohawk. I tried not to focus on the jaw, what it could do to me in an attack. I scanned the ground again and picked up a fist-size rock.

I aimed for the dog's throat, missed, and hit the paw. The dog yelped. I found an empty soda can on the ground and raised it over my head, ready to launch again. "Bad, bad dog!" I said in as deep and disapproving voice as I could muster.

The Rottweiler dipped its head, turned slightly. The first sign of retreat. In the distance, I heard a woman call, "Luda! Luda!" The dog took it as an out and ran away.

"Impressive," a male voice said. "Very impressive."

It was Dane Piedmont, in running shorts and a T-shirt, walking toward me from the path. He had a rock in his hand, and I realized he must have been ready to help me. "That hound was no match for you," he said, letting the rock drop to the ground and brushing off his hands.

My legs were still quivering in the limbo between fight and

flight. I took a deep breath and tried not to think about the dog's open jaw, the bared teeth.

"You all right?" Dane Piedmont said, touching my shoulder.

"Fine," I said.

He stepped back, respecting my show of independence. His bare legs were long and muscled. The socks were hidden in brand-new Nikes with neon reflectors. I became aware of my crummy T-shirt, which had a tear under the arm, and the shorts, with the slightly stretched waistband. I wished I'd thought to at least brush my hair or my teeth.

"Hey, have you been trying to call me?" he asked, making it sound like a pleasant surprise.

I nodded.

"Sorry for not getting back to you. I've been tied up in court all week."

I nodded again. But when lawyers *wanted* to talk to you, they found time in the courthouse hallway, or called you on the way home from their car.

"About Lizette Salazar, my secretary said?" He didn't wait for me to confirm. "What a shitty thing, her accident."

We were both silent, a moment of respect.

"What are you writing?"

"I don't know if I'm writing anything yet," I said. Until I had more proof, it was best not to spread around my murder theory. "But I'm looking into insurance fraud."

He waited for me to elaborate, and I decided to keep it simple. I told him about the questionable testimony from Anna Theresa Plummer and that Joe D'Anzana was representing Lizette's husband in a massive insurance claim.

He rolled his eyes at the mention of D'Anzana's name, revealing the proper disgust for the personal injury lawyer. "But how can I help you?" He sounded puzzled. "I don't do any personal injury law.

His T-shirt, which had a name of a basketball league on it, had the arms torn off at the shoulder, revealing arm muscles as defined as his thighs. It was hard not to stare. "I heard you volunteered your services at the Hispanic Center, and I figured you might have worked with Lizette."

Did that sound far-fetched? Because he still looked just slightly bewildered. Like, of all the people who worked at the Hispanic Center, why had I called him?

"She was a good interpreter," he finally said. "Very precise. But I only worked with her on one or two cases. I don't know much about her on a personal level." And then, "You might want to call Vergen. She's the director. She knew Lizette a lot better than I did."

I might have explained that I'd already interviewed Vergen, but that would have made my calling him seem even more pointless than it apparently was. And I was starting to question my motives. Why had I really called him anyway? Clearly, he was wondering the same thing. So I thanked him as if that tip were just so helpful, and started to move away.

But he stopped me. "Hey, you want to run with me? Fend off the canines together?" he asked.

"I'm not sure I can keep up with you."

"We'll run at whatever pace you set." He smiled. "Please? I hate those frigging dogs."

I laughed. And how could I refuse, since obviously I had plotted this moment. We started at a reasonable pace, heading through the park, following the path to its end near the cemetery. Dane had a great stride, long and effortless. As we progressed, I found myself ignoring the ache in my shins completely, pushing faster off my heels, trying to impress him by using everything I'd learned in speed camp. By the time we were on the return loop, I was going as fast as I could, my throat was getting dry, and my legs hurt like hell. But my head felt clearer and my nerves began to settle. Finally, when we were back where we had started on the path, I slowed my pace, shifted to cool down. Sweat was running from my forehead into my eyes, and I was dying of thirst.

I could tell by Dane's even breathing that he had never had to push out of low gear. His hair wasn't the slightest bit damp, and his T-shirt appeared perspiration-free. "You okay?" he asked again.

"I forgot to bring a water bottle."

The sun had dipped below the horizon, and the park was growing dusky and gray. My T-shirt was soaked through with sweat and I needed a shower badly. "I think it's time for me to head home," I added.

"I'll walk you home."

I had a sudden vision of Matt looking out the window of his condo and seeing Dane Piedmont escorting me to my door. "You don't mind?"

"Hell no." He was smiling again, his eyes holding mine just long enough to let me know that this was a move. His move.

It occurred to me that since he was clearly useless as a source on this story, it was perfectly all right for me to date him. I smiled back.

Turning down Angell Street, we made our way through Wayland Square. The sidewalks were mostly empty, but in the distance I could see people still sitting at tables outside of Starbucks. By the bus stop, there was a pushcart selling Del's Frozen Lemonade. "We gotta have one," Dane said. And before I could answer, he pulled a five-dollar bill out of a stitched pocket in his running shorts that was apparently designed for this purpose and bought us each a large.

The lemonade, sweet and sharp, with little flecks of zest, came in a waxed paper cup. Partially frozen into soft slush, the lemonade melted the moment it touched the tongue. We found an empty bench outside the CVS Pharmacy and sat down to slurp with abandon.

My head was tilted back, cup to my lips, trying to drain every last drop. Dane reached over and tapped the bottom of my cup, so that stubborn bits of ice slid into my mouth.

He was sitting close, his shoulder nearly touching mine as he watched me swallow. Our eyes met, and his, a dark, determined blue, did not flit away. Then he took the cup from me to show me the most efficient way to twist out the ice, wringing the cup like a rag. When he put the cup back in my hand, his hand lingered an extra moment on mine.

A couple of minutes later, as we were crossing Elmgrove, Dane asked me if I liked baseball. "You kidding? I used to practically live at Fenway before I moved down here," I said.

The Sox were on a two-week road trip, but he had season tickets to the PawSox, a triple-A team that played at McCoy Stadium in Pawtucket. He wanted to know if I'd go with him sometime.

Even if I hadn't been completely seduced by Del's Lemonade, or by the way it felt sitting next to Dane, I would have said yes. This was one of those Rhode Island experiences I hadn't had yet. And I loved baseball.

He asked for my phone number, but neither of us had anything to write with. He began reciting it aloud, like a poem he had to commit to memory. As we headed toward the lobby of my building, I saw Matt's Audi take the corner onto Elmgrove and pull into his driveway. I stopped, hoping that he'd see me with Dane. But he did not look back as he got out of his car. Instead, he seemed preoccupied by a woman with short blond hair who got out of the passenger door.

Every muscle in my face tightened and several moments passed before I could breathe. If Dane noticed, he made no comment.

"Oh, wait a minute. The PawSox aren't back in town until Tuesday. Any chance you'd see me sooner? Like this weekend?"

I suggested dinner Friday night and he asked if it was okay if he picked me up on his motorcycle.

I envisioned the motorcycle, loud and fast, roaring past Matt's condo as it sped up Elmgrove Street. "Definitely," I said.

The first thing I did when I got to my desk the next morning was to key Marcella's maiden name into the database.

Unwrapping my breakfast—a fried egg sandwich on buttered rye—I took several large bites in case I was about to lose my appetite. Please God, let Tito be lying.

Across the room, I saw Dorothy step off the elevator. She worked until after eight in the evening and almost never arrived this early. She marched directly to the city desk without stopping to chat with the receptionist. I shifted my gaze to Nathan's office and saw that he was also in early.

I'd failed to put first and last names within quotes and the system pulled up every Diaz in Rhode Island. I re-keyed the query and was able to finish half of my sandwich before my search narrowed to the text that made my stomach take a dive.

Three years ago, Marcella Diaz, twenty-five, of South Providence, was sentenced to two years at the ACI for attempted robbery, as well as possession of OxyContin, a synthetic morphine and a Schedule II controlled substance. I scanned down the story to the last paragraph—OxyContin, she'd been strung out on OxyContin.

I swung the monitor away from me and covered my face with my hands. Three feet away, Kira, the business reporter, clucked with joy over a dire quarterly report about a toy company she covered. Could it get any worse?

"You okay?" Kira asked. At a mere twenty-two years old, she had turned down a job at *The Wall Street Journal* to live near her boyfriend, a quahogger. We had absolutely nothing in common, but she was the only person in the department who ever talked to me.

"Fine." I tried to look as if I meant it. As if the rug had not been pulled out from underneath my feet. Then I swung the monitor back into alignment and forced myself to read on. I tried to take heart in the fact that although the prosecutor made an allegation of perjury, there was no actual reporting of the outcome.

But the second item, the arrest story, killed any attempt at optimism. It had made the front page of a Saturday paper, apparently because all participants, victim and perpetrators, were female. The working mom pharmacist at the Wheaton Apothecary claimed that Marcella attacked her while two accomplices ransacked the inventory. There was no mention of a weapon, but I found myself picturing a knife.

For several minutes, I could do nothing but stare at the screen and try not to feel that knife slicing through me. Did Marcella hold it to her throat? I finally began to wonder. I scanned back to the sentencing story. Why wasn't the charge armed robbery? Or even assault?

I was still trying to process my misjudgment of Marcella and where the hell it left my story when I looked up again and saw Dorothy heading across the newsroom toward my desk. I immediately quit the database program and tried hard not to look as if I'd just lost a lot of blood.

"You got a hold of Bennett this morning?" Her tone was difficult to interpret.

"He's going to run those names against DMV records this morning." We were talking about the names I'd copied from the mailboxes when I'd followed Riordan to the East Side medical building last week. "I'm sorry, I got held up. I had major car troubles yesterday."

She didn't say anything but stood with her arms folded across her chest, with that weird expression on her face, like she was containing an emotion, but what? Amusement? Anger? Frustration?

"That's not the only assignment you gave Bennett, I hear."

Shit. I'd *thought* it had gone too easily when Bennett agreed to chase down the DMV records on the license plates from Tito's. Then he'd gone and squealed. "Look, I got a family member, a sister, who thinks Lizette was murdered. By Tito. With a motive tied . . ." But then I cut myself off, remembering what Tito had said about Marcella's own motives.

"Tied to what?" Dorothy probed.

If Marcella was trying to destroy Tito, maybe she'd been telling me what I wanted to hear. Drug addicts were known to be manipulative. Involuntarily, the image rose of Marcella with the knife. "The car ring," I said weakly.

"But there's still no police investigation?" Dorothy asked.

I shook my head.

"And no one on the record?"

"Not yet."

Dorothy had every right to explode, but, oddly, she didn't. She stood silently, as if calculating what the hell to do with me. Then she glanced over her shoulder at the Fishbowl, and I noticed yet another group of business suits beginning to collect inside. "Obviously, you must believe in this story because you won't let it drop," she began, "but Ellen and Ryan are both out sick, and Jonathan is following a new lead on Riordan's campaign contributions, so I need you and Bennett to pick up the slack on the surveillance."

Despite the Birkenstocks, Dorothy was not a touchy-feely type. Her managerial style involved insulating herself with an extra foot or two of physical distance. But now she stepped around the computer so she could lean close to me, put her hand on my shoulder, and speak in almost a conspiratorial tone. "I've got *another* meeting, but listen, there's going to be a lot, I mean *a lot* of changes around here. Right now, it's critical that the team gets something big in the paper—ASAP. We need to impress the new guys *before* they make the final decisions about cutbacks. So if you can just hold off on this car ring story until after we get this Riordan thing in the can, maybe all of us can keep our jobs."

14

I was forced to devote the next week to the Riordan story, following him from his home to his office, to his dry cleaner's and back to his home. This went on for two days with no scandal to report. Finally, I got a break on Wednesday, when Riordan left work after lunch and spent all afternoon at a house in Rumsford with a little sign on the door that said *MASSAGE THERAPIST.*

I called for a photographer, who came and snapped a clandestine shot of Riordan leaving the house with the massage therapy sign in the frame. And then, the very next morning, I got another hit when Riordan went straight from his home to the golf course.

There was a palpable sense of elation in the newsroom when I went back that afternoon to type up my notes on the three hours Riordan had spent golfing. We had now amassed enough proof of Riordan's spotty work schedule that Jonathan could begin the last phase of the story, confronting both Riordan and the governor who'd appointed him.

Dorothy was optimistic that if Jonathan agreed to work the weekend, we could showcase the story in Sunday's front page—two weeks before the big meeting in which the new publisher was scheduled to make the layoff announcements.

I was doing my best to remain as upbeat as Dorothy, to try to believe that another Frizell success could actually help me, and that I would still have a job on the investigative team, or with the newspaper even. But anxiety fluttered in my stomach like a bird that couldn't escape. I'd spent three years between newspaper jobs after I'd left the *Boston Ledger.* I didn't ever want to waitress again.

I tried to take comfort in the fact that I'd had a positive first date with Dane. We'd had a great dinner at a restaurant called Olive's that turned into a dance club by the time we'd finished our desserts. Mr. Nike could not only run like the wind, but he was a fairly decent dancer.

Finally, on Friday, with my surveillance role in the Riordan story finally over, I got a chance to flip through the notes I'd made after my conversation with Tito. The shock of Marcella's criminal history had worn off, but it troubled me that I'd made so many naive assumptions. "Lover's Revenge???" I'd written up the side of the paper, with three question marks.

Maybe I *was* being naive, but I wasn't ready to believe that Marcella was using me to set up Tito. And I wasn't willing to write her off because she'd made mistakes in her life. Having rehabbed from a drug problem myself, I, of all people, knew that an addict could change.

But the allegation of perjury remained a huge problem. I closed my notebook and stared out the window at the city, wondering what possible spin I could give perjury so that it wouldn't be a total deal breaker for Dorothy.

And then it occurred to me that Marcella's credibility issues wouldn't matter so much if she were able to get me actual proof. If she could find the business records that detailed the income and expenses of a fraudulent enterprise or named the participants and the payoffs, it didn't matter if she was a convicted perjurer. A document was like a bar of gold in the newspaper business. Once in hand, no one asked too many questions about how you got it.

First I called Marcella, who insisted that she would not search Lizette's home until I held up my end of the bargain. I decided not to raise the issue of her criminal history until *after* I had the records. I had to demonstrate good faith by making good on my promise to ask Joe D'Anzana about why he wasn't pressing police to find the supposed car that ran Lizette Salazar off the road.

So at three o'clock on Friday afternoon, I got into my still-sparkling Honda and drove to Warwick, Rhode Island.

Warwick is south of Providence, and like nearly all communities in Rhode Island, on the water. But it wasn't so much a beach community as a high-density suburb, home of the airport and one of the major shopping malls, with mixed housing and a lot of discount outlets. Traffic on the highway was already heavy as people headed home from Providence. But luckily for me, the three-story office building was right off the exit, sitting in front of a Motel 6 and across from a Dunkin' Donuts.

I parked in a back lot that was jammed with cars and followed an arrow to the front entrance. D'Anzana's office was on the first floor. A sign on the door featured a caricature of a pit bull that appeared to be thrashing itself against a chain-link fence. Underneath, the caption read: *Joe D'Anzana and Associates: Attack law at its best.*

The canine theme was carried through inside. The lobby, designed for the masses, with plain white walls, low-grade carpeting in olive green, and several sofas upholstered in tweed, had two life-size ceramic statues of pit bulls guarding the reception desk.

Two of the receptionists were on the phone and a third was trying to calm a man who was complaining that he'd been waiting for more than an hour. There was a coffee machine on the end of the counter with a Post-it stuck on it that said *FREE.*

I ventured past one of the pit bulls, a murderous-looking lawn ornament, and up to the desk.

"You have an appointment?" One of the receptionists who had just hung up the phone asked me before I had the chance to give her my name. She was middle-aged and had two enormous diamond rings that almost reached her knuckles. By her outfit and the authority in her voice, I was guessing she was the office administrator. But given the size of the stones in the rings, she could also be D'Anzana's wife.

"I'm from the *Chronicle,*" I said. "Hallie Ahern, I'm doing a story on one of Mr. D'Anzana's clients."

She had Christian Dior reading glasses that slid low on her nose. "I *asked* if you had an appointment."

"No, but I'm on deadline, and I want to give Mr. D'Anzana an opportunity to respond before we go to press."

She hesitated. The deadline was a ploy, a time limit to suggest urgency. This could be her only chance to stop me from running something damaging in the newspaper. "He's got a very busy schedule," she finally said, but added, "I'll check with him."

I took a seat on the sofa beside a young woman with a four-year-old. "You never get to see him, you know," she said. "You always get some assistant."

Five minutes later, the office administrator came back out and asked me if I could wait. Twenty minutes later, she waved me through into a hallway, where I followed her to a large corner office with a view of the ramp to Route 95.

Sitting behind a large, plain desk, Joe D'Anzana was even stouter than he appeared on television, with a rounder, more florid face and deep circles ringing his eyes. The circles, which he must cover with makeup on the commercials, were so dark they were purple. They went beyond suggesting fatigue and etched a look of disappointment into his face, so that he looked more like a basset hound than a pit bull.

Maybe he was aware of this. Maybe that was why there was another small ceramic statue of a pit bull up on its hind legs, to remind clients of his attack-dog qualities.

I glanced around the office, which had stacks of legal files in piles on top of a credenza, his desk, and on the floor. I did a double take when I read the framed degree on the wall. Joe D'Anzana had gone to Harvard?

He studied me for a minute before offering his hand and gesturing for me to take a seat in an upholstered chair. "To what client do I owe this unexpected pleasure?" His Rhode Island accent pronounced it *plesh-a,* which managed to underscore the sarcasm.

"Manuel Salazar," I answered.

"Hor-ri-ble thing, his wife." D'Anzana had a tendency to

break up words into very distinct syllables. "Three young sons. Such a loss to her family." He dipped the bassett-hound eyes to the desk. A moment of respect.

I waited for his eyes to rise and meet mine. When they did, I saw little evidence of real sympathy. "I spoke to your witness, Anna Theresa Plummer," I began. "She said she saw a car, a Cadillac with one taillight, run your client's wife off the road." I strained to keep my voice level, as if I actually believed this. "I was wondering if you were concerned that police hadn't found anything that fit the description yet?"

I watched his face carefully, but there was no sign of alarm that his witness had been speaking to a newspaper reporter. "These things take time," he said, with all the patience in the world.

I poised my pen on the notebook. "So even though it's been almost three weeks, you don't have any complaints about the way this investigation is being handled?"

"I'm not going to say anything negative about the police," he said, but there was an emphasis that suggested that just because he wasn't going to say anything negative, it didn't mean he wasn't thinking it.

This prompted me to ask, "Is it possible that they aren't taking it seriously because she's a Dominican immigrant?"

This was an effort to get him to lower his defenses, by giving him a chance to rail against the injustices of the world, and blame ethnic bias on a lack of evidence to support his case. There was a long pause, as he seemed to weigh the pros and cons of this opportunity. But Joe D'Anzana decided not to take it. "Although Rhode Island's Hispanic community doesn't always get a fair shake, I think that in this case, it has more to do with the fact that we're dealing with a very small rural police department. They just don't have the staff. Un-fort-un-ate-ly."

"Have you tried to pressure them? Asked them to call in state police?"

He leaned forward on the desk, as if to share a secret. "Off the record, I've been on the phone many times to several different police departments, trying to turn up the heat."

I wrote this down, not only so I could relay it, word for word, to Marcella, but because I believed it was utter bullshit that future reporting could contradict. West Kent police clearly weren't under any pressure to investigate, and all it would take was a call to state police to verify that D'Anzana was lying to me.

I glanced at the files piled on the credenza and had another thought. "Have you represented Manuel Salazar before?" Like in his previous fraudulent car accidents?

But D'Anzana shook his head. "First time."

"Can I ask how he wound up coming to you, here in Warwick, instead of a Spanish-speaking lawyer in Providence?"

"I have quite a number of Spanish-speaking clients, which is why we employ several interpreters here." He waited a beat. "Including Lizette Salazar. Who we will all miss."

"You knew her personally?" This came as a surprise.

"Yes, she did quite a bit of work for me. As an interpreter. It was a terrible loss, her life. And a shock for all of us here." He made a vague gesture to express the condolences of his entire office staff.

I had to stop and regroup. Lizette Salazar had done work for the state's most notorious ambulance chaser. Her husband was a runner for a predator car ring. What were the odds Joe D'Anzana and his booming personal injury practice didn't get a cut of the action?

The trick was to prove a connection between D'Anzana and Tito Manaforte. I glanced at the stacks of files longingly. God, I wished that I could sift through them, collect the names of all the car accident clients and see how many had had their cars towed to the Big T.

The office administrator-wife appeared at the door. "You've got paying clients who have been waiting for more than an hour," she chided D'Anzana.

"Just one more thing," I said.

Joe D'Anzana's eyes met mine, and I knew that he understood that when a reporter asks for "one more thing" at the end of the interview, it's the entire purpose of the interview. He hesitated, as if trying to decide whether to take this escape hatch. But his curiosity must have gotten the better of him. "I'll be with you shortly," he said, waving the administrator-wife away from the door.

I waited until she left. "I wanted to ask you what you know about Tito Manaforte."

A smile played on his lips, as if he had anticipated this question. "Manuel Salazar works at his body shop, I believe."

"You've never met Tito?"

"I have not had the pleasure." There it was again, the exaggerated pronunciation, *plesh-a*. "I'm a personal injury lawyer, Miss Ahern. Not a criminal lawyer."

From what Eddy had told me about seeing them together at a PawSox game, I knew this was an outright lie. I made sure I got the lie down right, word for word.

He was staring intently at my notebook, as if he could read it upside down and across the desk.

"So Tito has never directed any business your way? Sent over anyone who needed a lawyer after their car got towed to the Big T?" I tried to make it sound as if this were an innocent question, as if this might be a commonly accepted practice among reputable lawyers. I didn't expect him to confirm it, but I needed to ask and get his denial.

My innocent ploy didn't fool him. His eyes blazed, as if he'd heard every ambulance-chaser crack anyone had ever made about him. "I've got a busy, thriving practice, Miss Ahern, enough business that I can afford to turn it away. I don't have to employ any body-shop runners to bring me car accidents, which is what you are suggesting."

I wrote down what he said, because the quote would look good as a graphic juxtaposed with evidence I hoped to collect about his deep involvement with the ring.

"So you've never gone to a PawSox game with Tito?" I said. And then, with just the tiniest bit of exaggeration to up the ante, I explained, "Because I have several sources who think you two are buddies."

"I have no association with Tito Manaforte," he said. He was now holding the statue of the pit bull and rotating it by the neck. He glowered at me and put the statue down on the desk between us. "And if you think you're going to write an article impugning my reputation by quoting some made-up sources—"

"I do not make up my sources."

But he wasn't listening. "Because if you should run such an unproven allegation in your paper, I'll make damn sure I subpoena every notebook in the *Chronicle* newsroom when I sue for libel."

This wasn't the first time I'd been threatened with libel. And I refused to be intimidated by this squat little man who thought he was a dog. With all of Joe D'Anzana's television ads and his radio talk show, he was easily a public figure. This made libel difficult to prove. "You wouldn't win."

"Maybe not, but I could sure cost Ian a lot of money to defend the suit."

Ian? This casual mention of the *Chronicle*'s new publisher, the CEO of the Ink and Mirror Corporation and boy wonder, Ian Clew, caused me to halt.

Seeing his desired effect, D'Anzana nodded to confirm. "Yes. You see, as a heavy advertiser in the *Chronicle,* I was recently invited to a luncheon to meet the new publisher. I had quite a long discussion with *Ian* regarding the future of journalism, what in this post–Jayson Blair era."

This was a reference to the *New York Times* reporter who got fired for writing fiction instead of fact. Now it was my turn to blaze with insult. "I do not make up stories, and I sure as hell don't make up sources," I said, stuffing my notebook in my backpack and swinging it over my shoulder.

"Turns out your new publisher has strong feelings about the use of unnamed sources in the paper. He thinks it encourages sloppy reporting, and didn't you already have a little problem with that?"

I nearly choked. Joe D'Anzana had been researching my career. He was talking about the Mazursky murder. Although the ultimate success of the story had gotten me the promotion to the investigative team, it had not been a smooth path. "A minor detail was wrong early on, but the source panned out bigtime," I said.

"Poss-i-bly," he said, dividing up the syllables again. "But if I were you, I wouldn't write anything about me or my client unless you've got ironclad proof to support it. Because I've already got your publisher's ear." Here he picked up the ceramic pit bull statue again, as if he might use it as a missile. "And if you fuck with me, I'll be at your throat."

15

It was drizzling again, and one of my windshield wiper blades needed to be replaced, so that when it scraped across the glass, it felt like it was scraping across every nerve. "Fuck you, you little man," I snarled at Joe D'Anzana. Out loud. As if he were in my car. "You don't scare me."

But unconsciously, my hand had come off the steering wheel to the base of my throat. The truth was that Joe D'Anzana did scare me. He almost scared me more than Tito Manaforte, who by comparison was almost starting to seem like an okay guy. And not because of the libel threat, but because he seemed to have the heads-up on the new publisher's rule book about the use of unnamed sources. It explained Dorothy's new and constant harping about getting everything on the record. And why she had pushed Frizell's Riordan piece over mine in the first place.

I was headed toward the I-195 split, where I'd have to decide whether to bother returning to the newsroom or head home and call it a day. I had a date with Dane tonight. I probably should get ready for it, anyway.

The hokeypokey began to play, and I fumbled a moment finding my cell phone in my backpack. It was Caspar.

"He's ready to talk."

It took me a moment. "Your cousin?"

"He says he'll talk to you."

"Right now?"

"Tonight. Or he change his mind. He leaves the country next week."

I'd have to call Dane and cancel our date. "Where? The bakery?"

"Away from the neighborhood. He wants you to meet where nobody will see. Where no one goes."

Another unnamed source I couldn't use, but I didn't care. A former runner in Tito's organization. This could be huge. I wracked my brain for somewhere private, where Tito's spies couldn't reach. Out of state somewhere. Some place in Massachusetts, not too far away. I thought of my Gambler's Anonymous meeting and the church parking lot in Foxboro.

It sounded like a good location to Caspar, so I gave him detailed directions. He was going to come along to make sure his cousin didn't back out. We agreed on six o'clock.

"No microphones," Caspar said, meaning tape recorders. "Or you scare him away."

They arrived in an ancient Ford Explorer, with Caspar behind the wheel. I recognized Franco immediately. He was the young, wiry man who had stormed out of Tito's auto body shop.

Up close, he was older than I thought, late twenties, and better looking since he had shaved the nub of growth that had divided his chin. I left my car in the parking lot and jumped into the backseat. I scooted over to the middle and leaned forward so we could shake hands. He had small, nervous eyes that met mine only briefly. There was no recognition or sign he'd even seen me the day at the Big T. He turned quickly to face forward again, underscoring that he was not the most enthusiastic of interviews.

I didn't expect him to be, and yet, despite Caspar's warning, I'd stopped at the newsroom to pack a tape recorder and two fresh tapes. This was risky. It could alienate Franco completely, cause him to abort the interview, but given Joe D'Anzana's warning, I had no other choice. The only shot I had of using any of this in a story without naming the source was if I had audio to play back for Dorothy, Nathan, and Ian Clew.

I left my backpack on the empty seat beside me, having decided against pulling out a notebook, which would remind him that I was a reporter. I had to move slowly, warm him up first. I tried to sound merely conversational as I addressed my first question to Caspar, who was pulling out of the church parking lot onto the road. "How's the catering business going?" I began.

Our eyes met in the rearview mirror. "Ten restaurants now. Ten! That article your friend wrote, was a big help." This was a reminder to Franco: A debt was owed.

Franco turned his gaze out the window. Known mostly as the home of the New England Patriot's football team, Foxboro was about halfway between Boston and Providence and an easy commute to the industry along both the route 128 and 495 technology belts. It was the kind of middle-class suburb that most Americans yearned for, a mix of center-entrance colonial houses designed to blend tastefully with the older more modest saltboxes and capes. Every lawn was nicely clipped, and there was the occasional church spire and stone wall. Franco stared at this landscape as if it were incomprehensible.

"No one uses my name," he said.

Although I knew this already, inwardly I groaned. "I promise, no matter what you tell me, I won't identify you in any way in the newspaper. Not by your name, not by any connection to Caspar."

I pulled out the notebook and pen and flipped open a page, which caused him to turn. Our eyes met. His were dark and deep set. I saw distrust. "Anything you tell me that you don't want me to use, I won't use it."

He made no response. I guessed that in his line of work, he'd outstared a few people. "You want to check my notes afterward. Cross out what you don't want me to use?" I offered.

He didn't glance at the notebook, which seemed to disturb him.

And then I had an idea. I tossed my notebook and pen on the seat and reached into my bag to pull out the tape recorder. In the rearview mirror, I saw Caspar's eyes dart, anxious under the wild eyebrows. But there was no point stopping now, so I turned the recorder on and leaned between the two front seats to thrust it into Franco's hand. "Here, you're in charge." I put my finger on the stop button. "You don't want me to use what you tell me, you can stop the machine. Or erase it. Throw the thing out the window."

Franco looked at Caspar, then at me, then at the recorder. It was a risky move; he might shut if off at the most critical time, inadvertently put a thumb over the built-in microphone, or throw the machine through the window right now. But I was banking on my ability to put him at ease, to get him to talk about himself and his world, and forget, as most people did after a while, that there was an electronic device at work.

He clicked the button off and on several times. It must have offered an illusion of control. "Okay," he said after a minute.

Rule number one of an interview: Ask a question the subject *wants* to answer. "Can you make a lot of money as a runner?"

"Better than driving a cab," Franco said, exchanging a look with Caspar. I guessed that at one time Franco had tried driving one of Caspar's taxies and rejected it as a career option.

I wanted to prompt for more, but decided it could wait. In general, people who made easy money liked to talk about it. They did not shrink from the numbers. Franco turned toward the driver's side, looping his left arm over the back of the seat, so that he could twist around to face me. I caught a hint of a smile on his face as he began to elaborate. "Two thousand on a good accident. Two, three a week, sometimes. Cash." There was both pride and wistfulness in his tone.

I played on the pride. "Good money, but hard work, right?"

At the mention of hard work, Caspar made a scoffing sound.

"It *is* hard work," Franco said, mostly to Caspar. "Not everyone can do it. You gotta find the drivers, the passengers, the locations. And you gotta know how to deal with the lawyers. And the guys in charge, they don't like no mistakes."

For the record, I wanted to ask him who the guys in charge were, but it was too early, too likely he would remember the recorder and snap it off. Instead, I said, "Tell me the hardest part."

Caspar scoffed again. I tried to meet his eyes in the rearview mirror, give him a look to shut up, but his eyes were on the road.

We were entering some sort of town square, with five major roads feeding into a rotary. There were a lot of little shops, a big pink building that looked like an old-fashioned movie theater, and a hardware store that didn't appear to belong to a warehouse chain. Caspar must have circled the rotary twice. I saw the big, pink theater a second time before we turned off onto one of the roads.

Franco was still giving my question some thought. "The hardest part," he finally said, "is finding the skilled drivers. These are the ones who drive the bullet car. They got to be good driver. Follow directions good. You got to get new drivers all the time, so no one gets suspicious. You need new policies. It's not easy."

"And the passengers?"

"Is easy. They sit in a car, fill out some forms." He made a dismissive gesture with his hand.

"But they can get hurt, right?" I asked.

"They can get hurt crossing the street. They can get shot outside their apartments. Here, they get hurt, at least they make money on it."

I nodded as if I bought into this argument.

"These guys, they know how to use the speed, how to hit with just the right angle. Is good skill. Is easy for them when they control both cars," Franco said.

"It's when they smash into innocent people—like me," Caspar interrupted, "that's when it's not so predictable."

"Hey, you didn't get hurt, either," Franco returned. But Caspar did not respond positively to this banter. He shot Franco a dark look, which seemed to sober him a little.

"We don't wanna hurt no one. Makes trouble. People wear

seat belts all the time, these days. We don't do no head-ons," Franco said.

As the road continued, we passed a big blue boardinghouse that looked as if it had been built as quarters for the more transient workers of the industrial age, a reminder that Foxboro had once been a bustling mill town. But quickly, the older working-class homes that sat along the road gave way to newer homes with impressive frontage.

"I bet they got some nice cars in those garages," Franco said almost wistfully.

"You use illegal immigrants for this?"

"As passengers only," he said. "They take less."

"How about their papers? Don't they need papers for the insurance company?"

"If the accident looks good enough, the insurance, it doesn't ask. Besides, you have a little cash, is no problem to get someone papers in Providence."

"Legal papers?"

He laughed.

"They *look* legal," Caspar explained.

"There are people who are very good at this," Franco said. "Is no problem." Illegal immigration was a huge issue in Rhode Island. This quote alone would get my story to the front page. My eyes veered to the tape recorder, which he was holding in his right hand, resting on his knee. He hadn't made a move to turn it off.

"Did you ever arrange accidents with innocent cars?"

"Me, I did mostly commercial policies. That's where the money is. Cabs are good because they're not so big, but we go after company vans, sometimes the rigs. The lawyers, they like those. They got real good policies, the commercial vehicles." The word vehicle was broken into separate and equally accented syllables. Vee-ick-culls.

"How many lawyers you deal with?" I asked.

"Two, three in Rhode Island."

"Joe D'Anzana?" I asked.

He didn't seem to hear this question. He was gazing out the window again, at what was now mostly a country road. "Another two, three here."

Caspar had turned into a high school lot, with a sign denoting *HOME OF THE WARRIORS*. "In Foxboro? You arrange accidents in Foxboro?" I asked.

"In Rhode Island, you gotta sue. You gotta know someone, you gotta make like you're gonna sue. The juries are good, but it takes long time. You gotta go with the no-fault. Massachusetts and New York. Is quicker."

An interstate operation? It was important not to reveal shock, to seem matter-of-fact. "So you've staged accidents in New York, too?"

"The Russians own all the clinics and the lawyers. They take too big a cut. Tito don't like that. Massachusetts. You can get eight grand each injury, no problem."

I struggled to show no response, no altered breathing. I wanted Franco to think I'd missed the reference to Tito, I wanted to distract him from the fact that he'd just fingered the guy on top for a multistate operation, on tape. "Do you know where any of this takes place in Massachusetts? Like where the passengers and drivers meet up? Where exactly they stage their accidents?"

"The accidents are never same place. Too suspicious."

"Where do the recruits meet, you know, beforehand, to get in the cars. Do they have to practice or anything?"

"You want to bust it up, yes?" He seemed amused by this notion.

"I'm not a cop. I can't bust anything up, I'm just curious," I said evenly, but my heart had begun pounding. All of a sudden it hit me, if the recruits met in a public place, I could get a photographer out there with a telephoto lens, maybe capture them as they loaded a car with passengers before takeoff. Get a few license plate numbers. If I had both photos and a tape, Dorothy and Nathan would have to let me do this story.

But Franco turned his gaze away again, out the window to the middle-class homes on the street.

"How about the names of the lawyers you use? Is it Joe D'Anzana?"

"We don't use the lawyers; the lawyers use us. They make the big money on this. The lawyers and the medical clinics." Then his expression became stony.

I didn't want to alienate him by pushing him on any particular point, so I shifted the subject. "So why did you leave? Were you afraid of getting caught?" I asked.

He scoffed at this notion. "Is safer than robbing bank. You get caught is only fine. No jail time."

"So why, then? Why'd you quit?"

He turned, suddenly hostile. "Because everyone cheats. The lawyers, the doctors, they take more than their share. The ones who do the hard work, like me. We get nothing, nothing but blame."

It sounded like Tito might have fired him that day at the Big T, which would explain the real reason he was willing to talk to me. I nodded my head sympathetically, trying to soothe him.

"He accuses me. Why? Because I'm Dominican." Franco was really working himself up now, reliving the injustice. He looked at Caspar, who nodded in understanding. They ranted to each other in Spanish. I caught the words *robando de Tito,* which I thought meant stealing from Tito. God, I wished I'd taken more Spanish in college.

To me, Franco said, "Everybody wants more. All the time. Is fucked-up business. That's why I leave. Get out of here, go home."

I took that to mean back to the Dominican Republic. Which also explained why he'd been willing to risk talking to me.

"Next week?" I asked.

He nodded, looking pleased.

I shook my head at the problems that seemed to be brewing in the underworld. But my mind returned to something he'd said about the greed within the organization. I was thinking of Lizette's theft. Maybe Marcella had been telling the truth. It sounded as if Franco thought people were cheating Tito. "Does anyone keep records of the business? A wreck script?" I asked.

Franco shot a look at Caspar for revealing this information. Caspar shrugged, refusing to apologize. There was a long silence and then Franco said, "There are wreck scripts, yes, but I don't know if the boss keeps them."

My mind started whirring. "You think any of the runners have them?" I prodded. Oh please God, let it be Manuel. Let Marcella find it and make good on her promise.

"I don't know who," Franco said. His anger at Tito spent, he seemed to be tiring of this interview.

"You know anything about Manuel Salazar's wife?"

Involuntarily, I glanced at the tape recorder, which Franco had laid on the console, and hoped to hell that the microphone wasn't too far away from his mouth to pick up his answer.

"I know that she's dead."

"You know anything about her stealing money from Tito Manaforte?"

Again there was no response, but now I noticed him looking at the tape recorder. He reached over and shut it off. "Manuel pay that money back the next day."

"He did?"

"That's what he say. Why he needed me to find him a loan on the street."

I took a moment to process this. Manuel had gone to a loan shark to get the money to repay Tito. Franco had no reason to make this up, no reason to want to protect Tito.

"You don't think Tito had anything to do with Lizette's death?"

He shook his head. "He need her. Everyone knows Manuel can't keep it straight himself."

I took a moment to process this. "You know of anyone else who would want Lizette dead? Who would have staged the accident as a cover-up?"

He said something in Spanish again to Caspar. To me, he said, "I don't know nothing about no accident."

A long, uncomfortable silence in the truck followed. In the rearview mirror, Caspar gave me a disapproving look. I thought about what Carolyn had said. I'd veered off course again, wanting badly to nail Lizette's murderer. I could wind up jeopardizing an important source and go empty-handed. "Look, forget that. All I care about is the car ring."

There was another brief exchange in Spanish between Caspar and Franco that I couldn't understand, but it had the cadence of a negotiation.

"Please," I added, "just tell me where they meet to set up the accidents."

Franco picked up the recorder, hit the stop button, and tossed it to me in the backseat. "The Cottage is a bar on Olive Street in Attleboro." Attleboro was only fifteen minutes away from Providence, but in Massachusetts, just over the border.

"After factories in the neighborhood close, they meet in that lot. I don't know what night. The recruiters, they send the new people there. They get maybe dozen, two dozen people who show up. All want a seat inside the cars. They have to choose which ones get to ride."

"You mean that many people want to do it? They have to turn people away?" I asked incredulously.

Franco shot Caspar a look that suggested irritation at the sheltered world in which I lived. "There are many people, they come here looking for job. They can scrub toilets for a hundred dollars a week, or they can sit in a car for a couple of minutes, make twice that much."

"But they can get hurt. Seriously injured—"

"A back pain? A broken leg—is nothing," Franco interrupted. "They need to eat. They need to feed their families. You can't understand. But for many people, a seat in a wreck is a good thing. Is good opportunity."

16

As I grabbed the newspaper from the hallway Sunday morning, I steeled myself for the nausea I generally felt at a front-page Frizell byline. I reminded myself that jealousy was a very small, very mean emotion, and tried to take pride in the fact that I had had a part in the story. Plus, if Dorothy was right, this exposé would help everyone on the team.

Still, I busied myself with other tasks to avoid the paper. I washed a week's worth of dishes in the kitchen sink; I examined the English bluebell bulbs I'd bought, and made a to-do list that included buying potting soil and clay pots. I snapped on the radio to the Sunday morning program of Myrna, a homemaker extraordinaire, and following her advice, I organized my fridge by throwing out two apples in the crisper that were bruised and brown.

Finally, I grabbed a cup of coffee and unfolded the newspaper on the bar. Leading the front page was a story of two teenage girls from Johnston who were arrested for child pornography after they posted pictures of themselves, naked, on their separate myspace.com Web pages. There was a weather alert about the threat of minor lowland flooding along the Blackstone River in Woonsocket. And a feature on a local gynecologist who had appeared on *Oprah* after writing what was sure to be a national bestseller on female frigidity.

There was no Riordan story.

Maybe Jonathan fucked up. Missed the deadline. Really pissed Dorothy off. I searched the inside of the paper just to make sure we hadn't been bumped to another section, even though that was highly unlikely. Then I got up and poured myself another cup of coffee.

Maybe it was the caffeine, but the warm, fuzzy feeling of Jonathan's failure didn't last long. I couldn't enjoy it, anyway, now that he was going to be a father. Then, as I was leafing through the Sports section, it occurred to me that there might have been another delay. Maybe Nathan looked at the two weeks of surveillance and decided it was an inconclusive sample. That we needed to follow Riordan for another couple of weeks.

I pushed the newspaper away and stood up. I didn't have more time to follow a low-life state bureaucrat around. I was desperate to jump on this insurance story while the info was hot. I had the location where the members of the insurance ring instructed new recruits on the basics of insurance fraud. A freaking Pulitzer, for Christ's sake.

As I turned to drop onto the sofa, I happened to glance out the window and caught a glimpse of a familiar figure on the street below. It was Matt, in his running shorts, heading out of his driveway toward the square. As if he sensed my gaze, he stopped in front of Starbucks and turned, looking across the street and up, toward my apartment.

I backed away from the window. He'd called my cell phone this morning, but hadn't left a message. I'd rescheduled my date with Dane, and he was taking me to a PawSox game Tuesday night. This new relationship seemed effortless, unencumbered by my career. I was determined not to let any lingering and misguided feelings for Matt get in the way.

The fourth floor of the *Chronicle* building held the executive offices: publisher, advertising, and the editorial board. The same marble found in the lobby gave it the imposing feeling of a courthouse and amplified the sound of my footsteps as I hurtled through the hallway.

I was late, this morning of all days, and I'd actually left my apartment early because I was dying to find out what had happened to the Riordan story. But a water main break tied up traffic on Angell Street for three blocks, and now I'd have to burst into the auditorium in the middle of the new publisher's presentation, calling attention to myself just as he was trying to figure out which employees should go.

Mercifully, the double doors were left open. I slid unnoticed into what was really an amphitheater with a small sunken stage. A man at the lectern looked to be about twenty years old. He was talking about what a great newspaper the *Chronicle* was, how well regarded in the field. "I have nothing but respect for the people who made the *Chronicle* what it is today," he was saying.

I spotted Dorothy sitting with the graphics editor and took a seat behind her. I leaned forward to whisper, "That *can't* be him."

"Where the hell have you been?" she whispered back.

I leaned forward to explain about the water main break, but she waved me off, righting herself in her seat to give her full attention to the new boss. On second glance, Ian Clew, chief executive officer of the Ink and Mirror Corporation, was probably in his thirties. He just looked younger because he was tall and lanky and had a long, skinny face that hung over the lectern like a half-moon. And the childlike enthusiasm. That didn't help.

He held note cards in his hand, but didn't look at them. He spoke as if all the information just welled up inside him, as if he were just bursting with good news. The new corporate owners of the *Chronicle* were growing exponentially through media acquisitions, nationally and internationally. There were challenges in the industry, but the corporation continued to believe in quality reporting, quality production, quality editing.

"Which is why they are going to lay off everyone," someone in the row behind me said.

Ian Clew had tremendous admiration for the thoroughness and accuracy of our news coverage. But most of all he admired the boldness of the reporting. "The way you guys go out there and explore new territory, uncover the scandals in this state. That's what sells papers," he said, "boldness."

But then, the silver half-moon above the lectern dimmed. The enthusiasm vanished. The publisher checked one of his note cards, halted, flipped the card over, and pushed it to the far end of the lectern. He needed to distance himself from what he was about to say. Sadly, immutably, there was a bottom line.

I didn't want to hear about how the newspaper business was in trouble nationwide, or the terminal case of declining ad revenue, the blood loss in circulation. I wanted to hear how Ian Clew felt about the use of unnamed sources, but he didn't seem to want to discuss that. So I leaned forward again and nudged Dorothy. "What happened to the Riordan story?"

She made a face and waved me to sit back in my seat.

Ian Clew knew that the news staff didn't like the idea of a bottom line, because we were journalists, idealists, pursuers of the truth. But businessmen like him had to wrestle with the practicalities as well as the ideals. Based on its ever diminishing circulation, the *Chronicle* had one of the fattest city staffs in the business.

I looked around the auditorium, trying to see if there was one single person who had been hired after me. Nathan's assistant. But he was an intern. Even most of the state staff, which was the entry level for reporters, had been around longer than I had.

Ian Clew steadied himself at the lectern, took a breath, and exhaled. Fifteen percent of the staff had to be cut. The corporation would offer buyouts, and there would be more transfers to the Web site staff, but the new publisher wasn't going to sugarcoat it. "There will be layoffs." And he was going to take the unusual position, an unpopular position. He was going to base his staffing decisions on productivity, not seniority.

I looked up swiftly. I'd just finished calculating the number: Fifteen percent of the news staff was almost thirty-five people. By union contract, the publisher could not ignore seniority. Or lack thereof. Could he?

Leaning forward again, I tried to catch Dorothy's reaction, but she would not meet my eye. And I realized by her steady, unwavering gaze at the lectern that she'd already known about this. This was why she wanted the investigative team to make such a huge impression.

The union president, a woman named Monica Collins, jumped to her feet. She reminded the publisher that the staff was represented by the Newspaper Guild, and that it had a binding contract with the *Chronicle.*

Ian Clew was quick to respond. Legally, the union had a binding contract with the Chronicle Corporation, which was no longer the owner of the *Chronicle*. Then he began to recite the list of newspaper cutbacks nationwide: 500 jobs at *The New York Times,* 130 at the *St. Louis Post-Dispatch,* 160 at *The Philadelphia Inquirer.* He went into every geographical corner of the country, and then began naming midsize newspapers that shut down entirely. "Because they couldn't resolve differences with the union."

I had no idea how Monica Collins managed to stay on her feet through it all. I held on to the armrests of my seat, hoping to regain my equilibrium. But all I could think was that if I lost my job at the *Chronicle,* there was nowhere else to go. No newspapers left.

Here Dorothy turned around. "He has cancer," she whispered.

"This guy?" I gestured toward the stage. Ian Clew looked pretty healthy.

"Albert Riordan. Bone cancer. Stage four."

"Oh." I was still a little too overwhelmed by the layoff threat to react. But slowly the logic of it snuck in. The repeated trips to the East Side Medical clinic. The massage therapy. Even the golf course. You couldn't fault a guy for blowing off work on the first sunny day when he had six months to live.

Dorothy was shaking her head in grief, and even Olivia, the graphics editor, turned to tip her head in condolence. Not over Riordan's failing health, but over the story, which was more of a goner than he was. A last-minute miracle might reverse Riordan's doomed medical condition, but the newspaper couldn't run an exposé on a no-show bureaucrat who was battling cancer. No way.

I felt bad, but I wasn't entirely sure for whom. Had two weeks of surveillance bound me to this man that I'd been stalking from afar? Was I actually feeling sympathy for Frizell, or was it more for Dorothy, who had the look of a desperate woman?

Around us, people were getting up, shuffling out of their rows to the door. The presentation was over. The lectern was empty. The overhead lighting was turned back up, making skin color universally gray as reporters and editors headed toward the newsroom. It was a slow, solemn march.

Dorothy pulled me aside as we followed behind Olivia toward the exit. "We need something we can go to press with in a couple of weeks. Did you ever get anyone on the record on that insurance thing?"

I shook my head, and quickly explained to her what I did have, emphasizing that the Franco interview was all on tape.

"But we can't use this guy's name?"

"We'd get him killed."

"Any other way you can prove this ring exists. How about that sister? Wasn't she supposed to be helping you?"

"I can't use her name, either."

"You've got to go see her, try to convince her to go public. Where does she work again, the dog track?"

"Right." I hesitated to tell Dorothy about Tito's man,

Norman, following me the last time I went there to see Marcella, but the recollection of Norman brought another thought to the surface. He'd been stationed at the dog track to recruit losing gamblers as passengers and drivers for the scam.

"Hallie?" Dorothy prodded. But my thoughts were racing in another direction. If the publisher wouldn't let us use unnamed sources, there was only one way to be bold.

"Hallie?"

If I could actually get inside a car, I could be an eyewitness. My own informant. My own source. Walter might know where I could get a fake driver's license. And if there was one thing I could convincingly portray, it was a losing gambler.

We were the last two people in the now-deserted auditorium, and Dorothy was standing in the aisle, arms folded, regarding me intently.

A first-person view of all the desperate people willing to risk life and limb for easy money. Ian Clew had said he valued boldness. Well, this would be bold all right.

"Can we call a team meeting this morning?" I asked Dorothy. "I've got an idea."

17

I'm not sure what exactly Marcella had hoped to gain from my interview with Joe D'Anzana, but clearly she had misunderstood the power of the daily newspaper.

"He lies," she said of his claim that he had hounded police to investigate Lizette's accident. I'd finally reached her on her cell phone late that afternoon.

"I know." I'd already checked with both West Kent and state police to confirm that they had received not a single phone call from Joe D'Anzana pressing for an investigation. I explained this to Marcella.

"So, now you make him."

"*Make him?*"

"Make this lawyer call police. Do the right thing for my sister."

I was at my desk, with every notebook I'd ever used on this story spread before me and the tape of my interview with

Franco ready for replay in the cassette. I'd just come back to my desk after the investigative team meeting, where I'd gotten the approval on the plan to go undercover. But I needed some key information from Marcella to make it work, and right then, I didn't want her to feel I'd let her down. "I can't make Joe D'Anzana *do* anything," I said as gently as I could. "The only thing I can do is write about it in the paper."

There was a long pause as this settled in. "So Tito gets away with it?"

The hatred in her tone made me worry about the real reason Marcella might hate Tito so much. "Tito told me that you used to go out with him," I said. "Is that true?"

"That was long time ago," she said. "When I was in trouble. All fucked up on the drugs."

"I saw the write-up about the armed robbery," I said softly.

"There was no weapon," she said. "I was fucked up, crazy. I threatened her with my fists. That's all."

"That's all?" We were robbing a pharmacy here.

"I serve my time. I change my life."

"Did you lie in court?"

There was a sigh of exasperation. "They thought I lie. But it was the cop who lie. Some Anglo. There was no weapon. He lost his job over many lies he tell. Woods. His last name. You check the paper. They never made a perjury charge. And I went into rehab. I got straight."

I'd have to check out the cop story, but it did explain why the sentencing story made no mention of perjury. And clearly Marcella had turned her life around.

"I had to get straight, too," I said, to soothe her. "I understand that people can change. But I had to ask you."

"Yeah," she said. There was a long, awkward silence.

Eventually, I'd have to ask Marcella about what Franco had said. That Manuel had repaid the money Lizette had stolen, which called into question Tito's murder motive. But at the moment I didn't want to say anything that further challenged her honesty. "Look, the way to make sure Tito goes to jail is to help me expose the ring."

There was a long pause. In the background, I heard some sort of announcement on the public address system and guessed I'd caught her either in a grocery store or a Wal-Mart. Finally, she said, "Manuel would not let me clean out Lizette's things. He says he is not ready."

This wasn't as big a disappointment as it might have been, now that I had a new plan. Now that I was going to pose as a losing gambler from the dog track, I needed something completely different from Marcella. "There was another favor I wanted to ask."

She waited.

"Norman. The guy at the dog track, what do you know about him?"

"Norman?" She seemed to scoff as she said his name. "He hangs around the lunch counter too much. That's what I know."

"What do you know about his operation? About what you told me last time, about recruiting the losing gamblers?"

There was a hesitation. "For the newspaper? You write about the dog track?" She sounded alarmed.

My plan was to stake out the Cottage and, posing as one of Norman's losing gamblers, pretend I was vying for a seat in the back of one of the crash cars. I wanted to meet the runner, the drivers, and other recruits to accurately describe what kind of people did this. I would copy down the license plate numbers of the bullet and target cars and see if we could use these to track the accident and insurance claims later. Because the lawyers insisted that reporters weren't allowed to take part in a crime, I'd have to bow out quickly if it looked like I was actually going to be chosen for the staged accident. But I wasn't too worried about that. Even without taking part in the actual accident, I'd have enough first-person experience in this grimy underworld to put together a hell of a story. "I need enough information to pose as one of Norman's recruits."

"You are going there? To the cars?" she probed.

I didn't answer.

"Is dangerous if they catch you, these people . . ." The warning drifted off.

"Don't worry. I'm not going to actually get into any of the cars. But if I see the operation for myself, there's no pressure from my editors to name other sources."

This must have appealed to her. After a minute she said, "Is what I already tell you. That Norman finds the big losers, down a grand or two. He offers them cash."

"Does he say how much he pays them?" It seemed to me that a gambler recruited to take part in a car accident would have this information going in.

"When he's done a few shots in the bar, he likes to brag about what a generous guy he is. Like it is his money. For the cars, the policies, he pay two thousand, he says."

I wasn't planning on even getting inside a car. I sure as hell wasn't going to let anyone smash up my Honda. "How about if they're just passengers?"

"They pay Anglos much better than Latinos. Five, six hundred, I think."

"Does Norman take any gambler who is interested? Or is he picky?"

The PA blared behind her again, with some kind of musical jingle. She waited until the announcement was over. "He likes the Anglos, and he says once that is gamblers from Massachusetts he wants. The insurance is better, I think."

That made sense. "Anything else you can think of?"

There was another silence as she thought about this. "He likes better they have no criminal records. And no other accidents. That part he talks about a lot."

My out. Once I got enough dirt on how the selection process worked, I could remember a minor fender bender that would disqualify me from the final cut. "Do you know if Tito or Manuel has to check these gamblers out first?"

"Lizette told me once that Tito uses different runners in different places."

This was good news. "How about Norman? Does he go with the gamblers? Or does he just send them along?"

"I think they just go. Norman gives them a name or some code word."

I was already flipping through a notebook for Caspar's phone number so he could get the name of the runner from Franco before he left for the Dominican Republic.

"You think this will put Tito in jail?" she asked.

"I think it's our only shot."

"I have been straight a long time now," she said. "I change my life."

"I know," I said. "I can see that."

There was a long silence. "I try to talk to Norman tonight," she finally said. "Find out more, so you don't get killed.

And I will go to Manuel's house when he is working. For my sister, I will take a chance. Like you."

An Italian sausage and pepper sandwich is not good date food.

Especially at McCoy Stadium, where the sausage is extra garlicky and the onions and peppers are cooked in so much oil that they slide out of the roll, drip into the foil, and can end up in your lap. But as I stood in line with Dane at the concession stand, inhaling the mix of popcorn, fried dough, and every happy moment I'd ever had at a baseball game, my willpower began to wane. What the hell, there had to be breath mints somewhere at the bottom of my backpack.

I was keyed up with my success. For once, things had gone easily. Caspar had been able to catch Franco on time, and I'd gotten the name of the runner: Sammy, who I also learned was Cambodian. Starting tomorrow, a staff photographer and I were going to stake out the parking lot at the Cottage in Attleboro every night until we caught the next meeting of the car crash recruits.

Although I was excited, this assignment meant I was going to be insanely busy for the next couple of weeks. I wanted to make the most of this night with Dane, since I might not be able to see him again for a while.

I grabbed about two dozen napkins while Dane carried the tray to our seats, which were in the box seats, behind the screen at home plate. I'd be able to feel the pitch coming at me, as if I were the batter.

The stadium was absolutely packed with fans. Luckily, our seats were on the aisle and we didn't have to climb over anybody.

As I slipped into my seat, I couldn't help but think that this would be Matt's nightmare, a place where any of five thousand Rhode Islanders might spot the two of us together.

Dane didn't seem to care. He'd been in a great mood when he picked me up on his Harley, and now, after he'd stashed our motorcycle helmets under our seats, he remained buoyant. He doled out my sandwich and his hot dog from the tray. "Great night for baseball, huh?"

I agreed. This was the first clear day we'd had in weeks. The game started early and there was still sun, which made it feel like a summer game. I wouldn't need the sweatshirt tied around my waist unless I spilled an embarrassing amount of oily onion on my shirt. I took a delicate bite of sausage and hoped for the best.

The game got off to a cautious start with neither team able to score in the first three innings. I headed to the ladies' room between the third and fourth innings to wash the greasy onion from my hands. As I walked back to my seat, I noticed that sitting a half dozen rows behind us was Joe D'Anzana. He was with two teenage boys, and his eyes locked on mine. We exchanged cold stares and I could feel him still staring as I slipped into the seat next to Dane.

Dane turned and saw D'Anzana. "Not exactly a friend of yours?"

"Not exactly."

"You still working on that story about Lizette?" Dane asked.

"Sort of," I said.

He seemed a little perplexed by this. "You think Lizette's accident was some kind of insurance fraud? Like she did it on purpose for the money?"

"Not really."

This did nothing to alleviate his confusion.

We were supposed to keep a lid on investigative stories, and it was only a second date. "Her husband works for Tito Manaforte at the Big T. And he's got a record of insurance fraud." This was public information, after all.

Dane seemed saddened by this. "It's depressing that so many poor immigrants see that kind of thing as their only opportunity."

"You come across any of the immigrants who do this? I mean at the Hispanic Center?"

"I take the civil stuff no one can pay for: tenant's issues, mostly, evictions, sometimes a divorce." On our first date, he had told me that he'd gone through a difficult divorce himself three years ago, and he made a face now to indicate that divorce work wasn't his favorite. "I used to be a public defender when I lived in Massachusetts. I was appointed to defend a teenager who got arrested for taking part in a staged accident in Mattapan. So I know a little about it. If you need legal advice, I have a little background."

"Really?" This could prove useful. It made me curious, though. "How come you don't do criminal law here?"

"It's a long story." His tone suggested it was not a story he wanted to tell. I shrugged to show him that I understood, that it was no big deal. After all, there was plenty about my own personal history—including the fact I'd gone out with Matt—that I wasn't ready to share. And then, luckily, we were diverted by a batter for the Mets' farm team, the Norfolk Tides, who slammed a ball into centerfield. We both forgot about insurance fraud and held our breaths hoping the ball wouldn't go over the fence for a home run.

It did, and the run brought home base runners on first and third, reversing fortunes and putting us down 1–3, with no outs. The crowd started screaming for a pitching change, but Dane was more patient. "He just needs a chance to get his curveball working again. He can still pull himself together." His eyes blazed with such clear blue certainty that even though I'd previously been thinking just like all the other booing fans, I nodded in agreement.

I was rewarded by Dane putting his hand over mine, a shared moment as we bonded over our coaching decision. "If we win, I'll take you to Fenway when the Sox get back from their road trip."

The next few innings became infinitely more exciting. I found myself rooting so loudly that my throat felt scratchy as I swallowed beer. Later, as Dane and I were heading back through the parking lot to his Harley, he said, "A client of mine can get us seats behind home plate at Fenway." He handed me my helmet. "You're coming with me, right?"

He looked so sweet, so earnest, as if I might refuse. I took the helmet and looped my arm through his.

And there in the middle of the parking lot, with packs of fans on both sides of us checking out the Harley as they headed toward their cars, Dane turned around and lifted my chin to kiss me. It was a sweet meeting of the lips that ignited some serious heat. I heard several people chortle and one drunk shouted, "Get a room!"

But I didn't care. Because clearly Dane didn't. He wasn't looking over either of our shoulders worrying about his career.

Dane lived in an enormous house, a Federal-style bowfront in the Historic District in the East Side—the kind of house that never went on the market but was passed down in a family. We parked the motorcycle in what looked like a carriage house, next to a snow-white BMW, another motorcycle, and a blue flatbed truck that he said he needed to transport the motorcycles when he raced in New Hampshire. Inside, I barely noticed anything besides the smell of furniture polish in the hallway as we raced straight to the bedroom.

Maybe it was pent-up frustration, or fear that I'd otherwise let myself do too much thinking and make comparisons to Matt, but I kicked my clothes off in record time, even before Dane had dimmed the lights.

"You want a glass of wine or anything?" he asked.

I shook my head. I'd had enough beer. Enough waiting for someone who really seemed to want me. Dane peeled off his shirt, and as he opened a drawer to search for a condom, I stared at his back muscles, which were broader and better defined than Matt's. Forget Matt, I scolded myself, as Dane undressed and came to the four-poster bed. I focused on the glutes I'd admired, free of Lycra.

His mouth went to my breast and I could feel the cultivated one-day beard scratching the tender skin of my nipple. I had to force myself not to squirm, or to long for Matt's bristle-free caresses.

Forget Matt, I told myself again. Stay in the moment. Engaged in this slightly muskier, male scent. Dane must have sensed that he was too rough, because his movements changed, grew slower. And I could no longer feel his beard, just his tongue sliding under my breast, drawing a line downward. I finally stopped thinking, stopped hearing sound. I got lost in the heat that traveled from my breast to my belly. Every muscle tightened, arched, waited.

He had me in some borderless, timeless place where he

wanted to keep me. His pace slowed even more. With thought gone, instinct took over. I tried to wrestle for control, taunting him to the same peak. And still he waited, fending me off.

Finally, he entered me and the room spun around. There was nothing else but the thrust, the long, toned leg muscles and the smell of our sweat on the sheets. He was a marathon man, full of endurance as well as skill. The thrusts went deeper until it seemed like all the cells of my body were stretched taut, begging for release.

Finally, the band broke. Sound returned. I heard moaning: my own. A fraction of a second later, Dane collapsed on top of me. It was a hell of a finish line, and it occurred to me later that, for once, I'd beaten Mr. Nike in a race.

I awoke to the sound of the hokeypokey playing inside my backpack.

I crawled out of bed and sat on the floor, naked and half asleep, scrounging through the bag, spilling my notebooks and pens all over the carpeting. The cell phone turned out to be in the outer pocket. I noticed that Dane slept through all of this, as I put the phone to my ear.

"You ask for the tattoo parlor in Pawtucket," a voice said.

"Marcella?"

"I tell Norman I had one of his gamblers at my counter today, looking for cash and I couldn't find him. I said he was confused about where to go and what to say. He said those morons forget all the time. Is easy to remember, he thinks. You go to the parking lot, you ask for the tattoo parlor in Pawtucket."

I was suddenly awake. "Tattoo parlor?"

"That is code, I think. It means you are on Norman's list."

"Do you know what night they're supposed to meet?" I asked.

"You want me to ask him?"

I thought about this for a minute. Any more questions from Marcella might get Norman suspicious. This didn't seem worth the risk. "No, that's okay. I'll figure it out. Just see if you can find those records." I thanked her again and clicked off.

Dane was still sleeping. For the first time, I looked around the bedroom, which had a lot of antique furniture and built-in bookcases. I found my underwear under some sort of upholstered chaise longue, threw on my sweatshirt, and after a trip to a nicely appointed master bathroom, headed downstairs to the kitchen.

The kitchen, which was in the back of the house, overlooked a beautiful garden of crocus and bleeding hearts that made me think of the English bluebells that I bought without having a real garden or place to plant them. It would be so nice to live somewhere with a lawn and trees.

The kitchen itself was less impressive. Too modern and sleek, with black granite counters and lots of stainless steel. Like astronauts cooked here. But there was a calendar pinned to the wall next to the cordless phone and I noticed on yesterday's date, Dane had put the time to pick me up with an exclamation point.

I found my backpack tossed on a chair. Seeing a notebook sticking out of the pocket, I suddenly felt anxious about the undercover plan, about what mistakes I might unwittingly make. I wanted to go home and run before I went to work, settle my nerves, and prepare for what could be a big day. But remembering how annoyed that had made Matt the last time I was with him, I decided I shouldn't seem so eager to skip out.

I searched for a coffee machine, but couldn't find one. Instead, I found a drawer full of teas.

I was trying to avoid all the weird, loose teas, and was plunging deep into the back of the drawer to find something that resembled Tetley when my hand touched metal. I opened the drawer farther and found a handgun. A sleek, solid, hunk of metal with a serious barrel.

There is something about a gun that makes your breath stop. Even when you see one on the holster of a cop, where it belongs. Here, hidden in a tea drawer, when it should have been a tin of cocoa, it made my hands start trembling. It was large, black, and military-looking, like something GI Joe might carry. This was why you should never sleep with someone on the second date.

What the hell was Dane doing with a handgun? I shut the drawer as quietly as I could and got the hell out of the kitchen.

I fled to the living room, which was an enormous room filled with several damask sofas and more antiques that smelled newly polished. I was standing in front of a glass-front bookcase topped with photographs, but I was afraid to touch any of them, my hands were still so shaky. A part of me wanted to run upstairs, get dressed, and get the hell out of here before Dane woke up.

But the other part told me that I could be overreacting. Walter had a handgun for protection, and that didn't freak me out. I glanced around the room, which had a half dozen gilt-framed oil paintings on the walls, and two separate sculptures on pedestals, one a bust of a statesman of some sort and the other an abstract that looked like a pregnant woman. With all the break-ins in Providence, maybe Dane needed a handgun to protect his artwork.

I directed my attention to the photos. They were all very normal family photos. A couple that looked the right age to be Dane's parents, taken at some sort of resort. A three-year-old boy lying in a hammock with a man who looked like he must be Dane's brother. Another family shot including the middle-aged couple from the resort, the brother again, and a woman with her arm looped through Dane's. This must be the ex-wife, a woman named Joanna, who had left him three and a half years ago. She was dark-skinned and exotic-looking, making me feel incredibly plain and Irish. I moved on to the last photo, which was the surprise. It was a picture of Dane with the attorney general, Aidan Carpenter, both on motorcycles at what looked like a motorcycle event, with a track behind them and a crowd milling around. They must be good friends, which was why Matt had been so freaked out when Dane saw us together at Al Forno.

"Early bird?" Dane was standing on the stairway with just a towel wrapped around his waist.

I backed away from the photos. "I was waiting for you to wake up. I've got to get to work. Got an interview this morning."

He came down the stairway and slipped behind me, putting both arms around me and fastening them at my waist. "Does that mean you don't want breakfast?"

"Rain check," I said. But his arms felt good around me, and I didn't pull away.

His eyes shifted past me to the bookcase, and I thought he must be looking at the photograph of his ex-wife, because suddenly he dropped his arms and turned me toward him. He opened his mouth to say something, stopped. His eyes darted to the bookcase again.

"What?"

"I owe it to you to come clean about something." His tone was apologetic. *He wasn't really divorced?*

"You got a minute?" he asked.

"Sure." I got a sick feeling in my stomach. Never, ever sleep with a guy on the second date.

"You asked me last night why I didn't do criminal work anymore. The reason is because I had a bad experience in Boston."

The long story he hadn't wanted to tell. He *was* divorced. This seemed something of a reprieve.

He gestured to the sofa, where we both took a seat. The handsome face was grim, serious. I folded my bare legs underneath me and leaned against the armrest, so I could face him.

"I was winning a lot of cases in Boston, so I wasn't a popular guy with the prosecutors there," he began. "They were dying to get rid of me somehow. I got appointed to represent a woman who had kidnapped her own newborn when it looked like the judge in New York was leaning toward granting full custody to the father. The father was a drug dealer in the city who had the judge in his pocket. He did a lot of methamphetamine and used to kick the shit out of Lisa." I guessed Lisa was the client.

"When the boyfriend showed up in Boston, Lisa freaked out, skipped on her bail. She fled to Vermont somewhere. She kept calling me, desperate. She needed some cash to live on until I could find something on the boyfriend to put him away. I made a fatal mistake of sending her a check.

"Anyway, the whole thing blew up in my face. My PI couldn't get enough on the boyfriend to bring charges in Massachusetts. And two months later the baby died of Sudden

Infant Death Syndrome. Lisa turned herself in, struck a deal with the prosecutor."

"What kind of deal?"

"She gave him copies of the checks I sent her. Got her time cut in half. I got charged with two felonies and a misdemeanor. Helping a client elude capture on a bail violation."

"Jesus."

He shrugged in a manner to suggest he'd long come to terms with the unfairness of the events. "They didn't have a strong case against me, so eventually they dropped the charges. I was disbarred in Massachusetts, though. I wanted to get the hell out of Boston anyway. I had enough of criminals. The drug-dealer boyfriend blamed the baby's death on me. Threatened to kill me. Twice outside of court, once in a phone call to my home. I took it pretty seriously. I moved back here. Even got a license for a handgun."

I didn't let on that I'd found it.

"Once the trouble started, Joanna flew the coop. Just took off and never looked back. Never gave me a chance to explain. The only time I heard from her was through the lawyers." Here there was less acceptance in his tone. It sounded as if it were still a fresh wound.

"I'm sorry," I said.

For a moment, he didn't see me. But then the bitterness in the blue eyes dissolved. He shrugged it off. "I was lucky, I guess. Because of my family, I didn't need the money. But I was bored out of my mind doing nothing. Aidan offered to help me out. He wrote a letter to the Rhode Island bar, attesting to my character. I got an okay from the bar to practice here. But I'm done with criminals."

He was searching my eyes, trying to gauge my response. For a long time, I didn't know what to say. He was expecting me to be shocked, but I was the last person in a position to judge people for their missteps. Mostly, I was relieved he had an explanation for the handgun.

"So you're not freaked out?" he asked.

I shook my head. I couldn't help but be struck by how similar our histories were. And it seemed incredibly unfair to pretend I didn't have my own transgressions. So I took a long deep breath, exhaled, and then, sitting there in just my sweatshirt, I told Dane something I'd never, ever considered confessing to Matt. "I fucked up in Boston, too."

I explained how I'd at one time been at the *Boston Ledger,* and how I'd gotten messed up on sleeping pills after my brother Sean died. When I was early in my recovery, I made a critical error of accepting an assignment to profile Chris Tejian, who was the hottest story in Boston at the time. He was a venture capitalist charged with murdering his business partner, a renowned scientist. He had also been a friend of my brother's, and my college boyfriend.

"I should have never taken the assignment," I said, "but I was trying to get my career back on track after my brother died. The editors knew that Chris had been my boyfriend; they didn't know that I'd never gotten over him. That he still had a hold on my mind. I thought I was tough enough to handle it. To handle him." I scoffed at my own pretensions.

"I'd wound up compromising myself and my career by doing the worst thing a journalist could probably do. I slept with the subject of my profile, a man charged with murder."

"Did you get fired?" he asked.

I shook my head. We'd beaten all the other media with a high-impact story. My editors had loved it. There was no confession. Only penance. "I quit."

Dane moved to close the gap between us on the sofa, and we looked at each other, a moment of shared understanding about the faulty decision making that can shift the direction of a person's life. I was thinking that Walter would like Dane, and that I should introduce them.

Dane put his hands on my shoulders. "So this guy? The college boyfriend. That's why you moved to Rhode Island. To start over?"

I nodded.

He gave me a funny smile and pulled me to his chest. "Then I should thank that asshole, I guess."

18

The Cottage was ineptly named. It should have been called the Bunker. Sitting between two industrial complexes, the bar was in a brick-faced building, surrounded on all sides by a moat of a parking lot and separated from the neighboring metal plants by a chain-link fence. The building itself was not much larger than a mobile home, with a flat roof hoisting a blinking bit of neon that advertised Budweiser. On either side of the entrance, there were two small windows placed high under the eaves, so no one could look in or look out.

I was in my Honda with one of the newest staff photographers, a young guy named Eldridge, whose car we had parked on the street a couple of blocks away. Eldridge had brought four different cameras with him that he kept fiddling with. By way of introduction, he told me that he hated hanging around these dingy neighborhoods working for a newspaper, and that his career goal was to get a job photographing wildlife for *National Geographic*. But he was a big guy, with large, square hands that looked like they could do damage, so I was grateful to have him beside me in the passenger seat.

Security seemed to be an issue in the neighborhood; both the warehouses and the bar property had numerous security lights. And there was a huge sign insisting that the parking was for COTTAGE CUSTOMERS ONLY. Another sign warned: YOU *WILL* BE TOWED.

I felt relatively secure about my own security. I'd come prepared with a fake Massachusetts driver's license that Walter had managed to pick up for me from some guy he knew in Boston. Dorothy and Nathan were nervous about the risk of someone recognizing me as a reporter, and had demanded extra precautions before giving me final approval. Besides the large and somewhat negative Eldridge, who was there not just to take photos, but to call the police if anything went wrong, I was also being monitored electronically in the newsroom. Although I hadn't realized it when I bought it, my cell phone came equipped with a GPS tracking device. Bennett Castiglia, the team's computer guy, knew all about this and had downloaded software that would allow the team to intercept transmitted data from my new phone. As long as I kept the cell phone turned on, he could track my whereabouts.

We were between showers during seemingly ceaseless April rains. The evening was clear, but a northerly wind felt wet and raw. Inside my Honda, I shivered with both cold and excitement that went right to the bone. I tried not to think about why Dorothy and Nathan had insisted on all this security. Of all the warnings about the miscreants I would be dealing with. Of everything that could go wrong.

After one spin around the empty lot, Eldridge and I decided

to park on the cross street in front of the entrance to one of the metal plants, which offered a decent view. It was still daylight and we had a good set of Nikon binoculars, but there was nothing much going on, no activity at all at the bar. Finally, at 7:30, a minivan showed up and six women, all looking sweaty and wearing softball T-shirts, got out and headed inside. A second minivan of teammates arrived ten minutes later. But there was no sign of Sammy, the runner, who according to Franco was Cambodian, and in his early thirties.

For some unlucky reason, my radio was working, and Eldridge had been flipping between stations, listening to only a few bars of music before changing the station again. Now, as he cut off Led Zeppelin for Coldplay, and back again, I felt like snapping off the dial. Did he have attention-deficit problems or what?

By ten o'clock, the only new activity in the parking lot was that the women's softball league had had enough to drink and was leaving. The women looked unsteady, and even from across the street I could hear them, loud and shrill, having a hell of a time climbing into the minivan. I put down the binoculars. "We should call police, or they're going to kill some innocent driver."

"Can we go home?" Eldridge asked.

Like this guy would ever have the patience to stalk a pride of lions on the African plains.

Then two cars, driving too fast for the side street, blew past us. The first car, some kind of ancient Mercedes, nearly hit the minivan as it turned into the bar parking lot. Both Eldridge and I grabbed for the binoculars at the same time. He got them first. "Three guys got out of an old Mercedes," he said. "Two others getting out of . . . I don't know, maybe it's an Impala."

He was silent a long moment.

"What are they doing?"

"Standing around."

I grabbed the binoculars from him and peered through the lens. There were five or six figures, but even with the overhead security lights, we were too far away to make out what anyone looked like. The Impala, or whatever it was, was souped-up, high on the back tires. I watched for several more minutes, but none of the figures made a move to go into the bar. I got a tight feeling in my stomach. This could be it. Sammy and his crew, meeting with the new recruits.

My stomach tightened the way it did on a high bet at the blackjack table, right after I'd asked the dealer to hit me. The world could change with this next card.

"You better get over there and check it out," Eldridge said. He was already packing his cameras into his bag, ready to hoist them over his shoulder. The plan was for him to stay behind, on foot and hidden, to surreptitiously get the pictures. Could I trust him to stay far enough away? What if someone saw him and spotted me as a fake?

Eldridge was getting out of the car. "Where are you going to be?" I asked.

"Right there." He pointed to a truck parked across the street just outside the gate to the metal plant. He would be less than twenty-five yards away from the bar parking lot, but under excellent cover.

There was a bright moon, and I could see Eldridge making shadows as he crossed the street and ran toward the truck. As I drove past him, he raised his cell phone to let me know he was calling the desk. Dorothy would call Frizell. Put him on alert. I checked to make sure my cell phone was turned on.

I pulled into the Cottage parking lot. There, I got a better view of the people standing around the cars, which were parked side by side along the chain-link fence. They were all male, and in their twenties or early thirties. Something passed between hands. And then heads swiveled toward my car, checking me out.

For once, I was grateful that my Honda was old and run-down, hardly conspicuous. Still, I felt out of place. An outsider. A woman alone. I hadn't seen anyone who looked Asian, but there were two guys in the back whose faces I hadn't seen.

There was a Dumpster at the side of the building, and as I passed, the smell of old meat and sour grease wafted into the car. I reminded myself that without sources, this was the only possible way to expose this story. This was my chance. My shot. I couldn't blow it.

I forced myself to park in a spot near the bar entrance and shut off the engine. I could feel the men watching me, trying to peer into the glass. I couldn't just sit there, but I needed a minute to find the courage that seemed to have deserted me.

Nearby, a train roared on its tracks, so close I could feel my bones vibrating. I took a deep breath and reminded myself that it was always harder to think about doing something than to actually do it.

As I got out of the car, I caught a glimpse of the men, all eyes staring. I couldn't see much else, except that there was something serious and furtive about the way they stood together, a little too close to each other, and silent, as if my presence shut them up.

I decided that I would walk into the bar first and buy a pack of cigarettes, as a cover. Inside, I was the sole customer. The bartender, a gray-haired man with a deep tan, looked up from an open dishwasher. "You want something?" he asked doubtfully, as if he suspected I'd wandered into the wrong building. There were a half-dozen empty tables along the exterior wall. And to the left there was a small room with a pool table and a couple of blinking video games making war noises. I guessed the cigarette machine was in there.

The bartender was not happy about making change. He grumbled when I gave him a twenty and slammed a pile of singles and quarters into my palm without counting them back to me. At the machine, I chose a pack of Marlboros, a cigarette my brother Sean used to smoke, but as I crossed back past the bar I stalled. I'd never smoked a cigarette in my life, but I wished to hell, right then, I could sit down on a stool and start. A long, deep inhale. A drink would be good, too. Maybe a couple.

This was not the kind of place where you ordered white wine. It would have to be a shooter. Tequila or some sort of cheap whiskey. Never a good idea.

Forcing myself into the night, I brandished my Marlboros in one hand as I made my way to the car. Then, as if it were an afterthought, I turned to the group of men still huddled around their cars. "Hey," I said, walking toward them.

"What's up?" One of the guys closest to me responded. But the others, I noticed, seemed to shrink away. I took another couple of steps and offered Marcella's code line.

"I'm looking for the tattoo parlor in Pawtucket."

The guy laughed as if this were a joke. "You guys know where this chick can get inked?" he asked his friends.

"I know a place on Federal Hill," one of the guys behind him said. This elicited more laughter. Then the other guy handed him a cigarette. He took a long drag while staring at the Marlboros in my hand.

Now that I was closer, I could see that these guys were younger than I thought. Very early twenties. One of them was wearing mismatched basketball sneakers of different colors. Another had a baseball cap on backward and a T-shirt that said: *Derek Jeter drinks Wine Coolers.* "How about a guy named Sammy?" I asked. "You know him?"

"Samm-y!" This time it sounded like a chant. The guy with the baseball hat passed the cigarette to the guy with the mismatched sneakers. He took a drag. A really, really long drag. He shut his eyes a minute before he expelled the smoke.

Sweet and pungent, a whiff of my college dorm. They were smoking pot. Hanging outside in the parking lot to smoke a doobie. That's why they were staring at me as if I'd just landed from Mars. They were high as kites, all of them. "You guys don't know Sammy, do you?"

"Samm-y!" They chanted. "Samm-y!"

"Never mind." I turned, headed swiftly to my car. All that anxiety over freaking stoners. I felt both stupid and relieved. As I pulled out of the parking lot, I could still hear them chanting. "Samm-y! Samm-y!"

The next night of surveillance I lucked out and Susan Tulanowski was assigned to work with me. She was about my own age, but she still looked like a teenager, with freckles across her nose and curly hair still wet from the shower. Unlike Eldridge, she would be of little use in a fistfight, but I had a feeling she'd be more dependable getting through to Dorothy or the police if something went wrong. She whiled away the time with her impersonations of the new publisher, Ian Clew.

But she didn't much like investigative stories, either. "They just take *forever,*" she complained. "You just sit and sit and sit, and you get what? One or two shots? If you're lucky . . . sometimes you spend all this time in the car and still miss the real action."

We were sharing a bag of potato chips and I felt a sharp edge stick in my throat. Susan was an experienced photographer who had many investigative team assignments under her belt. Her distaste for these assignments reminded me that sometimes, no matter how hard you tried, the story just didn't pan out.

I coughed hard and swallowed salt. I couldn't allow for that possibility. Although I'd explained carefully to Dorothy and Nathan that I had no idea what night these accident recruits would converge on this place—that it could be days or weeks before there was any action—I was banking on a miracle. A major break. A gift of timing from the journalism gods so I could launch this story onto the front page *before* cutbacks. My career was riding on it.

There were no miracles. No breaks. By the next week, there was still no sign of Sammy the runner, or even of anything nefarious going on in the parking lot. I'd rotated through three other staff photographers, who were obviously passing around the burden of this assignment, and was back to Eldridge.

It wasn't raining at the moment, but an on-again, off-again drizzle was expected to rev up into a torrent. Eldridge had left a message on my cell phone that he was running late, but now it was seven thirty, and he hadn't shown up yet. I told myself that it was probably a moot point. This was no night to stage an accident. How could anyone predict the physics of a crash with a downpour lubricating the streets?

But then two cars, a Bonneville and an ancient Chrysler

LeBaron, pulled into the Cottage parking lot and drove to the back of the building. Within ten minutes, six or seven other cars pulled in, all parking together in the back. I called the photo desk in a panic and told them that Eldridge still hadn't shown up. The photo editor assured me that he'd be there any minute.

I drove my car across the street into the parking lot, telling myself the whole time that these people were nothing but minor criminals who organized insurance fraud because they were too wimpy to rob convenience stores.

The Bonneville and the LeBaron were parked together in the corner of the lot where the bulb was missing from the security light. The rest of them, all shit boxes, were set apart in a line behind the building, with their noses against the chain-link fence. I parked at the end of the line.

I got out of the car, and put up the hood of my jacket. As if a thin layer of nylon could offer me real protection. I made my way slowly along the back of the building, which had an ugly corrugated metal door and a pile of empty cardboard boxes collapsing beside the stairs.

As I got closer, I could make out distinct groups. Four white men in their midthirties were huddled together. Standing close, but apart, were an anemic-looking white woman in her twenties and two older women, maybe late forties, one white, the other Latina. The women both looked tired and overweight, way too middle-aged to risk this kind of thing.

A fourth woman, an Asian and possibly pregnant, stood under an umbrella, near three Asian men. Leaning against the LeBaron, another Asian man, this one tall and thin, was conferring with a Latino man with a clipboard. They looked up as I approached.

The Asian man wore a black silk T-shirt underneath the jacket and pants so tight that they forced your eyes to return to his crotch. When the jacket swung open I noticed the square handle of what looked like a dagger and sheath in his waistband.

"I'm looking for the tattoo place in Pawtucket," I forced myself to say. "I'm Norman's friend."

He studied me a moment. I had taken pains not to look like a reporter, and was wearing jean capris, a Rolling Stones T-shirt under my rain jacket, and a pair of aquamarine Sketchers on my feet that I hoped looked trendy and cheap.

"Norman don't have friends," he cracked. From the fawning laughter this provoked, I gathered that he was indeed Sammy, the guy in charge.

"I met him in Lincoln," I said.

"You like the dogs?"

"Yeah."

"How much you lose?"

"A couple grand," I said.

He asked for my name. I gave him the name on my fake ID. "Irina Calek."

"You're not on Norman's list."

List? I felt a momentary panic. Then I remembered something Marcella had said about Norman's drinking. "Maybe he forgot about me. I met him in the bar. By the slots."

Sammy must have knocked a few back with Norman. "How much he tell you?"

"Six hundred."

"We got a lot a people here who want to be passengers," he said. "We only need four tonight."

Perfect. An easy out. But not yet. "I'll do it for five hundred dollars."

He seemed unimpressed.

"You going to use these two cars right here?" I wanted to know which license plates to memorize.

"That what Norman told you?" His eyes were set deep, swallowing the lids, so all you saw were the round, dark irises.

"He said I wouldn't get hurt too bad."

Sammy gave me a penetrating look. Was this something Norman would never have said? But then, the Latino guy, who was an assistant or second in command, caught Sammy's eye and gave a dismissive glance at the group of Asians standing together, suggesting some sort of problem in that quarter.

"Where you from?" Sammy asked.

"Milford." That's what it said on my fake license.

He and the Latino guy exchanged another look, and I understood that the Milford address was an asset. I knew that if they were going to stage an accident between two willing cars, they liked diversity in the separate cars—in terms of gender, ethnic background, and neighborhood. It was suspicious when all claimants in a supposedly random crash between two cars all came from the same city block.

I gave Sammy my fake license and he studied it briefly. He handed it to the Latino man, whom he addressed as Rodrigo, and asked him to check me out while he finished up with the others.

Rodrigo was a large man, not heavy, not jacked, just large, at least six three, with a huge head and chest, and legs that looked like they could support a small building. He had both eyebrows, both ears, and the recess of his chin pierced. He asked me what I did for work.

"Cocktail waitress."

"Where?"

"Skippers Landing." This was the job I'd had in the gap years between my reporting gigs at the *Ledger* and the *Chronicle.*

"In Boston?"

I nodded before I caught the look of puzzlement in his eyes. Stupid, stupid. I was supposed to be from Milford, more than an hour's drive to Boston.

"You go that far to wait tables?"

"The money's good," I said, and in case that wasn't convincing. "Plus my boyfriend lives in Dorchester, I stay there a lot."

"Dorchester, huh?" This was apparently another good answer.

I nodded.

"When you do this type of work, Irina, you gotta make time to go to the clinic," he said. "That's two or three trips to the clinic a week. For a month or so. You get a nice bonus if you string it out and we get the pain and suffering. You gonna be able to make time for that?"

What I wanted more than anything else was to nail the clinics. I needed some kind of paper trail to connect the ring to Tito. "Is there a clinic in Milford?"

Rodrigo evaded the question. "I tell you what clinic you go to *after*—" His sentence broke off, but I knew what he meant: after the accident. *If* I were chosen.

"I'll go wherever." I pointed to my battered Honda. "I got a car and my days are free."

"Good. Because you only get half the money tonight. You don't get the rest until the claim comes in, and we got no problems," he said.

Two of the white guys and the older women were walking away from Sammy toward their car. Dismissed. The Asian group was breaking up, too; the men began heading toward one of the cars. But the Asian woman remained. Please God, don't let her really be pregnant.

"You been in any other accident in the last six months?" Rodrigo was asking.

"What?" As if I hadn't heard. This was my out. Where I was supposed to confess a few recent fender benders. No injuries or anything, just a little damage to my windshield and front bumper. Small enough that I could think it didn't matter, but recent enough that they wouldn't want to make another claim on my behalf.

But if I did that, I'd never get the name of the clinics. This was the real action of the story. The shady doctors and chiropractors. Where the money got made.

"Pay attention now, Irina, this shit is important. Any accidents?" Rodrigo looked up from his clipboard, eyes intent. This was the million-dollar question. The clincher. In or out.

I was in front of that slot machine again, my nerves wired, my thoughts singular. "No. Never," I heard myself say.

19

What the hell was I doing?

Rodrigo had given me a thumbs-up and made a gesture for me to wait. Then he, Sammy, and one of the white guys who held his head tilted to the side as if maybe he'd already had whiplash, all climbed into the Bonneville for a conference.

It looked like everyone else had been voted off the island. The only other potential passengers left were a very young girl in velour sweatpants, an extremely doofy-looking white guy, the Asian woman who insisted on standing apart with her back turned so I couldn't see her stomach.

It was getting dark and, with the mist, even harder to see. There was still no sign of Eldridge or Frizell. I was here completely on my own. I thought of Walter and had a sudden image of that disapproving look he could get on his face. Was he right? Had I put myself in this kind of dangerous situation on purpose? For the action? The rush?

I was standing there silently repeating the license plate numbers of both cars in my head when the young woman in the velour sweatpants suddenly got talkative. She told me her name was Nini and asked me if I'd ever done this before. "You don't get too banged up, right?" she asked, before I could answer.

Nini was suspiciously thin, as if recovering from a drug problem, and her bones looked as if they'd shatter on impact. I tried not to think of the grandmother in Lawrence who had died in a staged crash. The car hit the intended target but kept going, slamming into a nearby telephone pole. The old woman's head snapped forward so violently that her brain began to hemorrhage.

We could die, I thought, and yet this produced that almost enjoyable tingling across my shoulders. "We'll be fine," I said.

"The worst part is all the forms you have to fill out," said the doofy-looking guy. He was a good two inches shorter than Nini and had really ugly sideburns and a halfway healed cut on the side of his face, but by the way he talked to her, I guessed he was her boyfriend. "How many times do I gotta tell you, the crash part is over quick. You'll be fine. These guys are pros. They know what they're doing."

This didn't seem to appease Nini, who moved another step closer to me. I wondered if she gambled with him or was just along to help clear his debt. "So if you're so scared, why you doing this?" I whispered, trying to make it sound as if I were just a concerned friend, but the motivation of why people did this kind of thing would be great insight for my story.

Her eyes darted to her boyfriend. "Greg's bailed me out a couple of times," she said. "At the park." That must be a reference to Lincoln Park. "This could help him—you know . . . get even."

I nodded, the whole time repeating to myself what she'd just said, trying to capture her tone, an odd mixture of resignation and hope, as I committed the quote to memory.

The security lights outside the back door of the bar suddenly clicked on and we were bathed in a sickly, yellowish light. "You've done this before?" I turned to ask Greg.

He nodded.

"What happens afterward?" I asked.

"One of us calls 911, and we got to fill out police forms. And then the insurance forms, that's the part that really sucks. The lawyer takes care of it after that. Don't worry, Sammy will explain it all."

Inside the Bonneville, Sammy sat in the driver's seat pointing to a piece of paper in his hand. It was small and square, a little bigger than a cocktail napkin, and Rodrigo had to lean left from the passenger seat to see and follow along. After a couple of minutes of instruction, he shifted back to allow the guy with the tilted head to lean forward from the backseat.

A wreck script? To stop from staring, I turned back to Greg. "You have any idea where we're going?"

"They don't tell you. But it's never the same place twice," he said.

Rodrigo emerged from the Bonneville and gestured for us to follow him into the LeBaron.

"I'm not sure I want to do this," Nini whined softly next to me.

I think she was talking mostly to herself, but Rodrigo had heard. He turned to Greg, shaking with anger. "What the fuck is this, man? I let everyone else go home and now she wants out?"

"She'll be fine." Greg turned to give Nini a cold look of

warning. "It's just the crash, man. She's scared of the crash. But she'll be real good with the clinic part." He gave Nini another look. "Tell him, Nini. You can keep your mouth shut when you have to."

"I'll shut up. I'll shut up," she said. "And I'm good at play-acting."

Rodrigo looked at his watch, a gold Rolex that might or might not have been a fake. I gathered it was too late for a change of heart. "Put her in the fucking car," he said.

Greg and Nini began piling into the LeBaron. It was at least fifteen years old with rust around the tire rims and some kind of fluid leaking underneath. I tried not to think about what Tito had said about rusting floorboards being a death trap as I slid into the backseat beside Nini.

I had to have faith in the newsroom. That Bennett was monitoring the transmissions from my cell phone. That someone could follow me to the accident scene and make sure I lived through it.

Inside the car smelled of vinyl and pizza grease. There was a hole in the dashboard where the radio had been removed. Was that to salvage the electronics in case of total destruction? The tingling sensation shot through my spine and into my limbs.

Rodrigo got into the driver's seat in front of Nini. He studied the square of paper in his hand that I hoped was the wreck script. Then he folded it in half, put it on the console, and reached into the glove compartment. He pulled out a cell phone, which he handed to Greg, who was in the front passenger's seat. Greg was assigned the task of calling the police. When the cops arrived, Nini and I were to tell them that we were sore but otherwise okay and refuse transportation to a hospital. Otherwise, we should keep our mouths shut.

Rodrigo put the key in the ignition. My fingertips felt hot and oddly agile as I quickly fastened my seat belt. I would not think of how it would burn into my chest on impact. Instead, I triple-checked to make sure there was no slack.

Just then, the hokeypokey began to play inside my backpack.

"What the fuck is that?" Rodrigo snapped off the car engine.

"My cell phone." I'd pulled it out of the backpack and saw the readout. Eldridge. The idiot. Quickly I snapped it off.

"You gotta be fucking kidding me," Rodrigo turned around in his seat and pulled the phone out of my hand. He double-checked to make sure it was off and threw it on the floor of the passenger seat, next to Greg's feet.

"He doesn't like distractions while he's driving," Greg said, without turning around.

I could not panic. Could not let on that my safety net had been pulled out from under me. I had to hope and pray that Eldridge, *fucking Eldridge,* was calling to say he was there, across the street, and could follow us. Sammy got out of the Bonneville, and the guy with the head tilt moved into the driver's seat with the pregnant Asian woman staying in the backseat.

I held my breath, willing her to change her mind and get out of the car. But no deal. I could see her fastening her seat belt, which I hoped slid around her waist and not her belly. As Sammy headed on foot back to the bar, the Bonneville headed out of the parking lot.

We followed close behind. The suspension of the LeBaron was past its prime. As we turned out of the lot, it felt like the whole back end shifted to one side. I could just imagine the state of its brakes. I thought of the fluid under our car.

"Are we going to get into an accident with the Bonneville?" I asked Rodrigo, trying not to let my voice sounded tinny and scared.

He made no reply at all. Nothing. This time Greg twisted completely around in his seat to give me a look. The look said shut up and don't ask questions.

There was no more rush. Now an interior wire connected and clenched every muscle in my body. The biggest enemy in these situations was panic, I told myself. I had to be cool. Not give anything away. Control my panic and I'd get out of this car with a few bruises and a hell of a story.

On the cross street, there was still no sign of Eldridge, who I now wanted to personally strangle with my bare hands. No one had any idea where I was. No one could follow where the cars were going. If anything went wrong, I was completely on my own.

Our car traveled behind the Bonneville through the industrial neighborhood. When we approached the entrance to Route 95, Nini reached over and grabbed my forearm. Was this going to be a high-speed highway accident?

Not with a pregnant woman in the car. Would they do that? But then it occurred to me that this wreck script might even target an innocent vehicle. Like the attack on Caspar. As we headed north toward Boston, the mist increased to a drizzle, and Rodrigo had to turn on the windshield wipers. Although it was cool inside the car, the back of my legs began to sweat, sticking to the fake leather seats.

We were in the fast lane, and Rodrigo slowed down so the Suburu to our right, in the middle lane, could catch up. "Who's inside?" he asked Greg.

"Two chicks," he answered.

This was apparently no good, because the driver increased his speed to pull away.

Several minutes of searching passed. "A couple. With an old lady in the back," Greg said. Maybe they had learned their lesson about old ladies dying in these crashes because Rodrigo passed on this one, too.

The highway felt smaller and narrower than before. Cars raced ahead of us on either side. A cell phone rang and Greg handed it back to Rodrigo. "Got it," he said, and increased his speed so he was directly behind the Bonneville.

To my right, I saw the chosen target. A lone man in the middle lane driving a Chevrolet, with the bumper covered with a disintegrating Pro-Choice bumper sticker. As we pulled alongside the car, I saw that he had longish hair and possibly a guitar case in the back seat. His mouth was moving, so he was either talking on a hands-free cell phone or singing along to the radio. Going less than fifty-five miles per hour, he didn't appear to be in any rush.

The rain began pelting the car, and I could no longer see anything but a blur through the windows. Rodrigo chose this moment to hit the gas. He passed the Chevy, then slid across a puddle to pull directly in front of it in the middle lane.

Now the sky hurled its water down at the road with such force that the highway was suddenly like the Narragansett Bay splashing up on both sides of the car. The only thing you could see through the windows was the diffused glare of lights. Nini reached over and grabbed my forearm again, this time digging in with her nails. This was it.

Walter was right. I'd gone after a bizarre new high and now I was going to get killed. My breath stopped. I deserved it,

I thought. For never paying attention at Gamblers Anonymous meetings. For thinking none of it pertained to me.

My shoulders hunched forward as I tried to huddle over my inner organs. My feet braced against the floor.

Anticipating the sudden cutoff, I closed my eyes. The moment refused to pass. I opened my eyes and saw Nini, her left arm up, as if to protect her face, as she stared at the back of the car seat, waiting.

From the left, the Bonneville lurched into the lane ahead of us, nearly clipping the front fender. We pitched forward as Rodrigo hit the brakes. The car began to slide, water splashed the car from all directions. The road dissolved, and there was no friction, no earth.

We slid for what seemed like forever.

There was a shriek as we stopped and the Chevrolet slammed into us. The force thrust me forward. The seat belt burned into my chest.

A blur of lights swirled past the window. My body stopped just short of the back of the driver's seat. I heard Nini scream and Greg tell her to shut up. I opened my eyes. My body was shaking. My arms were okay except for where Nini had dug in her nails before letting me go. I moved my legs and feet and felt no searing pain.

Rodrigo started the car again and pulled onto the shoulder, moving forward about fifty yards, and rumbling to a stop behind the Bonneville. The rain had let up and I could see through the rear window. The Chevrolet had pulled over, too.

Suddenly, Rodrigo leapt out of the car and ordered Greg into the driver's seat. "You're the driver, man." Then he took off, jumping into the passenger seat of the Bonneville and speeding off with the driver. Greg grabbed papers out of the glove compartment and climbed over the console into the driver's seat. The Asian woman who had been a passenger in the other car slipped into our passenger seat, her hair and clothes seemingly untouched by the rain.

"Are you all right?" I asked.

She looked at me as if this were none of my business, but nodded.

"Just wait until he pulls up closer, then we all get out of the car," Greg told us.

We waited several minutes. Inside, the muscles in my upper arms couldn't stop shaking, but my breathing began to slow. It was over. We were all safe, unharmed. All I had to do now was try to keep a low profile with the police. Get the name of the clinic from Rodrigo afterward and I was golden.

It was then that I noticed the fold of paper Rodrigo had left on the console was gone. I leaned forward and saw it lying on the floor near the Asian woman's feet. These were the instructions for the accident Sammy had given him, and they were lying right next to my cell phone. It might be a diagram, or even the whole wreck script.

"Now!" Greg shouted and jumped out of the driver's side door. The guy from the Chevy had gotten out of his car and was headed toward us, a newspaper held over his head.

The Asian woman immediately got out to follow Greg, and Nini opened her car door, but hesitated. "Aren't you coming?" she asked me.

The square of paper was just lying there. Ironclad proof to show the new publisher. Especially when we didn't have photos. Did I dare?

I told myself it was completely believable that it could have blown out of the car and dissolved into the rain. Besides, Rodrigo was gone now, and Greg did not strike me as particularly observant, or as any kind of a detail man. "Go ahead. I'm just going to grab my cell phone before I forget." I gestured to the front seat.

"Hurry," she said with new authority. But she left me, and when she was a safe distance from the car, I crawled across the console, fitting my body between the seats to lean far enough to grab both the square of paper and my cell phone. Quickly, I stuffed them in the bottom of my backpack and braced myself for whatever was left of the rain.

They were huddled together in the shoulder of the road. "You okay?" the guy from the Chevy asked as I approached. I put my hand to my back as instructed. "I'm having a little trouble walking."

"Fuck," he said. As if my injury was the final straw.

"That asshole cut us off and just kept going," Nini said. She was holding her right arm as if it were in a sling, cupping the elbow with her left hand.

"But I thought I saw it pull over for a minute," he said. I held my breath. Had he seen the drivers switch?

"Just for a minute," Nini said. "But when Greg asked for his insurance, the asshole just took off. Just took off . . ." Here she began to cry. I watched her in amazement, uncertain if she *was* shook-up, or, as she had claimed, just really good at playacting.

The guy in the Chevrolet stared at her. I couldn't tell if he was confused by her crying or still dazed from the accident. Then his gaze shifted to the Asian woman's belly.

"You sure you don't need an ambulance?" Greg asked him, flipping open his cell phone. "I'm going to call 911."

"No," the guy in the Chevy said swiftly. "Don't do that."

"I got to, man." Greg began to dial.

"Let's just exchange insurance papers. Don't get the cops involved in this."

Greg looked confused. Apparently, this was not a part of the plan. I noticed for the first time a thick, sour smell surrounding the guy from the Chevy. Beer? Maybe a little pot thrown in.

"We got to, man," Greg repeated.

"I don't want to take no fucking breathalyzer."

Greg continued to dial. Suddenly, the guy from the Chevrolet lurched forward, knocking the cell phone out of Greg's hand and onto the road. He turned and ran back toward his car.

"Get back here!" Greg said. The guy jumped into the Chevrolet with its crumpled front end and pulled into the slow lane, narrowly escaping an oncoming car that had to swerve to avoid hitting him.

"Get his license plate number," Greg instructed Nini, as he scrambled along the ground on the shoulder for his cell phone. It was raining hard enough that it was difficult to see, but Nini began reciting the letters and numbers to herself out loud.

Meanwhile, Greg found the cell phone beside the car and redialed. "There's been an accident," I heard him say. "We got hit by a drunken driver who just took off. Left us here. A hit-and-run."

20

"It's a felony," Dorothy had said when I called her last night after the accident to tell her what had happened. She was relieved that I was safe, but furious that I'd gone along on the ride. "The lawyers were very clear. In Massachusetts, it's a felony to take part in a staged accident." She seemed to think this jeopardized the whole story. That Nathan would not be willing to run a piece in which the reporter actually broke the law.

It was early the next morning. I'd awakened before dawn clutching my chest, which still ached from the seat belt, and I felt dizzy and anxious. As if from a major hangover.

I dangled my leg off the side of the bed and grounded my foot onto the floor. The room settled, and I could make out my backpack, a lump on the floor. After all I'd been through, there was no way I was going to lose this story on a technicality.

As the dizziness subsided, it occurred to me that I needed to talk to my own lawyer. For a moment I thought of Matt and had a nagging urge just to hear his voice again. But there was no way I was going to call him for any kind of favor. Then I remembered Dane's offer, and his criminal law expertise in Massachusetts. I waited until the sun was up to call him and ask if he could meet me for breakfast.

About an hour later at Rufful's, I chose the booth farthest in back. Only a block from my apartment, it was a favorite haunt, a narrow alley with a long counter that gleamed and with waitresses who remembered my name. No matter what time of day, it smelled of fresh coffee, warm baked goods, and smoked meats.

Dane appeared at the door only minutes later. He was wearing glasses that sat low on his nose and cut through the cool handsomeness, offering the first sign of any kind of physical weakness. Somehow, I liked him better in glasses.

Today he was dressed for business in a European-cut gray suit and a shirt that demanded gold cuff links. I felt a wave of both gratitude and power. Clearly, he had an important day ahead of him, but hadn't even mentioned it when I called. He'd actually put me *ahead* of his career.

I waved and he made his way over, weaving through the take-out line at the counter. He slid into the booth next to me, rather than sitting across the table. Throwing his arm over my shoulder, he kissed me. "I've missed you," he said.

Perhaps my underground relationship with Matt had warped me, but instead of enjoying his lack of inhibition, I felt acutely embarrassed. Especially when Livia, the waitress, coughed as if she had to break us up before taking our order. I pulled away slowly, trying not to look too uncomfortable.

Pouring coffee, Livia didn't bother to ask what I wanted,

since she knew it was a BLT on rye toast. She wrinkled her nose when Dane asked for an egg white omelet, as if this was somehow suspect, but she hurried off without comment.

"So if you're my lawyer, am I protected by lawyer-client privilege?" I began.

"Meaning?"

"Meaning that you're sworn to secrecy?"

"I can keep a secret without being your lawyer," he said, sounding a little offended.

"I know, I know. But my editor has a thing about secrecy. Especially when we're about to go to press. This is for her. Not me."

"Okay, I'm your lawyer." His tone was solemn, and he looked more lawyerly wearing the glasses. But underneath the table, he rubbed his thigh against mine. "Is this story almost over?"

"It runs Sunday. Then I'll be free."

"So tell me what's going on."

I explained it all in detail. That I was working on an exposé about staged accidents. That I'd gotten a tip about Tito Manaforte and the car ring in Providence and learned that the ring crossed the state line into Massachusetts.

"So you're planning to take Tito Manaforte down, huh?"

I nodded.

"A service to mankind, but—"

He was interrupted by Livia, who delivered our breakfasts. Starving, I immediately attacked my BLT, swallowing nearly half of it. But Dane, after only a single bite, put down his fork and knife. Checking over his shoulder to make sure Livia was out of earshot, he asked. "Okay, so how are you planning on taking Tito down without getting yourself killed?"

I explained about the Cottage, and how I'd wound up actually taking part in the staged crash.

"You got in the car?" His face paled.

"Hey, look, I survived fine." I decided not to mention the welt on my chest from the seat belt. "But what I want to know is if my participation itself is illegal. Is it a felony, misdemeanor?"

"Can you actually tie this to Tito?" he asked.

"I think so. I've got a former runner on tape."

He opened his mouth to ask something, but stopped himself. Then his expression grew grim. "You might want to think about whether this is worth it, Hallie. Tito is a very dangerous man who has done some horrible things to people. And you know he's on parole. So he's not going to just let it slide if you write a story that sends him back to prison."

"So is it a felony?"

He hesitated. "Not if you weren't driving, but if you gave the cop a fake license . . ."

I shook my head. "I gave him the fake name but not the license."

He thought a minute. "Believe it or not, just giving the cops a fake name isn't an actual crime, but it still might not be worth the risk."

I ignored the last part. "Really? It's not a crime?"

"But if you signed a statement—"

I shook my head. "No. I let Greg and Nini do all the talking."

He shrugged, then retreated to his omelet. After a couple of bites, something else occurred to him. "You must have signed some insurance forms, though?" he asked. "Because if you did . . ."

"I had to fill out some last night, and I'll probably have to fill out more at the clinic—"

"Clinic?"

"Sammy called me this morning. They made an appointment for me, at some shady medical clinic in Mattapan."

"How do you know it's shady?" Dane asked.

"That's why I'm going there, to find out for sure."

"You're actually going to go?"

"This is going to be the best part," I said. "If I can convince Dorothy."

"But what if they look up your name? Find out it's a fake driver's license? These people could come after you." He looked sincerely alarmed.

"Nah," I said, trying to soothe him. "The worst part is over, believe me. Now I only have to deal with chiropractors and receptionists."

His fork clattered to his plate. "Look, Tito Manaforte is no one to screw around with. You don't want to get him suspicious. Or make this guy your enemy unless you get him back in jail first. You should wait on this—"

"Hey, I've got a great story here, one that not only reveals the bottom of the food chain but the big fishes, too. The guys who really make money on this. The doctors. The lawyers like Joe D'Anzana—who don't give a shit as long as he makes his one-third off of Lizette Salazar."

Something flashed in his eyes at the mention of Lizette. "Are you going to put her accident into your story?"

"Off the record?"

He nodded.

"She was murdered."

This time all the blood drained from his face. "What?"

I told him that I'd gotten a tip she'd stolen money from Tito, and that I examined her wreck with a forensic expert who said she couldn't possibly have been driving the car because of the seat belt and the distance the seat was set from the steering wheel.

"Is this a police investigation you're talking about?"

I shook my head. "No. The cops aren't interested. Don't have the time for a Dominican immigrant. No, this is an independent expert who took me to the yard and explained why it was impossible for Lizette to be driving."

"Are you sure this guy knows his stuff and isn't just looking for the free publicity?"

Did he think I couldn't judge for myself? I decided to give Dane the benefit of the doubt. He must not realize that this question would be an insult to any reporter. "He knows his stuff," I said firmly.

He didn't seem to notice my change of tone. "Who *is* this guy?" he asked, with an intonation that still managed to challenge my source.

"I can't tell you that. I can't tell anyone. Not even my editor. He's doesn't want his name in the paper."

"You ever wonder why?" Dane pushed away his unfinished omelet, an anxious look growing on his face. I thought he was going to challenge my source's motives again, but now he had a new concern. "You're dealing with some dangerous people. Murderers, Hallie—maybe your life is more important than getting a story on the front page."

Had I asked for a lecture? His tone made me feel defiant. What was it about sleeping with a man that made him think he could tell you what to do? Still, I strove for diplomacy. "I'll be fine, really."

Dane put his hand over mine on the table, but it felt authoritative, rather than affectionate. "Hallie, don't do it."

There was an edge in his voice I didn't like, and I wished I'd thought of a way to get the information out of him without telling him about the assignment. "I'll be fine," I repeated, more firmly this time. I slid my hand out from under his and picked up what was left of my BLT.

"Maybe this *is* a felony," Dane said. "Maybe I was too rash . . ."

"What?" A complete turnaround? I didn't believe him for a second, and was about to tell him so when a voice at the coffee counter stopped me in my tracks. I looked up and there was Matt Cavanaugh, putting change in his pocket, staring at us.

My breath caught in my throat. But Dane followed my gaze, saw Matt, and waved. Matt continued to stare, his eyes taking in Dane beside me in the booth, the closeness of our bodies, side by side. Then he shook his head, as if he couldn't believe what he was seeing, and without waiting for his coffee, he turned around and walked out.

"What's wrong with him?" Dane asked.

This was the first time I'd actually seen Matt face-to-face since our breakup, and every nerve ending was issuing a response. The BLT dropped back to the plate. My hands were shaking, but that was the least of it.

"Holy shit. You used to sleep with Matt Cavanaugh," Dane said. This was loud enough for one of the women at the next booth to turn around and stare.

Dane's eyes were cold with accusation. For a split second, I wanted to slink under the seat, but then my own anger flared, and any guilt I'd been harboring for not revealing the relationship earlier dissolved. "You clearly mistake me for someone you can talk to like that." I tried to push past him to get out of the booth.

"I'm not moving." On the outside of the booth, his body was a block, and his voice a low command.

Two women sitting together at the counter turned around to see what was going on.

"Let me out," I said. "I'm on deadline."

His eyes met mine, resistant.

"Now."

Finally, he got up out of the booth to let me go.

I opened my mouth to tell Dane to fuck off, but halted. Standing face-to-face, I could see his anger was gone. Instead, he looked pained, and I remembered all that he had been willing to confide in me about his ex-wife. About her betrayal.

"It wasn't for that long," I said to try to soothe him. "And I haven't spoken to him for a month."

This last part seemed to appease him. His eyes met mine. "I'm sorry if I overreacted," he said.

"We can talk about this later." But I couldn't bring myself to kiss him good-bye. Instead, I grabbed my backpack and, over his objections, I tossed a ten on the table, leaving him to wait for the check.

21

Still shaking, I threw it all down on the conference table in the Fishbowl: a Ziploc bag containing the folded paper, which had a nice, neat, and amazingly legible diagram of the accident on it, the two hundred in cash I'd been paid so far, a piece of paper with the license plate numbers of the Bonneville and LeBaron scribbled on it, a helpful printout from WebMD about the symptoms of low back pain, and best of all, the name of the clinic where I'd been scheduled for treatment—the Holistic Joint Pain Clinic in Mattapan.

It wasn't even nine thirty, which is like the break of dawn for most newspaper people, but Dorothy and the rest of the team were already seated around the table, waiting for me. I was trying like hell to put both Dane and Matt out of my mind. When it came down to it, you couldn't rely on either one of them. The thing that mattered was this story, my career.

"You actually took part in the accident?" Ellen asked with a mixture of disbelief and awe.

"I couldn't get out of it," I repeated.

"Like anyone's going to believe that," Frizell said.

The table was divided up along boy-girl lines. Frizell was at the far end of the oval, next to Bennett Castiglia and his laptop on one side, and Ryan Skendarian and his laptop on the other. Since I had no use for men at the moment, I took a seat between Ellen and Dorothy.

I dropped my backpack under the table and gave a full account of what had happened at the Cottage. I put all remaining thoughts of Dane out of my head as I told them about Nini, the nervous passenger, and described Rodrigo's outburst when she tried to back out at the last minute. "I feared for my life," I said in a very deliberate manner, as if I were saying it on a witness stand, coached by a lawyer.

"You still took part in the accident," Dorothy said. "And it's still a felony. I checked this morning with the lawyers."

Behind her, the newsroom was beginning to fill up. Between two of the teal-colored fish taped on the glass, I could see several reporters peering into the Fishbowl, wondering what the hell we were meeting about so early in the morning.

"I checked with my own lawyer, this morning," I said, doing my utmost to dissociate Dane's legal advice from Dane himself. "Not someone who specializes only in libel." This was a slur on the *Chronicle*'s lawyers. "Someone who actually practiced criminal law in Massachusetts, who had handled this kind of case. And he has a different view on it. I wasn't the driver. And the cops didn't even take a statement from me."

"You gave them a fake name," Dorothy said.

"What was I going to do? Break role? Besides, according to

my lawyer, it's not a crime in Massachusetts to give cops a fake name, only a fake ID. And I didn't sign anything or give them a statement. I let Nini and Greg do all the talking."

"Who?" Ryan asked Frizell.

"The guy who switched into the driver's seat and his girlfriend," I called down to the end of the table.

"Who is your lawyer?" Dorothy wanted to know.

Here, in the interest of full disclosure, I had to explain that I had a "personal relationship" with him. But when I gave Dorothy Dane's name, she seemed impressed. "He's on my United Way committee," she said. "A cousin or friend of the AG."

"Is he the trust-fund guy? The one who's so good-looking?" Ellen asked. She sounded a little shocked, and by the way she looked at me, I gathered that my social standing had just risen. But since I couldn't bring myself to say anything too nice about Dane at the moment, I merely nodded.

At the end of the table, Ryan Skendarian was losing patience with this shift to my love life. "Were the police suspicious?" he asked.

I was grateful for the change in topic. "Not at all. Which was amazing. But mostly they were concerned about whether we were all right. They asked Greg a couple of questions, looked at his license, but they really wanted to know about the car that took off."

Ellen grabbed the Ziploc bag and peered through the plastic, trying to make sense of the cocktail napkin inside.

I was in full gear now, the morning forgotten, as I jacked myself up on my own story. I explained that it was the runner's sketch of how the accident was supposed to go down. On it Sammy had drawn, in neat, almost architectural rendition, three little boxes representing the cars, the three lanes of a highway, the shoulder, and arrows suggesting the angle of approach.

Frizell gestured to Ellen to pass the cocktail napkin to his end of the table. After a minute of studying it, he said. "So if police find this guy—the guy in the Chevy—they'll charge him with a hit and run. A crime he didn't actually commit."

That thought had also occurred to me during my period of early-morning sleep deprivation. "But he's a drunk driver who should be off the road," I said. "Anyway, he'll be cleared when the story comes out."

The long silence at the table suggested that this argument carried some weight. It was no time to back off. "And who knows how many more times these predatory drivers will hunt for suckers on the highway if we don't expose it?"

No one answered, so I kept going. "I'm going to call police this morning and get the report of the accident," I told Dorothy. "So we've got plenty of documentation to back up my first-person account."

She put her hand up, as if to say hold your horses. I pretended I didn't notice and passed her the paper with the name of the medical clinic. "This will help us get beyond the poor schnooks riding in the cars and get the real criminals," I said.

"You mean Tito," Dorothy said.

"Yeah. According to my source, Tito owns a good share of a couple of these clinics, but once we're on the paper trail, who knows who else we'll be able to bring down. Shady chiropractors and lawyers—the guys who don't get their hands dirty but make all the real cash."

There was no question, the lure of exposing white-collar

crime was a big a temptation for any journalist. This was a major story we were talking about. We all knew it.

"One problem," Frizell said.

I looked at him.

"Just getting the name of the clinic doesn't actually prove the clinic has done anything wrong."

"I can talk to my sources inside the insurance industry," Castiglia offered. "They keep all kinds of past claims data—that includes medical clinics. I can run an analysis against DMV records and see if there's a pattern of association with fraudulent accidents."

"That's good," Dorothy said.

"That's generic," I objected. "If we really want to make an impact with this story, we need to tie at least one of these clinics directly to this accident. Show the operation in narrative from start to finish."

All eyes turned on me. Ellen was already with me. Frizell was only mildly resistant. And Dorothy's expression could be read: Did I have balls or what?

There was no way I was going to back off. Maybe it was to prove to Dane that I wasn't about to take orders. But I'd already gone through the dangerous part; it seemed to me that I owed it to Marcella, to Lizette's memory, and to my own career to follow through on the details. Go for broke.

"Look, the runner already made an appointment for me at this clinic in Mattapan. Just let me go posing as Irina Calek. I can meet some of the doctors. See how the whole thing works. Give a blow-by-blow account about how easy it is to bilk the system."

Dorothy seemed to be considering this.

"He said he admired boldness."

They all looked at me in confusion. "Ian Clew," I explained. "He told us to be bold. And if we're not bold, what's the point of the newspaper even having an investigative team?"

"He told us to be bold. He didn't tell us to break the law," Frizell said.

Behind the glass, in the newsroom, phones were ringing like mad, and one of the copy editors was pacing between the rim and the city desk, probably waiting to ask Dorothy about something. Dorothy looked over and, seeing him, groaned.

At the same time, her pager began to vibrate against the wood of the conference table. She picked it up, stared at the number, and shut it off. Then she glanced at her watch.

By the way she pulled her bottom lip in and under, I knew she was still fretting about what to do, but I could also see from the glimmer in the eyes of the other reporters that they saw promise in the story, angles they could grab for their own, and success for the team.

Bennett, always the statistician, offered help from another angle. "We've been losing circulation in Southeastern Massachusetts. If the paper is serious abut trying to reach out to the readers, we need better coverage of that area. A series like this straddles the two states. It would draw in a lot of people."

"I can't let you commit another crime," Dorothy said.

"We can give the insurance company the heads-up the day before the story runs and stop everything in midmotion." I began innovating. "If the insurance claim isn't actually paid, the company isn't going to pursue it—especially if it's part of an expose that helps break up a criminal ring that's costing them a ton of money."

"And if you're worried about her safety, I can drive her to

the clinic," Frizell said. "I can pose as her boyfriend. Take down some details. Maybe talk to other patients while she's being treated."

Frizell had sniffed a change in the wind, but I didn't care. Let him horn in on the medical clinic story. As long as I got the approval.

Dorothy looked at Frizell a moment. Then she looked through the glass at the copy editor still pacing, still waiting to talk to her. She turned to me. "How long do you think it would take to get this story written?"

"The appointment is for one o'clock. I'll be back here by midafternoon. And I can write all weekend and have it ready for Sunday's paper."

Bennett chimed in by offering to call his insurance contact right after the meeting. He also said he could dig into the ownership of the clinic by pulling up corporation documents that were available online from the Massachusetts secretary of state's Web site.

Ellen wanted to get the story from the community level, talk to people at the Hispanic Center in South Providence and the Cambodian Center, to talk about the economic disadvantages that made insurance fraud so alluring for new immigrants. And Ryan Skendarian suggested another sidebar on rising insurance rates, which he could tabulate by city and town in Rhode Island and Southeastern Massachusetts and correlate with fraud rates.

"And you're *all* willing to work this weekend?" she asked us.

But she knew the answer. The cutbacks were going to be announced Monday.

When I got back to my desk my cell phone was ringing. It was Marcella. "I find what you are looking for," she said. "What we talked about."

"You found the accounting books?" I held my breath waiting for her answer. This could be the golden ring that linked all the elements of the story together. Profits and payments. Proof.

"Not the book. But my sister, she make copies. Of the numbers. These I find in a box under her shoes. I meet you."

"When? What time?" I asked.

Marcella was in the car on the way to her older sister's in West Warwick. She wanted me to meet her at the dog track in Lincoln at noon, before her lunch shift, but I told her I was going to the clinic.

"In Boston?" she asked.

"Mattapan. You know it?"

She didn't answer. "I will call you after my shift then. Six o'clock I get out." The connection got scratchy, and she said something I couldn't hear.

"I'm losing you. What?"

"I say maybe I was wrong, what I tell you. About Tito."

I figured that she had just learned what Franco had already told me. That Manuel had borrowed money from the street to pay off the money Lizette had stolen. But she had a whole new lead. "I think is someone who *steals* from Tito. My sister, she make notes of this on the copies. She adds up numbers and make circles in red. Her notes say there is problem. Money is missing."

This was what Franco had said. That someone was cheating Tito. Lizette had figured out that same thing. "Did she know *who* was stealing from Tito?"

Marcella said something that I couldn't hear, but it sounded like Spanish. There was a moment of static and the call dropped.

I dialed her back, but her voice mail immediately picked up. A no-service area. I left a message for her to call me and hung up. I tried again and got the voice mail a second time. I began rummaging through my backpack to find my tape recorder to listen to my interview with Franco again. I fast-forwarded through too much of the interview and then had to rewind. *"Because everyone cheats. The lawyers, the doctors, they take more than their share. The ones who do the hard work. We get nothing, nothing but blame."*

Then Franco and Caspar began talking to each other in Spanish on the tape. I stopped, rewound, and listened to a line in Spanish again. I made out *que está robando de Tito.*

I copied this down on a notebook as best I could, spelling phonetic Spanish instead of anything that approximated real Spanish. When Marcella called back, I'd ask her to translate.

Just then my phone started ringing. Thinking it was Marcella, I made a critical error. I answered without even glancing at the caller ID first.

"Tell me you aren't going out with Dane Piedmont." It was Matt.

At the sound of his voice, my stomach took a dive, landing somewhere underneath my chair. Like I had time for this now.

"Oh man, tell me you aren't going out with him," he repeated, but without the air of authority I'd gotten from Dane. Matt's tone was plaintive.

I was irritated by this intrusion and impatient to get Marcella back on the line. And yet I couldn't help seeing the hurt in his face, standing at the Rufful's counter. "I'm sorry, Matt," I finally said. "But we broke up, remember?"

"How long have you been seeing him?"

"That's really not your business anymore." Or ever, I might have added. We had never talked about being exclusive.

"Look, I know I have no rights."

"You got that straight." I might have mentioned the woman in his car that day I saw him pull up to his condo. But I didn't want to get into that argument. Or suggest my relationship with Dane was retaliatory.

"But Dane Piedmont is a complete asshole."

At the moment, I couldn't have agreed more, but I wasn't about to admit this to Matt. "I thought he was your basketball buddy?"

"He's a dirty player," Matt said. "Cuts out your knees when you go for a rebound. Complains about every foul."

Like that had anything to do with a relationship? "Matt, the thing is—He doesn't *mind* that I'm a reporter." I wasn't so much defending Dane as illuminating Matt's own defects as a boyfriend. "He's not ashamed to be seen with me."

"I was never *ashamed,*" he said. And then, "I'm really sorry about that night, Hallie. I'm sorry about everything. I was an asshole."

"Apparently I have a thing for assholes."

Matt did not laugh.

"Can I see you?" he finally asked. "Just once?"

I did *not* have time for this. But his voice always did it to me, warmed something deep under my skin. Now, with that pleading quality, it was hard not to respond. My heart turned over, revved, and raced down a familiar street. God, I was an idiot.

"How about lunch? Will you at least go out to lunch with me?"

I told myself that he was only this passionate, this determined, because a rival, a real rival had emerged. I couldn't get swept up in this right now. I had major leads to follow. I had to stay focused. Focused. "I'm working on a big story for Sunday," I said.

"I've heard."

This stopped me in my tracks. Was Frizell making small talk with his sources at the AG's office? "How have you heard?"

"The insurance thing, you were working on it before we broke up, remember? It was connected to that fatal you covered, right?"

Lizette. How much had I told him about Lizette that night at Al Forno? What could he know of my investigation now?

"Anyway. I've got something. Something you should know about."

"What?"

"I'll explain at lunch," he pressed.

"Is it connected to insurance fraud or the fatal?"

"Both, I think."

I don't know what was more shocking, that the state was looking into Lizette's accident or that Matt was so desperate to see me that he was actually willing to slip me information. But my heart had been getting an overload of stimuli lately, and now it felt like it was starting to skip rhythms. "Just tell me, please, I'm on deadline."

"In person," he said. "I promise I'll tell you, but I've got to see you. Please."

I felt both renewed irritation and the tingle underneath my skin. I wanted to demand that he tell me right then, and yet I wanted to see him, too. I reminded myself I didn't have time for this new desperation of his. I had an appointment at a medical mill. I had to find a time to meet with Marcella. And I had a deadline to meet. “I can’t make lunch. How about dinner? A late dinner, like maybe at eight or nine o’clock?”

“Even better,” he said.

22

The Holistic Joint Pain Clinic was on Blue Hill Avenue in a small office building on the corner of a city block with a thrift store, a nail salon, and a discount pharmacy that had iron gratings on its door and all its windows.

We'd driven Frizell's car, which was an inconspicuous four-year-old Camry that we parked three blocks away on the street rather than in the clinic's parking lot. But as we walked down the sidewalk together, I felt conspicuous all the same, a privileged white couple with perfect teeth in a seemingly homogenous black neighborhood, where both jobs and orthodontia were scarce.

There had been three shootings in this section of Boston in the last two months, and I could see Jonathan stiffen as we approached the corner where four boys in their late teens stood together outside the market. But I felt a rush again, this time in my legs, an energy that seemed to come out of the sidewalk.

There was nothing *wrong* with this kind of excitement about a story, I told myself. We were out there—on the front line of reporting—instead of holed up in our offices running computer analyses or thinking we were brave for taking on some lobbyist.

It was another humid day, warm as summer and airless. The boys were passing around a Gatorade bottle that looked diluted. Seeing us approach, they began to shift position, moving toward the center of the sidewalk as a unit. One of them crushed something in his hand.

When I worked at the *Ledger,* I'd lived in the primarily white neighborhood of Brighton, but not far from the projects, so I knew not to attempt any kind of eye contact with teenagers. I kept my gaze focused on something beyond them, determined and hurried, as I swerved to step around them into the street. Frizell followed my lead, but shook his head in annoyance, acknowledging their existence. A mistake.

"Hey, baby," one of them shouted. Another made a cooing sound to try to bait Jonathan. Frizell's hand went deep into his pocket, where I knew he had the cell phone, which was being monitored back at the newsroom to track our location, but he kept his eyes steady and said nothing. There was a lot of laughter as I quickened my pace.

We passed two boarded-up storefronts, where there had obviously been a fire, before we made it to the block where the clinic was housed. It was on the first floor of a small office building. The glass vestibule, which was unlocked, smelled of overactive sweat glands, but once we were buzzed inside, the linoleum floor reeked of ammonia. The small lobby had a grimy feel, with dark-paneled walls and fluorescent lighting that could not compensate for a lack of windows. A directory near the staircase was hand-printed. It gave the second-floor office numbers for an acupuncturist, a dentist, and a chiropractor, all with Russian surnames.

Suddenly I remembered that Franco had said something about *doctors* taking "more than their share." Maybe one of these doctors was the one who'd been stealing from Tito. Could a doctor actually have killed Lizette?

There were no windows or air-conditioning in the hallway. The heat and ammonia combined to produce what felt like a lethal gas. I coughed for air.

Jonathan was studying me carefully. "You want to bail, it's okay with me."

He was trying to be nice, understanding. Still, it pissed me off. There were reporters who begged for an assignment in Baghdad. We were two steps into a run-down office building and we were going to bail? "Of course not," I replied.

A second hand-printed sign pointed us down the hall to the Holistic Health Joint Pain Center on the ground level. There we found a window where we had to identify ourselves to the receptionist. I felt a flutter of panic that I would forget my fake name. But it spilled out of my mouth. "Irina Calek." I pointed to Jonathan. "And my boyfriend, David."

The receptionist, a young woman with long cornrows almost to her waist, shoved aside a novel she had been reading to gaze up at me. I felt myself tighten. Did I look too Irish for the name? Did it sound forced introducing my boyfriend? She glanced at Jonathan and without comment began to shuffle through papers. After what seemed like the most protracted moment in the world, she motioned us through the door.

Only three people sat in the waiting room, which was a disappointment to Frizell, who was supposed to chat up the other patients for info while I went through the exam. I was to act vague about my injuries to see how much prodding the medical staff offered, and how much real care I actually got.

All I really needed was a treatment plan, hopefully an extensive treatment plan that went right up to the limit Sammy needed to have the lawyers file suit for pain and suffering. All I had to do was act cool and go along with whatever the doctors ordered. I told myself to relax. It shouldn't be too complicated or take too long. I could be back in the newsroom in Providence and writing by midafternoon.

I thought about my phone call with Matt, about what he might have learned about Lizette's fatal. I doubted he had better information than Marcella. He'd said he *thought* it might be connected to insurance fraud, but he didn't sound certain. More likely it was something generic from a snitch, having to do with Tito Manaforte, who was always of interest to the state police organized crime division.

Whatever it was, I hoped to hell it was both specific and on the record, and that it didn't send me in a completely new direction, because I didn't have a lot of time to chase down extraneous and unconfirmed details. But I reminded myself that by the time I met Matt tonight, I might not even need his information. By then, I might already have the copies of the ledgers from Marcella.

My right knee was bouncing, as if it rode alone on an amusement park ride, and I had to put my hand on my leg to quell the agitation. Then, I realized that the receptionist was calling me. And that I was Irina.

The receptionist couldn't have been any older than twenty or twenty-one, and yet she stared at me as if she knew it when she met a liar all right. She pointed to a sheet of paper on the counter and told me to sign in. "You the hit-and-run?" she asked.

Frizell, who was studying a display of herbal supplements and vitamins on the far end of the counter, looked up sharply. Someone was keeping this clinic well informed.

"I feel lucky to be alive," I said as I signed the paper. The receptionist tilted her head and gave me a look that said: Spare me the bullshit. "Just take care of business," she said and passed me a clipboard stuffed with papers before returning to her novel.

That fueled another rush. *"Just take care of business."* It would make a great pull quote. I closed my eyes a second and tried to commit the expression of the receptionist to memory.

Then I took the clipboard with me to a small tweed couch to assess the paperwork. There were general medical forms, asking for history and inoculations, but also a form authorizing direct billing of medical claims to the auto insurance company. A copy of the accident report, which was now renamed a "crash data report," was at the back of the clipboard.

The receptionist looked thoroughly engaged in her novel, so after a couple of minutes I got up and headed to the restroom down the hall, carrying my clipboard and backpack with me. Hiding myself inside a stall, I scribbled the receptionist's quote and a brief physical description of the clinic in my notebook. Afterward, I pulled out my cell phone to see if Marcella had tried to call back. She hadn't. Then, after I had filled out the forms with my fake name and address, I photographed them with my cell phone camera. This gave Dorothy new options for graphics.

Back in the reception room, I found Frizell sitting on a plastic chair between an elderly woman with a back brace and a new patient who had just arrived, a man in his early forties wearing work clothes with deep sweat stains across the front of his T-shirt.

I sat waiting only a couple of minutes before the receptionist called for Irina Calek again. This time she directed me down another short hall into an examining room.

I was seen first by a man who introduced himself as Dr. Arlanov. Wearing a white medical coat and a stethoscope around his neck, he was a small, uncommunicative man, whose teeth smelled badly of plaque. He had a slight accent that sounded Eastern European. When I showed him where my back hurt, he touched it as if he really didn't like touching people. Then he told me that I had to see Dr. Wendy.

I was shuttled into the next room, which was larger and grimier, with yellowed blinds drawn on the window, an examining table of leather that was faded and veined, and a plastic skeleton hanging from a wooden stand in the corner. The skeleton's right foot was missing.

According to the cheesy-looking degree framed on the wall, Dr. Wendy, a heavyset woman with big, dewy eyes and almost no chin, was not actually a doctor but did have a graduate degree from a school that I'd never heard of in Nevada. I noted that there was nothing on the wall that spoke to her certification in the state of Massachusetts.

She had a scratchy voice and sounded both stuffed up and impatient as she ordered me to lie on my stomach. Roughly, she probed my spine with her fingers.

To my right, I could see an open door to a smaller room, some sort of consultation area with two wing chairs and a desk. A phone on the desk began to ring, but Dr. Wendy ignored it as she pushed into the valleys of my vertebrae.

After a minute the ringing stopped, and Dr. Wendy told me I had "extensive soft tissue damage" near my lumbar and that if I were good about making my appointments, I'd find relief over time.

"How much time?" I asked.

She slapped something warm on my back. "A couple of months. You have a big job or something?" she asked. "Because we have weekend hours and evenings." She also suspected that chiropractic treatment might be needed. "Are you sure you don't have any jaw pain," she wanted to know. "It's very common in this kind of accident."

God, I wished I could write this all down. Instead, I traced a line underneath my cheekbone. "It is a little sore right here," I lied.

"Right," she said, stopping to sneeze. She grabbed a tissue from a box, blew her nose, and said I'd need to see a dentist. Conveniently enough, the one in the office upstairs specialized in TMJ, which was apparently some sort of jaw condition that could haunt me for life. The chiropractor in the building was also very good. I could coordinate those visits with my physical therapy treatments.

The examination was over in about five minutes. I sat up and Dr. Wendy gave me a preprinted list of back exercises and said that I needed a cervical pillow and a lumbar cushion that my insurance would pay for. I could pick that up in the treatment area down the hall.

She had to stop, sneeze, and blow her nose again. "This weather," she said, referring to the rain, I guessed. Then she told me that I'd need an ultrasound immediately. She was explaining how this would help reduce the inflammation when a new, weird buzzing sound from the phone silenced her.

It was some sort of inside line. "I've got to take this." She walked over to the small office and picked up the receiver on the desk. I could see her eyes dart to me and back to the phone in her hand. Then she shut the door between the rooms.

I thought about what Dane had said about doctors and lawyers being the most dangerous because they had the most to lose. I worried that this woman, whatever the hell her degree, was on to me. Quickly, I turned my back to the closed door, pulled my cell phone out of my pocket, and hit Frizell on autodial. It rang twice and he picked up. "Get out and get the car," I whispered.

"I know," he said.

I snapped it shut just as Dr. Wendy swung open the door. "Carole has a busy afternoon. She'd like to see you right away." She picked up my chart, put it under her arm, and pointed me down the hall, telling me to take a right to the treatment room.

The hallway was narrow and windowless, with no sign of an exit or stairwell. I passed two vacant examining rooms on each side, and then a closed door with Dr. Arlanov's nameplate on it. Inside, I could hear male voices, and from the rising tone, it sounded as if one of them was chewing the other one out. I couldn't make out any words, but something about the cadence sounded oddly familiar.

"No, keep going. Take a right, you're almost there," I heard Dr. Wendy call. She was still standing in the hall, supervising my brief journey to make sure that I arrived at the assigned area. I waved a brisk thanks and scooted past the closed office door.

Carole, the assistant, was a short, ample woman in her mid-fifties wearing a pair of green scrubs. She stood waiting for me, a look of determination in her eyes and a johnny in her hand.

"Change into these," she said gruffly, pointing me toward a small changing area.

I pulled the curtain shut and tried to think. Maybe I was overreacting. Maybe none of these people were at all suspicious, and nothing was wrong. But the soft spot Dr. Wendy had probed around my vertebrae felt watery. And now every nerve in my body began to pulse.

The room shared a wall with the office next door and I could hear the male voice thunder. I put my ear right against the blue board wall and heard, "Fucking nimrod."

Tito Manaforte. It was Tito Manaforte.

The pulses radiated from my spine through my limbs. I had to focus on taking deeper breaths, not getting caught up in panic.

The changing room had a single, double-hung window that dropped down about four feet to a patch of grass abutting a small parking lot behind the office building.

"Ready?" Carole asked. She was standing just outside the curtain.

I heard movement in the next room, and the scraping of a chair. Tito could kill me. Suddenly I no longer felt panic, but that strange, eerie calm. This could be the moment before I died.

"I'm having trouble," I said through the curtain. "With my zipper. You have any lotion or oil of any kind I could use?"

"Just give it a tug," Carole said.

"I did. It's stuck. The jeans won't come off."

Underneath the curtain, I saw Carole's sneakers pad away and heard the sound of a cabinet door open.

I put the heel of my hand underneath the head of the lower window and pushed up. The window was old, painted over, stuck in the frame.

"We've got some massage oil, will that work?"

"Lotion won't be as messy," I called. I bent my knees, put my entire weight into my hands and pushed again. A small creak.

Underneath the curtain, I saw a new set of shoes in the doorway: the same ankle-height, red, white, and blue basketball sneakers Tito had worn that day in his body shop.

The moment stopped, expanded. Tito could kill me. And yet, here I was, very much alive. I had a weird clinking feeling in the back of my brain. I pushed a third time, and the window flew open.

I kicked the screen out with my foot and lobbed my backpack out the open window.

"What the fuck was that?" Tito shouted.

As if it were in slow motion, I watched my backpack land.

I threw one leg over the windowsill and struggled to pull the other one around. I was perched on the sill, holding on to the frame. Aiming for the backpack to help break my fall, I pushed off my butt and plunged to the ground. I missed the backpack entirely, landed briefly on my feet, and then fell forward on my hands and knees, ripping my palms and my jeans. I scrambled to my feet, got my bag, and ran like hell to the street.

"Are you sure no one is following us?" Frizell asked.

"I don't see anyone." I was twisted around in the passenger seat, on the lookout since Mattapan. We'd just gotten onto the Southeast Expressway, and there was no sign of a chase car.

"How are your knees?" Frizell asked.

"I need a couple Band-Aids, that's all." My palms were bruised, but barely bleeding.

"Someone ratted you out," Frizell said. He was hunched over the wheel, eyes darting between the rearview and side mirrors.

"What do you mean?"

"I was sitting there in the waiting room, listening to that old lady trying to convince me she had whiplash. The phone rings. I hear the receptionist say: 'What does she look like? Then she looked down the hall toward the room where she'd sent you, and then she looked at me. Real hard," Frizell said, without taking his eyes off the road. "I pretended I didn't see her, like I was listening to the old lady. Then she went down the hall, probably to tell someone else. I got the hell out of there. When you called me, I was already on the street headed toward the car," Frizell said.

"Jesus." Maybe Sammy did a little more checking with Norman this morning or figured out my driver's license was a fake.

My eyes searched the highway with new anxiety. The Southeast Expressway was full of bullet cars, aged and disposable. I watched cars whizzing by us on the left, expecting each one to veer over the yellow stripe. Each car was a potential predator, a weapon going at least sixty miles an hour.

A Dodge pickup with a muffler missing speeded up to cut ahead of us into our lane. "Watch the truck!" I yelled above the engine.

Frizell veered into the shoulder. But the pickup barreled off onto the exit ramp. A false alarm.

We took a minute on the shoulder, hazards flashing, trying to get ahead of our breathing as we watched the cars pass by us in the slow lane. To his credit, Frizell did not ream me out for overreacting. He reached into the glove compartment and found a Kleenex for me to clean up the blood on my knee.

We stayed in the slow lane for the rest of the ride, and both anxiously watched each car that approached in the passing lane or entered from a ramp. But by the time we hit the split, heading south to Providence, it was clear no one was following us. No one was going to follow us. For whatever reason, Tito Manaforte had let us escape.

I had to calm down. But couldn't. My throttle was stuck. Back at my desk, my muscle fibers twitched every time anyone called my name across the newsroom.

After we had briefed Dorothy, Nathan, and the investigative team about our escape from the medical clinic, it was decided that if Marcella called, I was not to meet her anywhere alone. Nor was I to go home alone to my apartment tonight.

I could go my mother's in Worcester to sleep, or spend the night at the Biltmore, where the *Chronicle* had an arrangement and could provide security. Since I still had to meet Matt to find out what he had on the insurance ring, and since Worcester was a good hour away, I chose the Biltmore. That seemed to make everyone happy.

I checked my cell phone. There was nothing from Marcella yet, but I had another couple of hours until she was off of her shift. There was a message on the desk phone from Dane apologizing again for this morning and checking to see that I made it back from my clinic trip safely. I didn't feel like talking to him before my dinner date with Matt, so I didn't call him back.

Next I decided to pay a visit to Bennett to see if he'd gotten anywhere on the medical clinic ownership, or finally run the license plate numbers that I'd gotten from Tito's auto body shop.

Reporters, in general, don't have offices, but because Bennett is the data guy, the one with access to the online services and a liaison to the computer department, he had somehow finagled one of the largest side rooms of the library as his own. It was a corner office, smaller than the library director's but larger than Nathan's, and with a door he could lock if he wanted to.

The newsroom was always buzzing in late afternoon. At four o'clock, politicians and corporate public relations were just beginning to fax over the bad news they had sat on all day. Sports reporters, preparing for the night's game, were starting their day, and a whole new shift of copy editors was reporting for work.

But as I headed through the newsroom, I could tell something big was going on. Marcy Kittner, the state news editor, was pacing in front of Dorothy's desk with a look of agitation, waiting for her to get off the phone. One of the bureau reporters, a new woman I'd seen but hadn't officially met yet, was standing nearby with one of the bureau chiefs, nervously watching one of those late-breaking news alerts on the television.

At the Rim, I stopped and asked one of the copy editors what was going on. "I heard they pulled a body out of one of the ponds stateside," he said. "I think it's in West Greenwich."

"You know who?" I asked.

He shook his head. "I think that's why Marcy is all fussed up. They're still waiting for a police ID."

I quickened my pace to the library and into Bennett's office. An envelope with my name on it was waiting for me on the corner of his desk. When I reached for it, Bennett, who was on the phone, held out his hand, asking me to wait.

I pulled a printout from the envelope and surveyed the names next to the license plate numbers.

Two of the cars that had been parked outside were owned

by rental companies. I guessed these were the ones that looked like they might have been towed to the Big T, but didn't need work. Another was owned by a pipe company and two were leased by dealers.

The Mercury Sable with the dented front fender, with the vanity plate, HAZEL1, was registered to Hazel McWhinney, fifty-five, of East Providence, who had no prior accidents and had not filed a claim on her insurance for the work Tito was doing, maybe because it was under the deductible.

The Passat on the hydraulic lift, 702 YYN was Miguel Esposito's. He lived in Providence. He'd already been in another fender bender earlier this year, in which he had claimed a back injury and had also filed for workers' compensation.

The last license plate number of any interest belonged to Paulo Laranjo of Cranston. The thing about Laranjo was that Bennett had managed to get the location of the accident, which had happened on Route 95, but right over the Connecticut line into New York. In handwriting that wasn't Bennett's, someone—presumably his insurance source—had noted that under New York State law, which applied to anyone who drove through, Laranjo would be able to make claims of $40,000 as well as the property damage. Apparently, he was claiming a neck injury.

Bennett was still on the phone, so I walked out to the bank of computers in the library, sat down, and plugged Laranjo into the newspaper database. The only Laranjo that came up was an eighteen-year-old from South Providence who had been named a high school valedictorian.

Miguel Esposito did not come up on the database, either.

Bennett hung up his phone. His long face, always pale, was heated. "You are never going to believe this one," he told me.

"Try me."

"This Dr. Arlanov you told me about. He practices at six different medical clinics in Massachusetts, and they are each managed by professional management companies that lease the property and equipment and pay the staff. I can't prove it, but I've heard that Arlanov came from New York, where he used to work at a shady medical clinic on Long Island that was closed down. I'm going to do a search on the management companies and see what I can get out of court records in New York."

"Speaking of court records . . ." I asked him to look up Paulo Laranjo and Miguel Esposito on the Superior Court database. Since this would only take him a few minutes, I grabbed one of the extra chairs from the library and pulled it up to Bennett's desk. Seated beside him, I saw very quickly that neither of the two men had criminal records.

Both did, however, have a civil action pending. Esposito had an action against workers' compensation for denying his last claim. When Bennett clicked on Laranjo's file, it turned out to be an action against Vasquez Taxi. Laranjo was the plaintiff. The suit was for unfair termination.

It took a minute to compute. Vasquez Taxi. That was Caspar's company. This guy must have worked for Caspar and gotten fired. This was the vendetta Caspar had talked about. The reason his cab had been targeted. Probably the reason he had dissolved his company and sold the cabs to Walter.

The printer, which was just behind us in the main part of the library, began to whir. Dorothy was going to love this: actual legal documents that backed up Caspar's story.

Although I didn't particularly want to, I knew that I should try to talk to Paulo Laranjo. "Does it give his address in the court documents?" I asked Bennett.

"Gotta be here somewhere." He began to scroll down the file. He stopped, squinted at something. "You want his lawyer's name?"

It was always easier to talk to the sleazebag's lawyer than to talk to the sleazebag. Especially when you were in a hurry. "Who is it, D'Anzana?"

Bennett shook his head. "No. Piedmont. Dane Piedmont. Has an office on the East Side." He scrolled back up to double-check something. "Yeah, and he was Esposito's lawyer, too."

"Christ."

"You know him?" Bennett asked.

"Sort of." All systems were suddenly on alert. I struggled to process this calmly. Dane represented the sleazebag suing Caspar, and both of his clients had been in car accidents getting their cars fixed at the Big T.

Bennett was studying me carefully. "Was that the guy you were talking about at the news meeting?

I nodded. Dane *knew* these people and never mentioned this when I talked about Tito Manaforte or the car ring.

"Don't you go out with him or something?"

"Sort of."

Bennett didn't seem to be alarmed by that. "Then I guess you know how to reach him."

The security guard from the *Chronicle* insisted on coming back with me to my apartment to pick up some clothes. He waited in my living room while I stuffed a gym bag with a few days' worth of work garb and running gear.

As I searched for my sneakers, I told myself for the third time that it was no big deal that Dane represented the two guys getting their cars fixed at the Big T. He wasn't their personal injury lawyer and might not even know of their car accidents.

I found my sneakers under a wet towel in the bathroom, and instead of stuffing them in the bag, I took off my shoes and put them on my feet. Sitting on my bed to lace up, I suddenly remembered how ardently Dane had tried to discourage me from writing this story at breakfast. I had assumed he was being overprotective, but could it be because some of the people involved were his *clients?*

I told myself I was being crazy. Irrational. That Dane represented the man who had sued Caspar Vasquez and helped drive him out of business was one of those "small world" coincidences that were rife in Rhode Island, a tiny state which had only a limited number of both plaintiffs and lawyers. And why should Dane have told me about it? I had never once mentioned Caspar Vasquez to him.

In the living room, Irwin Fontaine was waiting in front of the window, where he was watching the activity in Wayland Square below. He was an imposing man in a small apartment, about six feet and two-hundred pounds. But in addition to his size, Irwin had once been a Providence police officer, so he had a permit to carry a gun, which he did on this assignment. It was in a holster on his hip, only partially concealed by a jacket he wore over his brown and gray Chronicle Security uniform. It made me feel both safe and a little ridiculous.

We headed back to the hotel, where I felt even more ridiculous when Irwin wouldn't let me run on the street, and I had to resort to the hotel's health club. It was a small room with cardio and weight machines. I was alone, except for a guy in his late forties who was on the elliptical trainer, going like a hamster in a wheel. The window to the street was open and there was a decent breeze, but it couldn't cut through the sheer volume of this guy's sweat.

Waiting for Marcella's call, I'd brought my cell phone with me and put it in the cup holder of the treadmill. The guy on the elliptical was listening to an iPod around his neck and didn't acknowledge me at first. Then, probably to impress me, he pushed up his speed until he literally began to rain sweat. I felt a drop land on my forearm and recoiled.

Irwin, who had seated himself on the bench designed for the free weights, shot me a look, as if to say: What can you expect? But I desperately needed a workout to settle my nerves before my dinner with Matt. Since both my knees and my shins were sore, I began at a walking pace and grabbed the remote from the top of the machine to flick on the flat-screen television overhead.

I changed channels until I got Channel 10 News and caught the same footage of the divers collecting their gear after the discovery of the body at Card Pond in West Greenwich. "Police have just disclosed the identity of the victim," the news anchor said.

I turned up the volume a notch. The man on the elliptical reached for the digital controls to increase his incline. His machine chugged loudly as it began to pitch upward.

I had to hit the volume again to hear anything over the chugging. But I thought I caught the last name: Lopez.

My legs tightened and I almost tripped. There were a lot of Lopezes in Rhode Island, I told myself. It was a very common name. I snapped off my machine and walked it to a stop, waiting for the newscast to continue. Then I stood motionless as the TV flashed to a photo of Marcella posed in her wedding dress, her nose pressed into a bouquet of white roses.

"An autopsy by the medical examiner has revealed Marcella Lopez was killed by two bullets to the back of her head," the news anchor said. "A former drug addict who served time at the ACI for robbery, Lopez had reportedly been off drugs for three years and owned a successful lunch counter with her husband at Lincoln Park."

23

I grabbed a paper cup of water from the health club bubbler and sucked it down on the elevator as if it were vodka, as if it could numb the pain or maybe flush the fear out of my system.

Marcella had stolen documents from Manuel's home to give me. He must have figured it out and told Tito.

"You're pretty thirsty for such a short workout," Irwin commented.

"Yeah."

I was silent as we rode the elevator back to the fourteenth floor, but my mind was racing. Tito killed her. He could care less if those accounting records exonerated him and pointed to someone else as Lizette's killer. He'd want to whack Marcella for exposing his business. His highly profitable, multistate criminal enterprise.

"You okay?" Irwin asked.

I nodded. But he knew I was lying when I asked him to

check my room before I went in. He left me in the hallway, presumably examining the closet, bathroom, and even under the bed, because he took a while. He employed a fatherly tone to assure me that I was safe before gesturing me to come in. And he promised to wait right outside the door.

The high-pitched whir of the air-conditioning drilled through the room. I remembered the vicious look that Tito had given Marcella after Lizette's funeral. Then I thought of all the trouble Tito had taken to lure me to his body shop so he could convince me that Marcella was unreliable. How sure he was that she wanted to nail him out of revenge.

I turned on the television in the room and surfed between stations, hoping for more information about Marcella's murder—like an arrest—but the local news was over. I called the city desk to see if anyone there knew of any developments on the story, but learned that because it happened in West Greenwich, it was being covered by a bureau reporter. Marcy, the state editor, was already gone for the day. I called the bureau office but reached the machine.

I dropped my cell phone in my backpack and sat down on the bed to pull off my gym shorts. I only got them down halfway when I halted, overtaken by Marcella's own words: *For my sister, I will take a chance. Like you.*

Like *me.*

I sat there in my tank top and met my reflection in the gilt mirror over the bureau. My hair was pulled back and my eyes looked like they didn't want to stay in their sockets. I had pushed Marcella to get those accounting records, and now she was dead. Tito had killed her because of me.

"How long you gonna be?" It was Irwin.

"Ten minutes," I shouted through the door. I was going to

be late for my dinner with Matt if I didn't pull myself together.

I kicked off my shorts and running shoes, showered quickly, and started to change. As I was reaching for the fresh blue jeans in my gym bag, I suddenly had an image of Tito's sneakers again from underneath the curtain in the clinic dressing room. He'd been after me, this afternoon. Was this right after he murdered Marcella?

The air-conditioning must have been set on high. My blood felt like shaved ice. But this time, I wasn't crazy about the sensation. This time I knew that a woman had died because of me, and that unless the cops pulled Tito into custody soon, I could be dead next.

We left my car at the Biltmore garage, and Irwin drove me to the restaurant in a Chronicle Security vehicle. Since I was having dinner with a prosecutor from the AG's office, Irwin figured it was okay to go home and have dinner with his wife. I promised him that I would not walk home to the hotel, would not even take a cab. Matt would drive me back, and I'd call Irwin when I was on my way and meet him at the reception desk.

The Z-Bar and Grille was a nook of a restaurant on the corner of Wickendon Street, a funky retail area of secondhand stores and upscale coffee shops that straddled the downtown and the East Side. It had started to rain again, but Irwin double-parked and followed me to the sidewalk, holding a newspaper over his head as he peered into the window to make sure Matt was already there, waiting for me.

He was on the near end of the long bar. He had obviously come straight from work, still dressed from a day in court—a new gray, pinstriped suit. No cuff links, and he didn't cut into the room with elegance the way Dane had, but my heart made a pivot at the sight of him, anyway. And the deep breath I'd taken before I walked in the door stuck somewhere behind my clavicle.

"I was afraid you wouldn't show," he said, rising from his stool. I hadn't had the energy or focus to get dolled up, and had come without makeup, wearing a boxy cotton shirt and blue jeans that were wet on the bottom from the rain. Still, Matt looked at me as if I were descending a staircase wearing an evening gown.

He reached over and kissed me: a light kiss, a greeting you could give a neighbor, and yet, an amazingly public display of affection for him. His eyes were searching so intently that I had to look away. I was afraid he could be able to see both my guilt and my fear. That he would look though my eyes and see Marcella with the two bullets in the back of her head.

I sat down on the stool at the wooden bar that ran the length of the restaurant. The rooms had a lot of dark wainscoting, contrasted by a light wash of some sort on the walls. There was a greenhouse roof over part of the bar so that even inside, I couldn't escape the rain, which I could hear above me, driving into the glass.

"Are you all right?" Matt asked.

"Fine."

He ordered me a Corona with lime and I took a long swig to settle down. He was scraping off the label of his Michelob with his thumb, suddenly looking nervous. For some reason, this made me feel a little calmer. I was in a public restaurant with a prosecutor for the attorney general, I told myself. Right now, at least, I was safe.

He was studying me intently, still trying to figure out what was wrong. I decided to distract him with small talk. I asked him how the promotion was going.

"Okay," he said, looking pained.

"You don't like the new job?"

"I like the job," he said, without a whole lot of enthusiasm. Then he shook his head, looked down at his feet. He mumbled something that I couldn't hear over the bar chatter.

"What?" I asked.

He mumbled again, and I touched my ear to indicate I hadn't heard a word.

"It's what the job cost me," he said, finally audible.

His brown eyes were a dark lake of what looked like regret. I could see that although he had not technically apologized, this was the biggest apology of all time. I tried to relax, to absorb this moment, with poor Matt so uncomfortable. There must have been a window open somewhere or a draft from the door. A shiver began at the base of my neck.

"You want my jacket?" he asked.

I nodded and he helped me into it. When I stuck my hand in the pocket, I pulled out a piece of paper folded lengthwise. "What's this?" I asked.

He tilted his head, a gesture suggesting that I open it. It was from the *Chronicle* database with my byline on it. My story about Lizette Salazar's fatal accident. "So what do you have on this for me?" I asked.

"Is that the only reason you came?"

"You did offer it as a bribe, didn't you?"

"Right."

I relented. "No, it's not the only reason I came, but it's still probably a good idea for you to deliver."

"Can it wait until we get to a table?" His eyes darted to the couple sitting to my left to indicate that the bar was too crowded to talk there.

It would be too awkward to pull my notebook and pen out of my backpack there anyway, so I agreed. But apparently Matt forgot his concerns about being overheard when it came to Dane. He was smart enough not to make it sound like an accusation, but he wanted to know if Dane had looked me up immediately after that chance encounter in the Al Forno parking lot.

I didn't tell him I was the one who made the call. Instead, I countered. "Why is that important?"

"I'm just trying to verify to myself that it was all my fucking fault."

"Take it from me, it was all your fucking fault."

He nodded earnestly to show he was willing to accept the blame. That I could dish it out, and he would take it. But right then the hostess arrived to lead us to our table. Because of the rain, the patio wasn't open, and we were directed up a step to a small dining area opposite the bar. Maybe it was just the first available table, or maybe Matt had asked for privacy, but we were seated in the far back corner against an exposed brick wall.

Inside my backpack, the hokeypokey began to play. I pulled out my cell phone and checked the number. It was Dane. Matt watched me as I snapped it shut and slipped it back in my bag.

"Well, I know that's not your editor, or you'd take the call," he said glumly.

With my knee, I nudged the backpack under the table.

"There's a lot you don't know about him, you know," Matt said.

"Like?"

"Like he was disbarred in Massachusetts," Matt said.

I felt that I should have some allegiance to Dane, even though he'd pissed me off this morning. "He told me all about it," I said.

Matt set his chin and looked stubborn. So although it was completely uncalled for, I couldn't stop myself from saying, "And he never made me feel like a leper."

For a moment, Matt looked wounded. But then he squared his shoulders and accepted this with another nod of acknowledgment. This was followed by a shake of his head, as if at his own flawed behavior. Then he reached across the table and grabbed my hand. "I will never, ever do anything like that to you again."

This was more than a real, true apology. This was some sort of promise for the future.

"But I've got to ask you," he went on. "When you say Dane told you everything, did he give you that bullshit about protecting the woman from the abusive husband?"

"It's bullshit?"

"It's the story he gave Aidan. That's why Aidan wrote the letter. Turns out later, we learn that Dane was banging the woman. His client. Who also was caught with a shitload of stolen furs she was trying to unload."

"He was lying?" I got a sick feeling in my stomach, recalling how Dane's confiding in me had compelled me to reveal my own past failings. A flush of humiliation was rising up my neck.

"Don't feel bad. He fools everybody," Matt said, grabbing my hand and patting it. "He had Aidan conned for years, for Christ's sake."

But the blood flow increased, now full in my cheeks. The

waitress arrived, and, sensing an awkward moment, retreated from the table as if she'd caught us having sex. "I can come back if you're not ready." She was in her early twenties, and we made her nervous.

"We're ready," I said, slipping my hand out of Matt's to pick up the menu. The waitress began reciting the specials, and there was also a new dessert. "We've got that Tres Leches cake everyone's asking for," she added.

What did it matter what I ordered for dinner? I'd just found out I'd been had. Slept with a liar and bared my soul to the lawyer who had helped drive Caspar out of business. I chose the roast lamb shank because it was the first thing I read in the menu. Matt asked for some sort of chicken with penne and a bottle of wine. The waitress left and we sat staring at each other.

"That night at Al Forno, you asked me for a favor," Matt began.

Maybe too much had happened in one single day and my brain could no longer process. I tried to remember our conversation at Al Forno, how far I'd been into the story at that point, and what I might have needed from him. But it seemed so distant and vague. Our breakup must have eclipsed my memory of the earlier part of the evening.

"You asked me if I could get someone from state police forensics to check out the car—to test your theory that the woman might have been murdered," he continued.

Slowly, it came back. "You said you didn't have the resources."

"I called on a favor. The state police forensics unit went to the yard today," he said.

Silently, I absorbed this. Matt had actually used his position to help me. This was like other men sending roses or skywriting their love over the beach. "You're going to give me the lab results?" I didn't try to hide my amazement.

"That's the thing. There are no results. When they got there, they found out there'd been a fire."

"Are you talking about the car engine? That happened in the accident."

"No. The entire car. And four other wrecks were completely destroyed. A thorough torching."

Our eyes shared the knowledge that this was no coincidence. Someone had decided to get rid of the evidence, and only days before my story was to run. This was a major development that I should call into the desk for tomorrow's paper.

I was grateful, not just for the information, but for the urgency. With a sudden deadline, I had no choice but to put aside the humiliation of Dane and my guilt over Marcella. Temporary relief. Slipping into rote mode, I reached under the table into my backpack to get a notebook and pen. I wanted Matt to know that I considered the information to be on the record. "Are you calling it arson?"

He nodded.

I flipped open a page and wrote "ARSON. Five Cars. Impound lot, East Providence. Today."

He glanced at my notebook and pulled his chair back from the table, establishing more physical distance since I was now clearly in the role of a reporter. He gave me the name of the state police officer who had gone down to the yard and his cell phone number. "He'll be expecting your call."

"Any suspects?"

"Put down your pen for a minute," Matt advised. "This part is off the record."

One bit of information and he wants to jump off the record? For a second I considered refusing, throwing around my newfound power. But I put down the pen.

"With the fire destroying the wreck, I'm going to have to call you down for questioning. We're going to be after whoever let you into that yard and who knew enough about accident reconstruction to convince you that Lizette Salazar was murdered."

As I recalled, I never even confirmed to him that I had a source. Or that anyone had let me into that lot. And normally I'd remind him of that, but now I wasn't so full of myself. Now Marcella had been murdered, and my life was on the line. Now I just listened.

"I know all that bullshit you're going to give me about not giving up a source. But remember, you were the one who wanted us to investigate. And without an expert on the wreck, I don't have anything to go on. Tito, or whoever did it, will get away with it. You want that?" His eyes searched mine.

No. I especially didn't want that. And while I couldn't reveal a source to the AG, I could talk to Lester Wilson. Given the circumstances, I was highly motivated to convince him that it was the right thing to come forward.

"I'm on deadline tomorrow. I need every minute of the day to work, but if you can wait a day or two . . . I can't promise, but I'll see what I can do."

It was a major concession. He reached for my hand. "Deal."

As I slipped my hand into his, another thought occurred to me. "What would it take to arrest Tito right away? Take him into custody?" I asked.

"You mean in terms of forensic evidence?"

"In terms of anything." My heart started pounding, because

what I was contemplating was against all the rules. Reporters did not give law enforcement confidential information from their notebooks. Even when the source of that information was now dead.

Matt was studying me closely. "What do you know, Hallie?"

Reporters were not supposed to supply law enforcement with information that was not already in print. But this particular principle seemed a lot less important than, say, staying alive.

Still, I had to be wary of saying anything that would make Matt haul me down to state police headquarters right now. Get a court order to subpoena my notes, which he'd do without hesitation if he figured it was the only way to nail a murderer. I had to be cautious. Smart about it. The team had worked too hard on this. "What do you know about the woman they dredged up today in Card Pond?" I asked.

The waitress arrived with our meals, and I had to pull my notebook from the table and onto my lap to make room for the plates. I also had to wait until she had uncorked the wine and poured our glasses.

Finally she was gone. The table wafted of rosemary and roasted garlic. An enormous, prehistoric-looking bone of meat sat before me. I began to cut my lamb.

"Not much. I was busy all day in court. I heard she had some kind of criminal record."

So he didn't even know she was Lizette's sister. I took a forkful of lamb, which fell off the bone, but I was too distracted to taste it. Then I asked, "If you had a motive for Tito Manaforte to kill her, could you get police to take him into custody tonight?"

"He's still on parole." This meant yes.

"And can you promise me that you won't haul me down for questioning before Sunday, and that everything I tell you will be embargoed until then—meaning no one knows where you got any of this information until it comes out in my story? And none of these details get out to any one else in the media?"

He smiled. "I think you know I'm pretty good at stonewalling the press."

I ripped out a piece of paper from my notebook and handed him my pen. "You might want to take notes."

Not surprisingly, the rest of dinner was rushed. After Matt called in the information to the detective handling the investigation, he agreed to meet him at headquarters.

As he was driving me back to the Biltmore, he tried to talk me into coming with him "for my own protection," but I explained that I had Chronicle Security waiting for me back at the hotel.

"What, some ninty-nine-year-old retired cop?" he said.

"Irwin is very good. He's got a gun." What I didn't tell him was that I felt a whole lot more confident with Irwin as a protector, now that the police were planning to bring in Tito Manaforte tonight.

With Matt beside me driving, I had to call the information he'd given me about Lizette's car to the night editor, dictating a three-graph story, to make the deadline for Saturday's paper. Matt listened to me repeat the information about three times, as the editor questioned and triple-checked every sentence.

We turned the corner onto Dorrance Street, and Matt pulled up to the curb just before the hotel. Both doormen were helping a family with an enormous amount of luggage get out of a taxi. The rain was now a mere drizzle. I put my hand on the door handle, but Matt stopped me.

"Any chance you'd want to come home with me? I could pick you up on my way back from state police headquarters."

God, I wanted to stay with him. But not tonight. Not until this story was written and filed. And not until I'd sorted out my feelings and officially broke it off with Dane. "I've got too much going on right now. When I'm done with this story, and I can think clearly, maybe we can get together again and talk about us."

Matt looked up hopefully. "We can make this work. I promise. I'll come clean with Aidan. Tell him that you're my girlfriend and hand the investigation over to someone else."

My mouth fell open. "Really?"

"Look, for pretty much the entire time we went out, I tried to stop it from happening. I tried to forget you when we broke up, tried to go out with other women, but it didn't work. None of it worked. So now I'll just have to convince Aidan that we both can play by the rules. That, for the most part, we keep our professional and private lives separate."

These were words I'd dreamed of. A promise I'd yearned for. And I wanted nothing more than to drive away with him. But I knew Matt, and I knew he would ask questions all night. I didn't want to be tempted to spill anything else that could jeopardize my story, and I sure as hell didn't want to tell him that I'd slept with Dane.

"Call me when they get Tito into custody," I said. "And I'll see you tomorrow night. After deadline."

24

The lobby of the Biltmore was designed around a sweeping staircase that dominated the room and divided it into smaller conversation areas so that the layout was vaguely confusing. Maybe that's why I didn't see Dane at first. He was sitting on a leather chair near the window.

"How did you know I was here?" I asked.

"I called the paper. Your editor told me."

I wished to hell I'd never told Dorothy I was going out with him. She'd probably thought she was doing me a favor. But while I needed to break up with him, I wasn't sure I had the energy for it tonight.

But Dane appeared pleased with his detective work, and apparently expected me to be pleased as well. He'd changed and was wearing athletic gear: a sleek Lycra warm-up with a windbreaker and the signature Nikes on his feet, as if he'd run here in the rain. I eyed his gym bag with alarm. Had he actually thought that he could show up unannounced and spend the night with me in the hotel?

"Was that Matt who dropped you off?" he asked.

Had he seen this through the window? Man, he really *was* doing detective work. I refused to act or feel guilty. "I had dinner with him. We needed to talk," I said.

Perhaps he picked up on my coolness, because he responded without the morning's jealousy, taking a civilized tone. "About what?" he asked.

About the lies you told me, I wanted to say. Instead, I decided to give him something solid, something professional. "About Lizette's accident."

"Why now?"

Was that suspicion I saw in the set of his mouth? I didn't really care. But remembering again the way he reacted at breakfast, I decided that to avoid a scene here in the hotel lobby, it was probably best not to incite jealousy. I continued to play up the professional nature of my dinner date. "Because Matt's after one of my sources—that's all. He's trying to get information."

"What source?"

Did he not believe me? "Why does it matter? This isn't really a good time for me, I've got a really early day tomorrow."

Dane looked at me as if trying to gauge something, but he didn't answer. He shrugged as if to show that it really didn't matter, and said, "I was thinking that we should go back to my place."

I struggled not to physically recoil, not to show just how disgusted I was by him right now. I either did a good job of shielding my revulsion or Dane was so self-absorbed he couldn't pick up on anyone else's signal. It occurred to me that on top of everything else, I didn't want to be thinking about *this* all night, too. Maybe I should get it over with, get rid of him. I wouldn't breathe real air until then. "I can't go with you to your place," I finally said. "We've got to talk."

Every human who has ever been dumped knows what that means, but Dane looked at me with that same expression, the blue eyes meeting mine without a real connection. "Where did you park?" he asked.

"In the hotel garage, but I can't go back to your place with you."

"You want to go up to your room and talk?"

The last thing in the world I wanted was to find myself stuck in a hotel room with Dane, trying to get him to leave *after* I chewed him out for lying to me and told him to take a hike. A loud, busy, public place would be better for a breakup. "The bar?"

Dane thought about this for what seemed an inordinate amount of time. Finally, he nodded in a weird way.

I realized that I'd forgotten to call Irwin to let him know when I was coming back. I needed to check in at the reception desk to see if he had come back on his own. Dane rose from the couch to accompany me, brushing past a bellhop with a luggage car, without saying excuse me or acknowledging his existence.

At the desk, the clerk seemed to have caught this. Her professional smile of welcome faded as her eyes shifted from Dane to me. She was a very slight Asian woman with a French accent. Irwin hadn't returned yet, but she would call Chronicle Security to make sure they knew I was back. "You want an escort to your room, madame?"

Dane was right behind me. He put his arm around my waist. It felt like an act of possession. "We're going to the bar for a drink, then I'll walk her back to her room."

The clerk looked at me for confirmation, her red, glossy lips pursed. I nodded.

Her gaze shifted to Dane, and I saw what she saw. The well-tended physique, the chiseled features, and intense blue eyes. The guy you stare at when he blows by you on the boulevard as if you don't exist. You stare at him both because he's so handsome *and* because he's so self-absorbed. Halfway through a Corona, I would be free of him. A bar was a good place for a breakup. Dane would have no choice but to be civilized.

I gave the receptionist my cell phone number and told her to give it to Irwin or whatever guard the *Chronicle* sent over. I wanted someone to call me immediately when security was back on duty.

Crossing the lobby, I increased my step, trying to pull away from Dane's arm, which was now anchored around my waist. But Mr. Nike was not one to lose pace; his hand remained on my hip like a lever. He guided me through the first dining room and into the bar, which was busy enough for comfort, but not crowded. He passed several empty booths along the wall to the last one, by the outer door at the corner of Dorrance Street. But this was good. A quick exit for him. Because I had no intentions of letting him walk me back to my room.

Like the hotel, the bar was dark, with a lot of mahogany wood and leather, a saloon motif. There were booths along the windows that overlooked Dorrance and Washington Streets, but the blinds were lowered to keep out most of the city lights.

The restaurant, McCormick & Schmick, was a fish place,

with a raw bar on one side with littlenecks on ice. The faint smell of salt and lemon hung in the air.

Dane must have sensed my impatience, or maybe he was in a hurry for his own reasons, because he didn't wait for the cocktail waitress. "I'm not sure there is table service," he said, as he pulled back my chair for me. "I'll go to the bar myself. Corona?"

I nodded, grateful for the break his errand to the bar would provide. I shoved my backpack under the table and tried to prepare an opening. Maybe I shouldn't even let him know I knew about the real reasons he was disbarred in Massachusetts. He would probably just deny he lied to me. Maybe it *was* better if I was honest about Matt. Act like the breakup was entirely my fault. The waitress came over almost immediately to ask what I wanted. She was irritated when I told her that my friend had already gone directly to the bar.

I stared at Dane's back as he jammed his way between two people sitting at stools to try to get the bartender's attention. *I'm sorry if I've been confusing. I didn't mean to . . .* what? *Use you on the rebound? Fuck with your head?*

Although there were only a dozen or so patrons, they all were congregated at one spot at the bar. Dane took forever, trying to get drinks. Then, when the bartender gave him two beers, he carried them with him to the far end of the bar, apparently to catch the news on the television. I tried to get his attention, but his back was toward me, and he didn't turn around. The lights of the TV flashed as the news shifted to a new segment. I caught that same shot of Card Pond and the footage of the police cruisers and the yellow tape marking off the section of the beach.

I'd been so nervous about having to break up with Dane that I'd been able to put Marcella out of my head for a solid five or ten minutes. Now the guilt returned, along with the heavy feeling in my stomach. The accounting records she found would have spelled out the revenues coming in and out, documenting a criminal enterprise, a conspiracy to defraud. Published in Sunday's *Chronicle* series, they would spark immediate arrests. How could I not have realized Marcella's life would be in danger?

The camera shifted to a shot of Marcella's husband, Roman, distraught, and Manuel Salazar being shepherded out of state police headquarters by two men who looked like lawyers.

Could they be suspects? I slipped out of the booth and started walking toward the bar to find out what was going on, but the camera shot shifted back to the studio and a weather map. The weatherman was pointing to the air currents attacking the East Coast, the clouds hanging over Rhode Island and eastern Massachusetts.

Dane returned to the table with the beers. I asked him about the newscast.

"What?"

"The murder in West Greenwich," I explained.

"Too loud in here. Couldn't hear it." He handed me a beer with two lime wedges twisted inside the bottle and took a seat opposite me. "Cheers." He tapped his bottle against mine. For courage, I took a long swig. The bottle was so cold it hurt my palm. And the lime tasted weird. "Did they put Rose's lime juice in this?"

"Maybe. So why do you think that Matt is so interested in Lizette's accident all of a sudden?"

It was strange that he kept returning to this topic, as if he sensed it was the way to unnerve me. I tried not to think of Marcella again, but this time I couldn't help it. Tears welled up in my eyes.

"What?" Dane sounded impatient.

I gestured back to the television at the bar. "That body in West Greenwich. That was her sister."

"Oh," he said, but he didn't look either sympathetic or surprised.

I took another long drink of the beer. My throat was beginning to feel raw. I wanted to get this over with and get the hell out of here. "I hate to do this to you, Dane," I began. "And . . . it's just that, I guess I wasn't exactly over Matt. I thought I was but . . . I wasn't."

Dane didn't say anything. He just stared at me.

"So I can't see you anymore. I'm sorry. I'm . . . really, really sorry."

"Did you actually break up or were you seeing both of us at the same time?"

"No. We broke up that night at Al Forno—"

"And you didn't talk to him?"

"Not until tonight."

"Tonight." Dane turned so he could look over his shoulder at the television at the end of the bar. Then he turned back to me. "So was Matt trying to get the name of that accident reconstruction guy from you? Maybe that's his real motive."

This struck me as a very odd response. How did he guess this? It took me a moment to reply. "It's his job; he's got to ask. But that isn't what this is about."

Dane's expression remained dubious, insulting actually. Then he caught himself, shifted in his chair, and struck a strangely conciliatory tone. "No hard feelings. I should have figured it out about you and Matt," he said. "Or at least guessed. That night at Al Forno . . ." He let this sentence drift off. "So let's drink . . . to you and Matt."

I raised my bottle, not believing for a moment that he actually wanted it to work out with Matt and me. But I didn't care. At least he wasn't trying to play the guilt card—I had enough guilt already on my plate. In relief, I sucked down a quarter of the bottle.

A waitress passed by with two plates heaped with calamari. The smell of fried fish, which I usually love, was now making me feel queasy.

"Maybe it's time for me to get you back to your room," Dane suggested.

"Yeah." My head felt light, which was odd, since I'd skipped the wine with dinner.

Maybe it wouldn't be so bad if the beer knocked me out. At least I wouldn't have to think about Marcella. About the cinder blocks and the bullets in the back of her head.

Dane grabbed my backpack from underneath the table and hoisted it over his arm with his gym bag. I stood up slowly. My body felt heavy. Like in the old days, when I swallowed three Serax. What the hell was wrong with me?

I took a few steps and the carpeting undulated beneath my feet. I looked at Dane beside me, a strange, determined expression on his face. I swallowed and tasted sour lime. Could he have slipped me something?

He guided me back through the dining room into the hotel lobby, where I searched for Irwin. There was no sign of him or anyone from security. I waved in the direction of the reception desk, but Dane caught my hand and pulled it to my side. "You're drunk, Hallie," he said, his arm tight around my waist.

"I'm not drunk," I argued. Two middle-aged women walking with an elderly man skirted around us. One of the women shot me a dagger of reproach and looked around, as if searching for someone to take care of the riffraff exiting the lounge.

Dane shushed me and pulled me toward the elevators, his arm practically holding me up now. I was growing too tired to argue, too unsteady to shake him. I needed to get to my room.

Two other couples were waiting for the elevator. When the door opened and they got in, Dane held me back. "You don't want to puke on anyone," he whispered in my ear.

I hadn't thought about puking before, but now I was definitely nauseous. Where was Irwin? I turned toward the lobby and saw someone who looked like him in some sort of uniform in the revolving door. But I couldn't make out what kind of uniform. Another elevator door opened, and Dane pulled me over the threshold. The door shut. I found myself leaning into him. My room was all the way up on the twelfth floor, but the elevator stopped after only a floor or two.

When the door opened, I fixed on the carpeting, which had some sort of nautical rope design that looked like a noose. This wasn't my floor. I refused to budge. "Get away from me," I said.

"Shut up." He pushed me through the empty corridor to the skyway, and I realized we were headed to the parking garage.

"Where are you taking me?" I asked. He didn't answer.

Inside the parking garage, the air smelled of urine and exhaust fumes. Dane had given up trying to keep me upright and was now carrying me in both arms, past all the empty spaces reserved for the rental cars. Somewhere an engine ground and stuttered.

"Did you park on this level?" Dane asked.

I remembered the rental cars and nodded my head. He planted me upright, against the cement wall, and the floor began to weave. I stared down at Dane's Nikes and puked. There was an awful smell of garlic.

"Stop that!" Dane commanded.

I bent over trying to heave again, but he pulled me up. My hair smelled and my throat hurt. I wanted to go back to my hotel room and sleep.

The next thing I knew we were beside my Honda. Dane leaned me against the car, as he wiped his sneakers by scraping them under the chassis. Then he bent down and began rifling through my backpack.

"What are you doing?" I asked.

"You're not checking in."

I heard the jangle of my key chain. The low ceiling seemed to dip. Then he was stuffing me into the passenger seat of my car. The back of my head fell onto the headrest, and my eyes must have closed. I heard the driver's door slam shut. I opened them again as Dane slid the car in gear and began to back up.

He didn't give the engine enough gas, and the car stalled. "Fuck," he said. And then, "Where's your ticket?"

I didn't feel like answering him, so I didn't tell him it was a token. He began rummaging through my bag again, "Fucking mess in here." He threw my cell phone onto the floor by my feet. My wallet sailed into the backseat. He was about to toss my notebook, but halted. He flipped through the pages, scanning my notes with a look of intense concentration.

"Who was the expert who checked out the car?" he demanded. "Is his name in here?"

My stomach twisted with pain. Why? I wanted to ask, but I couldn't get the words out.

Dane flipped my notebook shut and threw it in the back of the car. "Tell me who he is, Hallie. What's his name?"

He was interrogating me with a new intensity. My stomach cramped a second time, and through my fog I got the first glimmer. This was why he'd always been so interested in my work. He knew something about Lizette's accident. Something he didn't want me to find out.

I lunged for the door, trying to find the handle. I was clumsy, slapping at it. My fingers gripped the plastic, but without real strength. I tried to push my weight into the door. But it was locked.

I foraged for the unlock button, but couldn't find it in my own car. Dane laughed at my efforts. "You're a real tough reporter now." Then he reached across the console, grabbed my arm, and pushed me back in the seat. "I tried to stop you, but you wouldn't listen. You had to be so fucking macho, had to keep pushing into everything."

My tongue felt thick. It was tough to talk. And I was confused. Why did he care so much about my story?

"These people, these people . . . Some of them are dirt poor. They've got nothing. No papers. No way to get a job. This is the only shot they have at making a little cash to tide them over. You ever think about that? You with your big investigation?"

Was he defending the car ring? My brain was addled.

"I always tried to pay them more than Tito, you know. He was so fucking cheap, but I always slipped them extra cash when they came to the clinic. I cared about their lives. But you wanted your front-page story. For what? You screwed everyone. Me. Yourself. Lizette's sister, too."

"Let me go. I want to get out of here."

"You're not leaving, Hallie. You fucked it all up. You've got too much shit in those notebooks that will fuck up too many lives. You've got too much information the cops need. That your fucking boyfriend needs."

"Let me go. Matt is checking on me. He'll know you did this—"

Dane slid his hand behind my neck, as if to get a good grip on me. "Don't worry about me, Hallie. I'm real good at making it look like an accident." Then he jerked my head forward, into the dashboard.

I awoke in the passenger seat, riding along on a dark road, my head pounding. My back was sunk low in the seat with my legs sprawled out in front of me. The driver was wearing a race-car helmet, a neck roll, and padding on his chest and his shins.

Dane? I wanted to ask. But my mouth was dry, and I tasted vomit. The rain was pouring down now, pounding on the sunroof. Where the hell were we going? I could barely see through the windshield. And why was I in the passenger seat?

One of the windshield wipers was tattered and flapped against the glass. My forehead felt bruised, and my neck ached. I remembered Matt dropping me off at the hotel. Dane in the bar. But this guy with the helmet? I thought of Lester Wilson. The protective gear he wore for crash tests. Was I still asleep and dreaming about my story? I wanted to ask the driver who he was, but I was so tired. My arms lay like weights across my waist and my legs felt as if they were very far away. The rain against the window began to lull me back to sleep.

I drifted off, thinking of Marcella that day in the back of the church. The mascara running under her eye. *"I am so happy you come."* I felt the surprising force of her thin, birdlike arms hugging me. *"So happy you take the time."*

Pain splintered through my head, pounding at my temples. My eyes opened wide. Marcella was dead.

Suddenly crowd noise roared from the car radio. Joe Castiglione announced that Ortiz had hit another home run and the Red Sox were up on the Yankees 6 to 1. "What the fuck!" It was Dane's voice coming from beneath the helmet.

He leaned forward to try to shut off the radio. I had a sudden recollection of him flipping wildly through my notebook. Interrogating me. He poked at the air-conditioning control by mistake. A shot of static screeched through the speaker. Then the radio cut off by itself.

Dane slapped at the knobs, trying to make sure it was off. I tasted vomit again in the back of my throat. I saw the bottle of Corona sitting before me, the double wedge of lime. Dane had drugged me, slipped something into my beer.

I saw the helmet begin to turn and shut my eyes again, trying not to breathe. I remained completely still, trying to look dead. My heart was pounding like crazy, and I prayed to God that Dane couldn't hear it. God, I wished I could brush my teeth. Garlic vomit. Corona. And somewhere there was gasoline.

I had no idea where we were, but I couldn't hear any traffic noises. Through the floorboard, I could feel the road vibrate: it was smooth, unpitted. And we were driving too fast for a city road and too slow for a highway. A country road somewhere. A dark country road. Like the one . . .

My limp limbs began to tense, and I had to struggle not to flinch. The helmet. The padding. Just like Lester Wilson had said. Just like Lizette.

A slide show sped through my brain. I had that same memory again, Dane rifling through my notebook demanding to know the name of my source. And then, the day on the boulevard: *"She was a good interpreter. Very precise . . . I only worked with her on one or two cases."*

Why kill her?

And Marcella? Her, too?

Several minutes passed as I lay back in the seat, this question pounding at my temples, the scrape of the windshield wiper hurting my ear.

Then I heard a new sound behind us. A car engine. "Fuck," Dane said. Then he must have laid on the gas pedal. Our car speed increased. I wanted to grab on to the seat with my hands, but forced myself to lie limp. I couldn't let Dane know that I was awake. Maybe it was the adrenaline, or maybe it was because I puked, but I was starting to feel a little clearer. I strained to hear the engine behind us, praying to God it was help on its way. But the harder I strained, the more I could hear only the rain pounding on the sunroof and the windshield wipers scraping faster and faster against the glass.

Dane must have been trying to lose the car behind us. He made a sharp turn and the centrifugal force pushed me hard. I allowed my body to fall into the door, my temples against the glass, the door lock under my chin.

I heard a thud and then a sloshing sound in the back seat—the gasoline smell suddenly grew stronger. I could feel it at the corner of my eyes, taste it inside my head. I had a sudden image of Lizette's car, the engine burning. I wanted to jump out of my seat, but I had to remain perfectly still, breathe the fumes slowly through my nose and swallow this new information. Dane was going to make sure the car went up in flames quickly. All the evidence destroyed.

Something Tito said came back to me. Something about my floorboards being a death trap. Could the gasoline leak through the floor? I had to get the hell out of this car.

It had been a long time since I'd spent round-the-clock days abusing Serax, functioning with an excess of mind-altering drugs in my blood. But I knew all systems, especially motor skills, would be slow. I had to think, come up with some kind of plan that didn't require a lot of physical speed or power.

I could tell that we were going at least forty miles an hour, too fast to jump out of the car. I'd kill myself. Plus, with my slow hands and heavy arms, I wouldn't be able to reach the door and unlock it before he grabbed me.

I thought of the stash of pens I kept in the glove compartment. Was a ballpoint sharp enough to do any real damage? I opened my eyes halfway. Dane's attention was on the road.

Even if I could get the pen out of the glove compartment fast enough and had the strength to pull it off, it was doubtful that I could hurt him with it. It had looked like he was wearing padding everywhere.

Several minutes passed as I remained still, my cheek on the door lock, trying not to twitch as my mind raced, desperate for a way out. The fumes permeated the car. I could taste the gasoline inside my head. I opened my eyes an eighth of an inch and looked down. In the door pocket, I saw the aerosol can of air freshener Tito had given me.

I remembered something Walter had said, outside The Big

T. *"Anyone tries anything, go right for the eyes. If they can't see you, they can't kill you."*

Desperation cut through the last of my haze. This was my best chance. I slipped my hand into the pocket and quietly stretched my fingers toward the aerosol can.

I felt a drop of water on my cheek and froze. I couldn't flinch or turn and see where it came from. "Shit." Dane must have felt it, too. And then, "Fucking Tito."

The sunroof. Leaking. I tried not to breathe, afraid Dane would now be hyperaware. That he would look over and see my hand in the door pocket. There was a long silence. I thought I could feel his eyes drilling into me.

Suddenly, I felt the car take another curve and heard water splashing up from the road onto the windshield. "Shit," Dane said.

A distraction. I inched my hand deeper into the pocket and closed my fingers around the aerosol can. I'd have to move fast. Surprise him and squirt right into his eye.

I risked a glance over. Dane was hunched forward, trying to see through the windshield. I lifted my chin and shifted my gaze out the passenger window. I could make out that we were on a narrow country road. To the right, the woods disappeared abruptly and there was a vast clear-cut area, what looked like an Amazon of a housing development under construction. I thought I saw backhoes and cranes looming in the dark.

All the construction equipment must have pitted the road, because there was a sudden, dramatic change in terrain: I could feel the ruts and potholes in my hips. "What the hell . . . ," Dane said. Out my window, I could see that on my side, at least, the road was engulfed in water, a lake of water.

I had to pray that it was deep, deep enough to force Dane to slow or, given my Honda's electrical system, even stall. I took a silent breath, trying to summon all my physical strength.

Another drip seeped through the sunroof and landed on my shoulder. The radio speaker screeched. I slipped the air freshener can up, out of the pocket, and positioned my finger on the spray nozzle. With the other hand, I lunged for the steering wheel and pushed up, forcing the car to swerve. Dane pivoted toward me. I aimed for those cold blue eyes and sprayed.

"What the fuck!" He started flailing, trying to knock the bottle away with his right hand, while wiping at his eyes with this left. The car swerved again and began to slide through the water. I ducked, dodging Dane's arm, and continued to spray. My finger was pressed so hard on the button it felt like I was going to crush the entire can.

Water splashed over the side of the car. I pushed every ounce of strength I had into that aerosol can. My eyes burned with lilac mist. I aimed up this time, into Dane's nose. He started coughing, still swatting wildly at me.

I was coughing, too, trying not to choke on lilac mist and gasoline. He knocked the air freshener out of my hand. It hit the dashboard and then rolled to the floor.

"Fucking bitch!"

Both Dane's hands were off the steering wheel, trying to clear his eyes. He must have taken his foot off the gas pedal because the car slowed through the end of the water. I hit the unlock button on my door and grabbed the door handle on my side. With one push, it was open. I plunged out of the car.

I landed on a mound of mud, rolled into a gully of some sort and came to a stop in about a foot of water. My lungs felt winded and my body bruised. My knee and ankle hurt like hell. I felt mud wedged between my fingers.

I caught my breath, sat up, and pulled myself out of the water. Staring anxiously into the darkness I spotted the faint taillights of the Honda.

The car was still moving. Away from me, down the road with the passenger door hanging open. It went about twenty feet and dipped. The taillights disappeared. There was a loud crash. It had hit something that loomed overhead. Maybe a backhoe.

I heard Dane shout. My radio speaker screeched a couple of seconds. And then, a blast. I held my ears as fire plumed toward the sky.

The air filled with a horrible chemical stench that hurt my eyes. The shouting had stopped. I inched back into the gully, hiding in case Dane had escaped from the car and came looking for me.

I sat there a long time, searching the road, inhaling the fumes of my engine burning and hoping to God that Dane was pinned inside. I was soaking wet, shaking with cold and crying silently in pain. I cupped my twisted knee with both hands, and held still in the rain.

Finally, from the other direction, I saw lights and heard a car engine. The car slowed down as it passed me and pulled up alongside the road. It was too dark to see the car make, but it looked like a big car.

A figure jumped out of the driver's side, slammed the door. Another figure jumped out of the passenger side and rounded the car. He was running toward the wreck. "Oh my God, Hallie? Hallie?" My name rang through the air, reverberated with agony.

It was Matt.

"Here!" I said.

He didn't hear me. "Hallie?" He was wild. "Hallie?"

"I'm here!" I shouted. "I'm okay."

The other figure turned, shouting something to Matt. I looked up and saw Irwin in his Chronicle Security uniform.

"She's over here!" Irwin shouted.

Matt turned abruptly from the wreck and ran toward us. He slid through mud, caught himself just at the edge of the gully. His eyes sought mine and I could see him try to brace himself. "Are you all right?"

"I'm okay. I'm fine."

25

I was not fine. My ankle was sprained, and my knee was swollen to twice its normal size. But that was nothing compared to my emotional state, which the hospital emergency room was not equipped to treat. In the course of a sleepless night, I traveled out of shock into anger, guilt, and utter humiliation.

Dane was dead. Paramedics knew that as soon as they pulled his body from the remains of my Honda. We hadn't gotten the results of the official autopsy yet, but at the hospital last night one of the nurses told me that in the length of time he was trapped in the car, smoke inhalation probably did him in.

I felt no grief, only shock. Not just at Dane's capacity for violence, but at this weird twist to his life. His connection to Tito Manaforte and his bizarre sense of purpose.

The fact that he had almost killed me was not as hard to deal with as the fact that I had been played. I'd made the incredible mistake of leaving that message on his machine, which must have delighted him. He sensed my attraction to him and exploited it.

He had charmed me to keep tabs on my investigation, and I had fallen for it. Kept him abreast of the latest. In the end, I'd even sought his legal advice. I'd spilled it all.

But there was something else. Something Dane had said in the parking garage that I couldn't remember. Something that was stuck in the corner of my mind like a scratched disc. Voice over voice, both sharp and unclear.

"Forget it," Matt said. He had insisted on taking me back to his place, and had spent most of the night awake, trying to console me. "The man had lost it, completely. Whatever he said, he was just trying to justify what he was about to do."

Matt tried his best, but there was nothing he could say that made me feel any less culpable, less stupid, or less used. In the end, it was the deadline that forced away the remorse and self-doubt and made me rise to my feet.

So against his better judgment, Matt drove me to the newsroom Saturday after I'd caught up on some sleep.

That's the beauty of a deadline. The urgency of it trumps all. It gives you an excuse to shelve everything else about your life. Your laundry, your unpaid bills, your fractured relationships. Even your trauma and guilt. These will all be dealt with later or not at all.

Maybe that's the real reason I'm a journalist.

I was at my desk by eleven o'clock the next morning, with my foot propped up on a chair wheeled over from the sports department. Wound up in Ace bandages, my ankle and knee hurt like hell, but the pain was actually a good thing. I preferred to focus on physical pain instead of my wounded ego.

The entire investigative team had reported to work early, not only to get the scoop on my near-death experience and new developments, but also to follow the attorney general's investigation into Lizette Salazar's accident. We were all hoping nothing bad happened in Iraq, because we needed every inch of tomorrow's front page.

Because it was the weekend, with only a few reporters and a skeletal editing crew on shift, the newsroom belonged to us. Since I couldn't get around too well, Bennett, Ryan, and even Dorothy had relocated to a desk near mine in financial or sports and were typing with a manic determination. Jonathan was off covering the press conference state police had called to deal with Dane Piedmont's fatal, and Ellen Felty was on the East Side trying to interview anyone who had ever known Dane—his surviving family members, his neighbors, even his friends at the health club.

Jonathan came back just before noon. Police had released the statements I'd given them last night at the hospital—about Dane's motive in trying to stop my investigation into Lizette's death, which meant the phone would be ringing soon with television and radio looking for me to comment. But there was also new evidence. Early this morning, police had discovered Dane's Harley-Davidson two miles from the accident, hidden in the brush on a dirt road. Investigators had also been able to match tire tracks in the area to the flatbed truck in Dane's garage, leading them to believe that he'd used the truck to ferry the motorcycle over earlier that day.

Which he must have done after the scene at Rufful's, when

he realized how well I knew Matt. Fearful that I might start feeding my investigation to the AG's office, he panicked.

Off the record, one police source speculated that after I'd called Dane about Lizette's accident, he and Tito might have decided together that Dane should personally keep tabs on my investigation. But clearly Tito was kept in the dark about Dane's real interest—covering up Lizette's murder. And the source also believed that Tito was genuinely pissed off that Dane had tried to murder me himself. "If Tito wanted to get rid of a reporter, he sure as hell wouldn't send a lawyer," Jonathan said. "He'd hire a professional who wouldn't botch the job."

Dane's plan, to ram my car into a tree, douse it with gasoline, and take off on his motorcycle, was foiled when I made the car swerve back and forth. "The gas tipped over in the backseat and seeped through the floorboards to the exhaust pipe, and . . ." Frizell was about to smash his palms together to enact an explosion, when with his new, uncharacteristic sensitivity, he stopped himself.

Dorothy was horrified, but I kind of liked the idea. I'd been saved by my own spotty car maintenance.

Later, Bennett, who had been searching through the secretary of state's records all morning, was finally able to document Dane's connection to the insurance ring. His name appeared as treasurer of the management company that owned the Holistic Joint Pain Clinic where I'd been treated, as well as a similar clinic that had been shut down in New York.

Bennett, who was sitting at Kira's desk, opposite mine, rolled his chair around the desks to pull beside me. "I'm guessing that he was the brains behind the operation—at least the medical end of it."

He searched through his papers until he found another printout he wanted. These were from a five-year-old court case from Massachusetts in which Dane had represented Dr. Arlanov, who had been charged with Medicaid fraud and acquitted on a legal technicality.

"But how did he hook up with Tito, do you think?" I asked.

Bennett gave me a look. He was a database guy. Personal relationships were clearly beyond his area of expertise.

We would not have any clue about this until later that afternoon, when Ellen Felty finally came back to the newsroom.

She'd had a long, hard day. The rain had not abated outside, and her blond hair was disheveled, most of it escaping from a knot she'd pulled together on the top of her head. The bottoms of her blue jeans were soaked from going door to door, and her jacket had been splashed with something that looked like car grease. But she was exhilarated, glowing with information.

Despite the impression he liked to give, Dane had *not* been related to the well-to-do Piedmonts in Providence. From a neighbor, Ellen learned that Dane had not owned, but rented, the fancy Federal-style home where he lived on the East Side. Arthur Piedmont III, in particular, wanted to make clear that Dane wasn't even a distant cousin. Apparently, his family had been French Canadian immigrants who settled in Woonsocket, where his father had worked in one of the wool mills.

In Woonsocket, Ellen learned that both of Dane's parents were dead, but she had found a surviving sister, Marie Claire, who told her that Dane had financially supported both parents until they died. Eager to defend her brother's memory, she had gone on and on about his work at the Hispanic Center. "She said he was just really committed. After his divorce, he didn't have much else except a real passion to help these people."

"Some help," said Dorothy, who was listening in on this. "He couldn't find another way?"

"Well, actually, yes," Ellen said. "I talked to Vergen Jiminez. The woman who runs the center. I know her from an internship I used to have there, when I was in college. Anyway, I tracked her down at home. She says that Piedmont didn't just go through the motions. He really got involved in his cases. Apparently he worked with Lizette Salazar quite a bit."

"Maybe she introduced him to Tito," I said, more to myself than to anyone else.

Ellen shrugged. "Couldn't tell you about that, but Vergen said something else that was interesting. She said Piedmont made financial contributions to the center on a fairly regular basis, and"—here, in deliberate mimicry of Jonathan, she paused for effect and read directly from her notebook—"in cash."

"Quote, end quote," Bennett said with a snicker.

But Dorothy was fascinated. "Maybe he was donating back some of the ill-gotten gains from the clinic. A misguided philanthropist, that's a great angle," she said.

I was left feeling vaguely disturbed. My temple throbbed again, as I recalled part of what Dane had said: *These people, these people . . . some of them are dirt poor. They've got nothing. No papers. No way to get a job. This is the only shot they have at making a little cash to tide them over.*

"I think he meant it," I heard myself say.

Ellen, who was settling in at a nearby computer, looked over. I told her, as best I could remember, Dane's exact words in the garage. Excitedly, Ellen typed them into the computer to use in her story.

There was something else Dane had said, something I didn't want to deal with. I pushed the memory of the garage aside, and focused on Ellen, watching her type. After a minute, her remark about her internship finally filtered through my discomfort. "Hey, how long did you intern at the Hispanic Center?"

"Three semesters."

"Speak any Spanish?"

"A little," Ellen said.

I dug through my backpack, pulled out the tape casette, and after much fast-forwarding and rewinding, played that part of my interview with Franco for her. Her eyes lit up immediately, but she insisted on listening to it three times to make sure she got it right.

Even before she gave me the word-for-word translation, I knew what it would be. Why Dane would kill Lizette. Why he'd kill Marcella, and why he'd wanted to keep such close tabs on my investigation.

El abogado del centro es él que está robando de Tito.

"The lawyer at the center is the one who is stealing from Tito," she said.

26

THE PROVIDENCE MORNING CHRONICLE

Two Murders Linked to Insurance Fraud

Tangled Web Worth $10 Million a Year Spurs Creation of a New England Fraud Task Force

BY HALLIE AHERN AND JONATHAN FRIZELL

Chronicle Investigative Team

Eighth in a series

PROVIDENCE — Passengers were recruited from the back of welfare offices, job lots, and the Lincoln Dog track. They met in the parking lot of the Cottage, a bar in Attleboro, and vied for a seat in a car destined for a highway accident.

The payoff for the poor immigrant or losing gambler

was $300 to $500 and the chance to spend months getting treatment at fraudulent medical clinics for fake injuries. But the payoff for the Providence-based fraud ring that ran the multistate operation was millions in insurance money.

In fact, a month-long investigation into the ring by the attorney general's office, triggered by the *Chronicle*'s Staged Accident series, has revealed that the enterprise raked in $7 million a year in personal injury and inflated collision claims. It was so lucrative that police now believe it was the motive for two murders.

The first victim was Lizette Salazar, the Providence woman who appeared to have died in a one-car collision two months ago. Her body was exhumed in early May after Lester Wilson, an accident reconstruction expert who examined her car after the crash, came forward to say it was impossible that she was driving the car at the time of impact. The autopsy revealed that Salazar died of poisoning.

The body of her sister, Marcella Lopez, was found at the bottom of Card Pond in West Greenwich last month, with two bullet holes in the back of her head. State police believe the same man, Dane Piedmont, the Providence lawyer who died in a fiery crash a month ago, was responsible for both murders. Police have a witness inside the fraud ring who will testify that Piedmont, who along with convicted felon Tito Manaforte ran the insurance ring, ordered Lopez's murder when Manaforte informed him that she was providing information to the *Chronicle*.

Piedmont, who had been a friend of Attorney General Aidan G. Carpenter, was known as a philanthropist who donated his time and money to the Centro Hispanico in

Providence. He also worked on various causes throughout the state to benefit the poor and homeless.

But a recent search of his office by police provided evidence that he had gone to various Web sites to learn both about poisons and how to cover up a murder with a car accident. Police theorize that he may have killed Salazar himself to keep her from revealing to Manaforte that he'd been skimming the profits from the operation while Manaforte was still in prison.

Manaforte, who had his parole revoked and is being held at the ACI, is awaiting trial on insurance fraud and conspiracy charges. Manuel Salazar, the husband of the victim, is out on bail. He was charged with fraud stemming from the operation of the predator car ring, but has reached an agreement with prosecutors in exchange for his cooperation in the case.

***See* Two Murders, page B-15.**

"You should feel better about the series," Walter said. He had the Sunday paper in a pile in the backseat of the cab. It was just before noon, and we were on our way to the Gamblers Anonymous meeting in Foxboro, which I was attending regularly these days.

"I know." The series was credited with a boost in circulation, especially in southeastern Massachusetts, and it was the primary reason the investigative team had been spared through the first round of layoffs.

But the very first day the series had run, the whir in my brain finally stopped, the disc settled, and unbidden, Dane's words in the parking garage came back in force. *But you wanted your front-page story. For what? You screwed everyone. Me. Yourself. Lizette's sister, too.* And although part of me knew that he was justifying his own insanity, a part of me knew he had keyed right into mine.

"You stuck on what that guy said to you again?" Even with his eyes on the highway, Walter could read me.

"I'm trying to deal with it," I said.

"Hey, it was her own brother-in-law who ratted her out to Tito. Not you." We were talking about Marcella, a conversation we'd had many times before.

"I know," I said again. But I couldn't be sure Dane hadn't heard me say her name when I'd answered my cell phone in his bedroom. That maybe he hadn't really been asleep.

"Your stories helped break up that ring," Walter said. "They had an impact. Who knows how many other people might have been hurt or killed by one of Tito's cars?"

"I know. I know." This is what Matt said, too.

"You also keep forgetting the other part of it."

"What other part?"

"The part where he says you screwed yourself up, too. Maybe you keep focusing on what you think you did to Marcella because you won't think about what you almost did to yourself," Walter said.

There was a long silence as we exited onto the ramp. As we turned onto Mechanics Street, a car came up fast from behind. I shuddered, bracing my body for a hit.

Seeing my reaction, Walter reached across the seat to put his hand on my shoulder. "Maybe you should bring this up at the meeting."

I'd been going to the meetings for four weeks and had remained silent, hogging my mistakes and misgivings, afraid of the story that would come tumbling out once I stood up to share. But bottling it up was clearly not working very well. Sometimes the only thing that helped was the absence of condemnation from a group of total strangers.

"Maybe I will."

It was a warm, sunny day, which made it easier to be in a cemetery. The grass, a brilliant green after all the rain we'd had, blanketed the endless plain of graves.

I was on crutches. The ankle injury had only been a sprain, but the twist I'd taken as I leapt from my car had torn the cartilage in my knee, and I'd had surgery two days ago. Matt helped me out of the car and carried the bag for me. Inside was a bottle of water, a spade, and the English bluebell bulbs wrapped up in the morning's front page.

After my brother died, I'd taken solace in planting French thyme on his grave. Now, I'd finally found a spot for the bluebells I'd sent away for.

Even with directions from the groundskeeper, it took us a while to find the graves. We found Lizette's first. It had a white limestone headstone that looked small beside the fresh mounds of earth where she had been buried, exhumed, and reburied. It had not yet been engraved, but I knew it was hers. Someone had saved the ribbon from the funeral flowers that said "Mother" and it flew it like a small flag at the head of the grave.

I said a prayer at Lizette's grave and moved on to Marcella's, still unmarked, which was two graves to the right, according to the groundskeeper. I winced at the sight of the turned earth.

Matt put his arm around me. "You've got to keep reminding yourself that Marcella was a grown woman. She wanted to do the right thing. It was her decision."

He took my crutches and helped lower me down so that I was sitting on the ground, the good knee folded underneath me, the bad one extended. I dug a four-inch-deep trench across the grave, just before where the gravestone would go, and fitted a dozen bulbs into it.

My mother had suggested that the bluebells were the proper memorial because they would bloom every year around the anniversary of Marcella's death, and after they were spent, would be easy to mow by the cemetery grounds crew. I combed through the dirt with both hands and tried to think of Marcella somewhere else. I closed my eyes and let my hands linger in the earth. What was it about dirt that made me feel settled inside? That made me feel that I'd dug into something that mattered.

"Tito will never come out of jail," I said to the grave. I looked up to Matt, who was still standing over me, for confirmation. "You're going to put him away for good this time? Right?"

"Hopefully, they'll never let him out." He extended an arm to lift me up. "But it's not going to be my case anymore. I've asked Aidan to reassign me."

"What?" It took me a moment to balance myself on the crutches. My hands, caked with dirt, were a little slippery on the grips.

"The Newport office. I'll manage the division down there."

Although Newport had a generous share of state crime, it was still a small office. "A demotion?"

"Same salary. Technically the same level job."

"But why?"

"I was sort of hoping that you'd get reassigned after the staff cuts, but since it looks like you're going to be on the investigative team for the long haul . . . It'll just work out better for us if we don't have these conflicts."

Our eyes met. His were serious. "You'd do that for me?"

"I want to get rid of the roadblocks," he said.

I'd pretty much been living at Matt's condo since the night of the accident. At first because of my injuries, then because I didn't have a car, and most recently because of my knee surgery. Last night, he'd made a remark about how silly it seemed for me to keep my own apartment.

"But even with me in Newport, we have to be careful," Matt went on. "I can't always be the one removing myself from cases. You get some big story that leads to some millionaire crook in Newport, you'll have to bow out, let Frizell do the story alone."

Matt saw my hesitation. My automatic revulsion at the notion of letting Frizell cover a high-profile story without me. But the ache in my knee, mitigated only by Tylenol, helped me to catch myself. I'd followed ambition and an adrenaline thrill a little too far this time, and where had it gotten me? I'd kept my job, but almost lost my life. Matt was only asking for a fair compromise.

I put my hand in his. "Okay."

We shook on it. I inadvertently transferred the mud on my fingers to his, but Matt didn't seem to notice. He poured the rest of the water over my planting, and we stood silently, watching as the earth drank it up.

ACKNOWLEDGMENTS

I must begin by thanking my writers group, Barbara Shapiro, Floyd Kemske, Hallie Ephron, and former members Thomas Engels and Judith Harper. Without their help, support, and patience with my misspellings and double periods, I'm not sure I could pull this off.

I want to thank my agent, Dan Mandel, at Sanford J. Greenburger. And I especially want to thank my editor, Kelley Ragland, at St. Martin's Press, who offered her enthusiasm when I needed it the most.

A huge thanks to Officer Donald Mong, who generously shared his expertise in automobile accident reconstruction; to insurance investigator Mark Connors, who also provided insight and information; and to Matthew Dawson, deputy chief of the criminal division at the Rhode Island Attorney General's Office, for his many good ideas.

Also at the attorney general's office, I'd like to thank

Attorney General Patrick Lynch and Assistant Attorney General Patrick Youngs. On other legal issues, I'd like to thank Judge Thomas Brogan, attorney Richard Bremer, and Sergeant Paul Sicard of the Westwood Police Department.

I'm grateful to Patricia Comella, LouAnn Pastore Porter, and Carl Steele for their help with insurance information, and to Mike Stanton, Thomasine Berg, and Laura Meade Kirk for help on reporting and newsroom issues.

A big thanks to Seth Leibson for help on immigration issues and to Victor Mejia, Ilsa Diaz, and Ivelis Fuentes for translating my dialogue into Spanish.

For their gambling expertise, I thank Joe Healey and Lee Pearson. For their help in site research, thank you to the Matarese brothers at Matarese Towing, Inc., to Sharon and Paul Norton, and to the folks at the rectory at St. Michael's Church.

Thanks to my brother, Bob Brogan, for help in brainstorming; to my good friend Beth Kirsch for help with galleys; and to my early readers, Naomi Rand and Laurie Mocek.

I want to credit as background sources the *Lawrence Eagle Tribune, Fortune* magazine, and *Accidentally On Purpose* by Ken Dornstein. I also want to thank Linda Henderson at the *Providence Journal-Bulletin* library.

As always, a special thanks goes to my husband, Bill Santo, for his love, support, and creative solutions. And to my children, Lannie and Spike Santo, who are always an inspiration.